Northern Ireland
Edited by Lynsey Hawkins

 Young**Writers**

First published in Great Britain in 2004 by:
Young Writers
Remus House
Coltsfoot Drive
Peterborough
PE2 9JX
Telephone: 01733 890066
Website: www.youngwriters.co.uk

SBISBN 1 84460 594 9

Foreword

Young Writers was established in 1991 and has been passionately devoted to the promotion of reading and writing in children and young adults ever since. The quest continues today. *Young Writers* remains as committed to engendering the fostering of burgeoning poetic and literary talent as ever.

This year, *Young Writers* are happy to present a dynamic and entertaining new selection of the best creative writing from a talented and diverse cross section of some of the most accomplished secondary school writers around. Entrants were presented with four inspirational and challenging themes.

'Myths And Legends' gave pupils the opportunity to adapt long-established tales from mythology (whether Greek, Roman, Arthurian or more conventional eg The Loch Ness Monster) to their own style.

'A Day In The Life Of . . .' offered pupils the chance to depict twenty-four hours in the lives of literally anyone they could imagine. A hugely imaginative wealth of entries were received encompassing days in the lives of everyone from the top media celebrities to historical figures like Henry VIII or a typical soldier from the First World War.

Finally 'Short Stories', in contrast, offered no limit other than the author's own imagination while 'Hold The Front Page' provided the ideal opportunity to challenge the entrants' journalistic skills asking them to provide a newspaper or magazine article on any subject of their choice.

That's Write! Northern Ireland is ultimately a collection we feel sure you will love, featuring as it does the work of the best young authors writing today. We hope you enjoy the work included and will continue to return to *That's Write! Northern Ireland* time and time again in the years to come.

Contents

Kyle Clarke (12)   40
Ryan Mairs (12)   42
Andrew Purdy (14)   43
Jayne Cluff (14)   44
Sarah Tilbury (14)   46
Catherine Vennard (14)   47
Philip Saunderson (14)   48
Adam Sharratt (14)   49
James Spence (14)   50
Emma Gault (11)   51
Grace Kennedy (12)   52
Julie McCormick (15)   53
Emma Montgomery (15)   54
Emma Wilson (14)   55
Amy Camlin (13)   56
Graeme Farquhar (12)   57
Alison Crothers (12)   58
Rosie Ramsey (12)   59
Kate Aisling Jones (11)   60
Ruth Young (12)   61
Ryan Glass (14)   62
Becky Archbold (12)   63
Rebekah Buchanan (12)   64
Rebecca Hamilton (13)   65
Stuart Crawford (12)   66

Belfast High School, Newtownabbey
Matthew McKnight (13)   67
Sehyeon Kim (12)   68
Claire Rea (13)   70
Hannah Scott (13)   71
Lynsey Pritchard (12)   72
Michael McCullough (13)   74
Rebecca Neill (13)   75
Amanda Ritchie (13)   76
Victoria Patton (13)   77
Shona Mulholland (13)   78
Emma Murphy (13)   80
Emma O'Neill (13)   81
Peter Mackey (13)   82

Foyle View Special School, Derry

Larne High School, Larne

Andrea McNally (14)   159
Julieann Houston (15)   160

Limavady Grammar School, Limavady
Sinead Corr (12)   161
Niamh McCann (12)   162
Hannah Jack (12)   163
Chelcey Douglas (12)   164
Joanne Reay (12)   165
Hannah Neilly (12)   166
James McCaffrey (12)   167
Pamela Nicholl (12)   168
Clare Henderson (12)   169

Newtownhamilton High School, Newry
Stephen Nelson (12)   170
Lynsey Dodds (13)   171
Lauren Henry (12)   172
Lesley-Ann Hanna (10)   173
Jennifer Stoops (12)   174
Laura Nesbitt (12)   175
Jenna Smyth (13)   176
Gareth Scroggie (13)   177
Sarah Foster (13)   178
Neil Hughes (13)   179
William Geary (13)   180
Norma McClenaghan (12)   181
Aimée Chambers (12)   182
Ryan Martin (12)   184
Merlyn Hughes (12)   185

St Ciaran's High School, Ballygawley
Enda McElvogue (13)   186
Marie McKenna (12)   187
Emma O'Neill (13)   188
Megan McDonnell (12)   190
Ciara McGoldrick (13)   191
Edward McClenaghan (13)   192

St Patrick's Academy, Dungannon

Pearce Cullen (14)	193
Shane Telford (14)	194
Daniel Toner (13)	196
Richard Fox (14)	197

St Patrick's College, Maghera

Fearghál O'Baoill (13)	198
Lauren Agnew (12)	199
Ryan Conway (11)	200
Marianne Carey (11)	201
Michael Corrigan (11)	202
Rachel Gribbon (12)	203
Eoghan Mulholland (12)	204
Michael Diamond (12)	205
Turlough Hendry (12)	206
Ryan Convery (12)	207
Kevin McKeefry (12)	208
Mandy Scullion (13)	209
Stephen O'Kane (14)	210
Claire Rice (14)	211
Odhran Scott (13)	212
Michael A Toner (14)	213
Shéa Flanagan (13)	214
Stephen Quinn (13)	216
Rose-Marie Murphy (12)	217
Áine Quinn (12)	218
Kevin O'Kane (13)	219
Kevin O'Neill (12)	220
Caitlín Kelly (13)	221
Áine Kelly (13)	222
Siobhán Barry (12)	223
Joseph Bradley (11)	224
Donna Toland (12)	225
Christina O'Hagan (13)	226
Orlagh O'Hare (12)	227
Karen Diamond (13)	228
James Laverty (12)	229
Caroline O'Connor (12)	230
Naoimh Glass (13)	231
Conall Halferty (13)	232

The Creative Writing

A Day In The Life Of Britney Spears

I get up at 8 o'clock every morning of the week, even if I don't have a concert that night. I go down to my kitchen and get a tasty bowl of Special K and, as they say, it makes me feel special. After breakfast I go out to my big swimming pool and swim for about half an hour. Then I go inside again and have a shower and scrub, scrub, scrub.

After all that I go to the gym for an hour or so. I truly enjoy this as I used to be good at sports in my old school. I personally prefer going on a bike ride but I don't like going out alone. Next, I drive home in my convertible (my Monday car) and dinner is always ready for me. My cook, Martha, is absolutely excellent, she always has a delicious meal waiting for me.

Next comes work! My singing tutor comes in and I have to sing for about two hours non-stop. It really is a nightmare, since she is cross. But I suppose she is very good at it. Now I go to my dance tutor and dance for an hour or two. I enjoy this because it keeps me fit.

After all that comes the fun bit! I go to my private hair salon and get my hair done. I usually get it washed; cut, blow-dried and either pinned up, straightened or curled. Then I go and get dressed. These have to be my two most favourite activities of my day, they're so much fun. Just a really girly activity!

Now I'm ready for the concert!

Rachel Coote (12)
Aughnacloy College, Aughnacloy

New Album, New Masks, Slipknot Are Back For More!

The band, who have been on hold for two years, have unveiled their third series of masks which won't be coming out until May 24th.

Joey Jordison said, 'The masks are just an extension of what we wore last time, they just have more detail, you can still tell who is who'.

Slipknot's UK fans will get the opportunity to hear tracks from Vol 3 'The Subliminal Verses' live for the first time when the band head across the pond in June to play the Download Festival, which takes place at Glasgow Green on June 2nd, 3rd and 4th and then in Donington on June 5th and 6th. The masked metallers join Metallica on June 4th. The band have spent the second half of 2003 in a Los Angeles studio with producer Rick Rubin recording the follow-up 'Iowa'.

For the upcoming release, Slipknot have recorded over 25 tracks in the Houdine Mansion with producer Rick, thirteen of which will make the final cut. Outside of 'Pulse of the Maggots' and 'Duality', other tracks expected on the release include 'Vermilion', 'The Blister Exists', and 'Circle'.

Timothy Law (12)
Aughnacloy College, Aughnacloy

Is Charlie Quitting Busted?

The boy band Busted is doing very well in the charts, but will all this change? Read on to find more . . .

Charlie from boy band Busted has been surrounded by rumours that he might be leaving the band in 2005. All of the fans are devastated, wondering are the rumours true, or just idle showbiz gossip? Maybe it's a publicity stunt?

It seems that the boys don't get on very well, but in the public eye they always appear to be the best of friends, this picture helps to make them a successful band. The three boys have three very different personalities.

I had a chat with Charlie to find out what was on his mind. He told us, 'I am bored with having fans screaming at me all the time and losing my privacy. I just want to spend more time with my family and my girlfriend'.

So the question is, with Charlie planning on leaving, will the other two boys make it in the pop world? It is hard to say what will happen; the boys will struggle with Charlie's absence to keep their music in the top of the charts. The other two boys, James and Matt don't care about Charlie leaving because he always got the attention so they think they will do even

better than before. The fans don't want Charlie to leave, and I don't think the band will ever be the same again.

Charlie is a very good singer and he has a strong voice, perfect for a solo career but there has been speculation that maybe he is not going to quit pop as he has been spotted secretly going to another rock band!

So, readers do you think he may quit because of his family or is he going to join another band? Be sure to get next week's paper as we keep you updated on the lives of the *Rich and Famous*.

Jill Stewart (12)
Aughnacloy College, Aughnacloy

The Best Day In My Life . . .

I was away shopping in Belfast when I met the one and only Matty from boy band Busted! He was dressed differently so no one would notice him, but he would never get away from me, Leanne Taggart!

I ran over and started screaming with excitement. I started hugging him and asking him questions. He took me to somewhere a bit more quiet and said not to make it so obvious that it was him. He then offered to spend the day with me and take me shopping to help him pick his outfit for his concert that night, and also promised me dinner. What an offer, I could not refuse!

I was so happy. Then we drove off in his limousine and he wouldn't tell me where we were going, it was a surprise . . . The next thing we arrived at a photo shoot and he even asked me to pose in some of the pictures.

We got back into the limo and when we stopped, the door opened and there were hundreds of screaming fans and people take photographs, I felt like a film star! We had arrived at The Odyssey for Busted's concert, Matty arranged for me to get a front row seat, everyone was so jealous of me!

The band started performing their songs, and I was singing away. Matty asked me to come up on stage and I got to sing with the band, my dreams had come true. I sang along and danced with the band. I was having so much fun and smiling from cheek to cheek. It was such an amazing feeling performing on stage, the crowd were screaming and cheering like mad.

After the concert was over, I headed backstage and Matty came over to me and asked me to be his girlfriend. Of course I said yes, and now he is my fiancé!

Leanne Taggart (12)
Aughnacloy College, Aughnacloy

S Club Reunion

Yesterday evening Rachel, Tina, Hannah, Jo, Jon and Bradley announced that they were getting back together. S Club told our reporters that they are going to LA in a couple of years to shoot a film called 'S Club Reunion'.

During those two years they hope to sell all their old singles to get enough money. One of our reporters asked them if they were still going to do S Clubbers in LA. They answered, 'Probably'.

Tina told us that she had had the idea after she had heard Brian McFadden was leaving Westlife. She decided that because Westlife will probably spilt up soon and then she won't have any good music to listen to. The first person she phoned was Rachel. Rachel said she would phone Jo and Jon so Tina could phone Hannah and Bradley They decided they would go to Hannah's house in LA.

The next day they were all there at 7 o'clock in the morning. They went straight to Hannah's house. She was waiting at the door for them. 'We were really keen on the idea', said Rachel. After they got in they sat down to think of when they should announce it. 'I think we should leave it for a couple of weeks because we will need to get ourselves a good agent', said Hannah. Everyone agreed. 'We are so happy to be back!'

Naomi Abraham (12)
Aughnacloy College, Aughnacloy

Busted Go With Local Girls

Busted were out in a nightclub about fourteen months ago and met three girls from the Aughnacloy area. Read on to find out more . . .

Matt is dating Ashton Wylie, James is dating Nicola Jones and Charlie is dating Jill Stewart. James and Nicola have been dating for a year and James told us that he is planning on proposing to Nicola tonight at their concert in Belfast in front of millions of fans.

Charlie has already popped the question to Jill. Jill visited Pop Magazine to tell us the exclusive news; they are buying a house in the country to get away from city life, and are hopefully tying the knot in the next few months. Jill says Charlie wants to have a family so he might leave Busted!

Matt and Ashton are leaving to go to Spain for four months and have already bought a flat in London.

The managers of the band are not too keen on all this marriage talk; they don't want the band to break up. They have even told other newspapers that our local girls are no good for the boys! But our girls are just as talented as those boys and have been on stage with the boys singing and dancing along.

We wish all of the couples every happiness for whatever the future holds.

Ashton Wylie (12)
Aughnacloy College, Aughnacloy

A Day In The Life Of J-Lo

I begin my day by getting up at 7.30am and heading downstairs for my breakfast of a yummy cereal bar and a glass of pure orange juice, delicious! I get myself dressed in my favourite velvet tracksuit - I think I'll wear my pink one today with my matching Gucci pink-tinted sunglasses!

After I'm dressed I head into downtown LA to the sauna to relax for half an hour before I go and work up a sweat in the gym where I usually workout with my personal trainer for an hour and a half. Then I have time for a quick shower before driving to the beauty parlour.

It's now time for my daily tanning session, this helps to keep my skin glowing. I also get my make-up done and then I go next door to the salon for my hair appointment, I think I'll get my hair all bouncy and curly today . . .

Sometimes I meet up with some of my girlfriends for a bite of lunch, today I'm meeting my sister in a little Mexican café. Yummy!

After lunch I have to go to my vocal coach for singing lessons which usually last two hours. This is really tiring but can be good fun; I have to sing in many different styles. I have a concert tonight so I have to practise my songs. Getting ready for a concert is always nerve-racking and hard work. Doesn't matter how many times you perform in front of an audience!

I get home for my tea about 5pm and my cook, Susan, always makes me a delicious meal to keep my strength up for the concert. Then it's time to have a relaxing bath before my stylist comes over with my outfits for my concert. I get picked up at 8pm by my manager and then off I go to sing and dance for all my fans. I'm a busy lady but I love my job!

Kirsty Thompson (12)
Aughnacloy College, Aughnacloy

Going To LA

Rebekah and I were getting ready to go and meet Mary-Kate and Ashley Olsen over in Florida. We were so excited. But all of a sudden a big storm came and we had to turn off onto this strange, long, dry road with no shops.

Three hours later it stopped raining and it started to get really hot. We were so hot, and then we saw a sign. it said *LA Left and New York Right.* So we turned left to LA, we were so happy because we were going to LA but sad we would not get to see Mary-Kate and Ashley.

Then we saw the big LA sign and shouted like mad as we drove passed all these cool big houses. Then as we were going through the streets, we saw a lot of famous people, it was so cool! We met Rachel Stevens, Sam and Mark, Gareth Gates, Westlife and Queen of the Jungle, Kerry McFadden.

We stopped and asked her for the way to Florida because we were going to see Mary-Kate and Ashley. She said it was a long way so we could go stay at her house overnight. It was so cool. We got a big bed each, king-sized and there was a big pool outside just for us. Maids and servants were there! We got up in the morning and we said our goodbyes and headed on our journey to Florida.

We finally reached Florida and met up with Mary-Kate and Ashley. We stayed there for three weeks before returning home. It was brilliant fun! Next year the girls are coming to Ireland to stay with us.

Jemma Hanthorne (12)
Aughnacloy College, Aughnacloy

Madrid Bombings

On Thursday 11th March 2004 10 bombs were planted on 3 different trains, they exploded when the trains arrived at the station. The bombs killed 100 people and injured 1,000 people. The emergency services did not have enough staff to cope with the explosions.

The hospitals were packed so the doctors had to treat people lying on the streets. The Spanish government immediately started to blame the Basque Separatist group ETA for the bombings but ETA said that they were not responsible for the attack.

Two weeks later the Spanish government found out that the terrorist group, Al Qaeda was responsible for the attack. Officials believe that several people boarded the trains and left the bombs onboard. The bombs were made up of dynamite. The people who planted the bombs are believed to have been standing by and they detonated the bombs by remote control. The police have arrested five people in connection with the bombings.

One week after the bombings, Al Qaeda made a threat against America. People in Madrid had three days mourning for the people killed, that was the plan, but two weeks later Madrid was still mourning their dead.

The wreck of each train is being examined. The trains are completely wrecked. Three bombs was the amount put on each train. The trains were completely blown apart; the carriages that the bombs were in were cut in half. Police say there is still a threat.

Matthew Crawford (12)
Aughnacloy College, Aughnacloy

Bin Laden In The UK

This disturbing headline, London police have just confirmed it. Bin Laden is in the UK. He's fooled us all. We thought this would be the last place on Earth he would go. But he will never get out of here. *Never!*

We're not 100% sure of his position but we're sure that he came into Heathrow Airport on Wednesday evening with a number of the wanted suspects on the USA's list. He then stole a car, which was unlocked with the keys hanging in it, we lost him from there but an eyewitness spotted the car at the ship port of the Stenaline HSS so there is a good chance he is in Ireland.

The UK and the USA have joined heads and five of America's top detectives are on bin Laden's tail.

Nevertheless bin Laden could still be in England, Scotland or Wales. The army has moved in. Soldiers are on all A and B roads with helicopters combing and landing troops all over the UK. Tanks have been put at all docks (even small ones) and airports have been prepared, also armed officers at all boarding points and luggage is being opened with sniffer dogs searching too.

To add to the trouble, he has made a threat telling us to stop trying to find him or else. 'Watch your airports'. Warning, if seen, stay well clear. Remember if he thinks we are on to him he'll be away in a minute, he is dangerous.

Stay clear!

James Bleakley (12)
Aughnacloy College, Aughnacloy

A Day In The Life Of David Beckham

I start my day off by getting up and taking a shower or a bath. I get dressed and Victoria makes me a bowl of Ready Brek porridge at 7.30am. Then I put my hair up in a ponytail!

I have to look my best for the match tomorrow so I go and get a manicure, a pedicure and a massage. Then I go for my dinner at The Red Palace where I usually get a Sirloin steak and chips, yummy. I also always drink my two litres of water every day.

After my lunch I go home to get my football kit. I drive off in my big convertible. On the way to training I see lots of screaming fans. I train for about three to four hours. It is hard work. At training we practise our skills and play a few games.

After I go training I go home and relax in my jacuzzi for a couple of hours then I spend a couple of hours with my kids before reading them a goodnight story.

Gemma Wylie (12)
Aughnacloy College, Aughnacloy

Children Of The Sun God

The *'Ancestors of Mankind'* were alive in the fourth world, below this one, when the great flood came, with waves as high as mountains. The *Ancestors* made a giant hole in the sky we live in now.

One day the people heard from afar the faint 'wu hu hu u' of Hastseyalit, the taking god. Slowly the noise grew louder, until they could hear his moccasin tread, and at last he stood before them. From a piece of turquoise, he made Estanathlehi, Changing Woman. From two ears of corn he made White Corn Boy and Yellow Corn Girl.

Changing Woman married Tsohanoai, the sun god, who carries the sun on his back and hangs it on the west wall of his house at night. He built her a home on an island far to the west, where she now lives. It is from there that the fresh breezes of spring blow and the Navajo country.

Changing Woman had two fine sons, Killer of Enemies and Child of Water. However their father, the sun god, refused to have anything to do with them.

When they had grown into two strapping lads, they got married and had children. Then they decided to seek their father's help in overcoming the many evil spirits that were tormenting mankind.

Gillian Robinson (11)
Aughnacloy College, Aughnacloy

It, The Clown

Once upon a time, I had a clown called 'It' and it sat on the end of my bed. One cold and dark night the clown got hit by lightning as my bedroom window was opened.

I was terrified in case anything happened to my bedroom, the thunder roared and the lightning was so bright. When the thunderstorm was over, my clown began to walk towards me. I was so scared that I threw a book at him. It fell on his toe and he went mad! He threw a piece of paper at me and started chanting I'm going to kill you in ten days'. I was terrified and ran downstairs to tell my dad. He came back upstairs with me but the clown was lying on my bed as if it was not alive. As soon as Dad left the room the clown woke up and started saying 'I'm going to kill you in ten days'. I screamed and ran into my mum's room. She marched me back into my room and lifted the clown and took it with her.

Suddenly I heard a scream! I ran downstairs and found my mum had collapsed on the carpet; Dad was standing beside her holding the clown. Mum came down to show Dad the clown and it spoke to her saying 'I'm going to kill you in ten days'. So, Dad decided the best thing to do was burn the clown. Dad put the clown in the fire; I don't think I'll be buying any more toy clowns!

Hayley McGettigan (12)
Aughnacloy College, Aughnacloy

A Day In The Life Of A Soldier

My name is Billy and I was picked to serve in the First World War. I was picked when I was just 18. The colonel took me on intense training to fly a jet plane called the tornado.

The Germans were building a dam to make more power for them to make more bombs to bomb London. When all my training was over they let me bomb a small village to practise for the big dam.

On our way there, I met this man and he said, 'I'm really scared of this.'

I said, 'It will be OK.'

We were on our way there when a few Germans tried to shoot us down. My plane got hit on the wheel, which meant landing would be very difficult.

We got there and my friend's rocket hit right off the dam. Now it was my turn to drop my bomb. My lever to pull up the jet would not go up and my plane just followed the rocket. I began to panic but remembered the ejector seat. I pressed it and I landed in a big forest. I remembered we had a base in an underground hole, which I quickly began to look for.

I had to go into a small village and get a goon uniform so I could steal a big truck out of the Germans' base.

I got to the Germans' base and stole a lorry. The Germans were shooting at the wheels and they burst one. I just had to get to the south when I was in the north.

When I was there I said, 'Private Billy,' and when I got in I said, 'Thank God that's over.'

Aaron Eagleson (12)
Aughnacloy College, Aughnacloy

Once Is Enough

Once upon a time there was a boy called James. Now what way can I describe James? Oh yes, a liar. Sit back and relax because you are going to hear my one and only story of 'Once is Enough'.

One day James' dad bought a Ford Focus 2000 and James' dad warned James not to go near it or else! James' mum and dad were going out with their parents and had to leave straight away because it was a bit of a drive.

When they left, James said goodbye and straight after he treated himself to a good noisy drive on the tractor. While he was driving he did not know there was a helicopter taking pictures of houses and in the picture of James' house you could see the new Ford Focus and inside it, was a small figure.

The next day the door knocked and a salesman was offering them a picture of the house. James' dad bought it straight away and showed it to James.

The moral of my story is: Don't lie to your parents!

Stacey McKeown (12)
Aughnacloy College, Aughnacloy

Busted, Will They Return?

Busted's heartbreaking news: they have split up.

It was the 11th January, 1999, when Charlie announced they were splitting up and nearly everyone busted down crying!

They have released a goodbye song and the tears came down like Niagara Falls. They made a big speech saying how everyone had helped them get together and without all their support they wouldn't have become a band. They said a big thank you and told everyone how grateful they were. The crowd gave them ten cheers and even Busted were crying. They have decided to split so they can spend more time with their families because they were always on tour and hardly ever saw them!

One year later, my friends Ashton, Jill and I met them in Hollywood and asked would they get back together. They said they missed being in a band and were thinking about starting again . . .

James is now married to Rachel Green, Charlie to Leanne Berton and Matt to Holly Brown. They love their families but they miss being a band. They are all enjoying family life but there is a possibility that in the next year we could hear a Busted number one hit . . .

Keep your eyes and ears open readers!

Nicola Jones (12)
Aughnacloy College, Aughnacloy

Young Writers – That's Write! Northern Ireland

The Swamp Legend

One day there was a boy called Jack Sprat, he was out for a walk around the local pond, nobody hated him or bullied him. Now he was walking around a cave, he didn't notice but somehow he had walked into a cave. He came to sort of a junction, there were three tunnels. He chose to go down the middle tunnel which had footprints down it, so he hoped that there would be somebody down it that would help him get home.

He walked and followed the footprints, the end of the footprints led to a swamp.

Jack Sprat was standing at the edge and some kind of a monster's hand came out, grabbed him by the leg and pulled him in.

The boy known as Jack Sprat was never seen again.

Charlene Johnston (11)
Aughnacloy College, Aughnacloy

Who Gave You Those Orders?

As Boris Kessel, a Russian agent, working for the KGB, stepped out of his taxi onto Oakridge Drive, he was fatally hit on the side of the head.

Back at the MI6 headquarters in London, the sniper, David Royce, had just arrived back from his mission, it was now nearly midnight. As he walked through the office door, leading into his boss' room, Captain Sam Lawther, Royce had a contented grin and the feeling of a job well done.

'What's with all the smiles David?' asked Captain Lawther.

'Sir, I have just taken out Boris Kessel, the Russian spy we have been tracking for about eighteen months.'

'Who gave you those orders?'

'Sir, I was given a package two days ago, which instructed me to stay on a roof top beside his south London apartment, this I did. I was also informed to bring a weapon of my choice, which I took to mean take him out.'

'No Royce, you idiot, the weapon was for self-defence and self-defence only and Kessel left this morning for Russia. Your job was to tell us when he left his apartment. Did you not read the whole briefing?'

'No Sir, sorry Sir,' said David.

'So who did you kill? Because we really don't need this kind of embarrassment at the moment.'

'David, in the light of what has just happened and for your own safety, I request that you stay at home until further notice.'

Some weeks later, Kessel was caught in Poland and was forced to talk. He held out for sometime but finally cracked under the pressure. He explained how he had got a fellow Russian by the name of Braten Backofen, wanted for numerous war crimes and major drug smuggling, to dress in his clothes and return to his London apartment, so that the neighbours would not think anyone strange was about.

The next day David Royce was telephoned and congratulated on accidentally killing an even greater enemy to the British, and the man responsible for a quarter of all drugs in Britain was now gone. David was awarded the medal for outstanding achievement in the field of accidents.

Murray Dalzell (13)
Ballyclare High School, Ballyclare

The New Babysitter

Alana had just turned five and was becoming a bit of a handful, especially for her single mum. Her mum wanted to go back to work, so she needed to hire a babysitter. She posted adverts around the local shops and in the newspapers. They said, 'Babysitter required. Must be child friendly and willing to work days and nights. Will be paid five pounds per hour'.

She had many replies, but all the people were unsuitable, some were just strange. One person in particular, was quite scary. She had no recommendations from all twenty-one families she worked for. She carried guns and knives in her handbag and had a criminal record.

Just when she thought she was never going to find a babysitter, the doorbell rang. A handsome young man stood under the porch, with a dripping wet application form. Alana's mum was speechless. It was like an angel had fallen from Heaven and landed on her doorstep. She invited him in and gave him a towel to dry himself off. He handed her the form and sat down. Quietly she read it, it said:

Name: Jack Magee.

Age: 23 years old.

Recommendations: Brilliant with children. Good fun for kids.

Other jobs: Worked for 3 other families.

She looked up at him as he dried his face. He was tan, tall and thin, he had fair hair and blue eyes. Alana's mum thought to herself, *yes, he's perfect, Alana will love him!*

Nicola Rodgers (13)
Ballyclare High School, Ballyclare

Prince Richard The Frog

Once upon a time there was a prince. He lived in a lovely house with a beautiful wife, a cook and a potion lady. He lived happily and you would think him to be tall, dark and handsome. In fact he was small and looked somewhat like a frog! His personality wasn't anything to go by either. He was lazy and made everyone do everything for him. If the prince wanted something, the prince got it immediately!

One day the prince wasn't feeling himself so he demanded that Gladys the potion lady was brought to him. 'I want a potion to make me feel myself!' he ordered.

'I'm sorry but I don't think I have the right ingredients that I need to make the potion work,' she said.

He replied, 'Use other ingredients instead because I *must have that potion now!'*

Gladys went to her room and got out her cauldron. She gathered the ingredients together and started to add them to the cauldron supplementing other ingredients for the ones she didn't have. As she stood over the cauldron stirring the ingredients she spoke this rhyme. 'Cats' whiskers and butterflies' wings along with one of his favourite things. A nail, a snip of his hair, not forgetting a tooth from a bear!'

Gladys put the potion into a bottle and took it to the kitchen. She told the cook to take the potion that said 'Fairness' on it and to stir it into the prince's soup. However the cook accidentally lifted the wrong potion and gave it to the prince!

He ate all of the soup and then said, 'I do feel a bit more like my . . . ribbit!' The cook had lifted the one that said 'Frogness'! The prince sat trying to complain but all that came out was 'ribbit.'

His wife fell in love with another prince and when they were about to get married a frog came bouncing down the aisle saying, 'I up . . . ribbit!'

So the moral of this story is to learn how to talk when you become a frog!

Emma Jayne Ferguson (13)
Ballyclare High School, Ballyclare

Is Your Brother Really Identical?

The identity crisis

There was once a man with an identical brother. This man was called Andrew Jackson and he was a peaceful and law-abiding man. His brother, Mark, however was the opposite, an unruly and reckless person. The unusual thing was, they were identical in their outward appearance.

One day a squad of police officers broke into Andrew's house and said, 'You are under arrest for serial killing.' He was unable to take in what was happening before he realised that he had been handcuffed and forced into a police car.

His court case was going to begin today. While there Andrew saw a video and some pictures and realised immediately that it was his twin brother Mark. He then suggested to the judge that if he was released for a period he would be able to find his brother. The judge then released him for a month.

The next day he set off to find his brother. When he got to where his brother was living, he found out that there was a man who had been frequently to his brother's apartment. He decided to follow this man back to his brother's so he could give the police the address to come to.

The next day he did this and once he reached the apartment he realised that Mark had already left. He then telephoned the police and told them to find his brother.

The police despatched a helicopter, which found the car. The police in front of Mark had also laid spikes and these burst his tyres, which sent him skidding into a lorry at 100mph. There was then a fatal crash and Mark died.

Evan Cusick (13)
Ballyclare High School, Ballyclare

War!

'Who gave these orders?' shouted the commander at the battle briefing.

'Commander, they want us to retreat immediately and return to base,' said the messenger.

'Why was this order given at such short notice?' asked the commander.

'It appears there was a glitch in the original orders,' replied the messenger.

The Russians were ahead of us in technology and in producing their army of tanks and navy vessels at a very fast speed.

'Alright, tell the troops to load themselves into the trucks,' said the commander to his second-in-command. *Saluting, the second-in-command left the room.*

When we were heading for the base we met heavy resistance. We sent out our spies to check out the surrounding area and found that we were surrounded. So, at dawn, we attacked not noticing the plane flying overhead.

Quiet as a mouse, the Russian spy plane had spotted us and had warned the enemy army that we were coming. We got over the first hill and found a sprawling army in the valley below us.

Before we could react a battalion of tanks started blasting us with long-range shots. After this we decided to launch an offensive. We all grouped together and ran towards them. We rushed through them, managing to break through. We then drove as fast as we could towards the base.

In the end we were given a leave of absence so that we could go home because of our 'exemplary service in the midst of battle'. The war was going badly for the Russians and we were gaining ground.

I found out from a newspaper report that we had broken through the main Russian army! This eventually led to a peace treaty being signed.

Matthew Hunter (13)
Ballyclare High School, Ballyclare

Not Always A Happy Ending . . .

On a fine sunny morning in June, Rose Meadows got out of bed and stretched. Her room smelt of flowers as there was a vase of them sitting on her dresser. A golden light shone on her face as she looked out the window and smiled at the rabbits playing amongst the wildflowers and wheat that were swaying from the gentle breeze in the field below her window. Then she sat on her stool and brushed her long, wavy, hazel-coloured hair as she looked in the mirror. Today she was going into the town with her friends and so she got changed into her trendiest outfit - her denim three-quarter length jeans that were turned up at the bottom with her new trainers, and her new pink top that just sat below her shoulders. Before she left the room she sprayed some perfume on herself, then went to the bathroom to clean her teeth.

Finally, when she was completely ready to go, her friend Alana's mum pulled up in front of their house, a converted barn.

'Ready to go, Rose?' said Hazel, Alana's mum, smilingly.

'Yes,' replied Rose. She got into their car, a small but able one and buckled her belt.

'What do you want to buy?' asked Alana interestingly.

'I don't know yet, I'll just wait and see what's there,' answered Rose.

She returned with a new top, pencil case, hair accessories, earrings and a box of chocolates for her family to eat while watching the DVD her mum had rented. The situation was cosy, Rose and her parents sitting on their comfy sofa with the open fire lit. Rose enjoyed the film and went to bed happy, having had a great day.

It was 2am in the morning and Rose woke up to the sound of barking. She sniffed the air - it was smoke. She rushed to her parents' room - it was on fire! Crawling and coughing at the same time, she went into the flame-filled room and found her parents weren't there. She moved quickly to the window and saw people gathered, trying to save her. The window was jammed. Desperate and intensely saddened she lay down on the ground, hugged herself and prayed.

Three days later Rose was buried at the local churchyard. Both parents were crying and their emotion was felt by all. But there was something that everyone was thinking - how could such a perfect situation become such a disaster . . . ?

Joanne Williamson (13)
Ballyclare High School, Ballyclare

A Day In The Life Of Tanya!

I wake up to the sound of the family coming down the stairs. I get put outside for a while and then I get let back in. The family leave the house for a while and then only Kim comes back in and cleans the house, I usually get into the living room to lie on my comfy cushion. Kim leaves after a while and comes back with Kathryn, they have their lunch at this time and I always get a bit.

After lunch Kathryn would watch TV or play with her toys. Kim leaves again with Kathryn and comes back a little later with Ryan, he usually watches TV or sometimes goes up to his friend's house or his friend comes down. Soon after Ryan comes in Dawn comes back, I love Dawn and always wait at the door for her. Dawn would go upstairs but comes back down soon and takes me out for a walk with her friends and these other dogs. I usually have a nap once we get back in.

When I wake up the family are usually having their dinner and once they've finished, I get mine.

After I've finished mine, I get into the living room and lie on my cushion. When all the children are in bed, Paul takes me out and then puts me into my bed, after a while Paul and Kim go up to bed and then I fall asleep thinking about my day and what will happen tomorrow!

Dawn Comins (12)
Ballyclare High School, Ballyclare

A Day In The Life Of George Best

After thirty-five years of alcohol abuse, I have finally realised I owe it to myself to be fit and healthy. With a past like mine, you do not cut down, you stop. So now I am teetotal and vegetarian. Before I start the day's activities, I work out for an hour. Three years ago, I was a sixteen stone mess with a worn out liver. My wife, Alex did not think I was a real person anymore and threatened to walk out on me. I bought a cottage in the countryside away from all temptation, had a liver transplant and embarked on a new life.

Despite my good intentions, alcohol won and I hit the bottle again. My wife left and the haven in the country had to be sold. I am like a kind of life commando. I like life to hurt. Some would call it self-destruction. I have got nothing to prove these days except to myself. I used to be a big spender, now I will haggle over the price of a cauliflower. I am not interested in splashing it about anymore.

I am not really a moralist; I just make the assumption that certain things we do lead to catastrophe. I am trying to find out why people destroy themselves the way they do. I have no formal religion, but there is a space in my head for it. Maybe I would believe in God if he believed in me. Uncertainty seems to be the only true principle.

Christopher Williamson (13)
Ballyclare High School, Ballyclare

The Fatal Orders

In 1024, there was a battle between 2 towns in north Germany, near Hamburg.

In a hole in the ground was a small man, about 5'' 2' with black hair and quite bushy eyebrows. He had been sitting there watching for 2 days with a loaf of bread and 2 pieces of ham. His name was Kopfmark. He was armed with a sword and was heavily armoured. A man came over to him. He recognised him and said, 'Hann!'

'I am not Hann, I am his brother Frankle Toes!'

'Oh right, I didn't know you had a brother, well I mean I didn't know he had one, is your brother really identical?'

'Who gave you these orders?' he shouted.

'Sergeant Cromwell!'

'Well it's pretty pointless of you being here now.'

He attacked hard with his axe but Kopfmark quickly blocked it!

Kopfmark said, 'Why are you attacking me?'

'You know my brother Hann?'

'Yes, why?'

'We had an argument and I changed to the other clan and you are in our territory so I am sorry, I must kill you!'

They fought for one hour until the head of him was lying in the hole. Kopfmark got out and ran to the control tower.

He arrived and said to Cromwell, 'Why did you send me to the other clan's territory?'

'Of course, to die,' replied Cromwell!

'Traitor!' he yelled.

He gripped his sword and swung it out and killed Cromwell.

Lee Coupe (13)
Ballyclare High School, Ballyclare

My Dream - Gone Wrong!

The tiger prowled silently through the undergrowth, his massive paws refusing to make a sound, his stripes blending into his background. This was it! This was paradise!

The hot sun was blazing down on my bare shoulders. The huge cat took long strides through the thick grass. Here I was, looking at an endangered species. This was a once-in-a-lifetime experience!

I was a cameraman for a top animal documentary company. This footage would be worth a lot - after all, tigers are an endangered species.

I was in complete amazement. I was staring at a huge animal, capable of killing me! This was my dream, seeing a tiger, filming a tiger. Tigers were one of my favourite animals, were.

I don't know exactly what happened next but suddenly, I sensed a streak of danger in the tiger's eyes. Then it disappeared into the trees. I searched frantically for a glimpse of orange and black but it could not be found!

Somewhere behind me, a twig snapped. I jumped round - there was the tiger! In a sudden burst of energy, he leapt, leapt at me. I tried to run but the tiger's strong grip held me fast. I struggled, then stopped, it was obvious I wouldn't escape.

I'm now dead, that tiger killed me. I'm up in Heaven. This was my dream. It went wrong!

Ashleigh Holmes (13)
Ballyclare High School, Ballyclare

A Day In The Life Of An African Woman

I woke up one morning and I looked over at my 21st birthday cards. Most of them were from my friends but some of them were from my racist enemies with nasty messages inside them. I looked at my clock and it said 9.30am. Reluctantly I got out of my bed and went into the kitchen, my flatmate, Anne, was already up.

'Hey Nadia, what do you want for breakfast?' she asked, tying her sleek blonde hair up.

'Umm, nothing, I'm too nervous,' I replied. 'I'm leaving for a job interview today. Anne would you drive me there?' I asked. I'm 21 and I still can't drive; I've failed my test twice.

'I personally think your driving instructor is racist,' said Anne.

'I agree, I don't think he likes me at all,' I answered.

A couple of hours later, I'm outside the Art College. My white enemy comes up to me and said, 'They're not going to give the job to a black person and I'm going to make sure of that!'

I was first to go into the interview with the boss so in I went. He asked me some questions like what my qualifications were and stuff like that. He was very pleased with me because he was smiling a big broad smile. I walked out of the room feeling very happy. Anne was there to take me to a restaurant for lunch, while waiting for all the others to get interviewed. For lunch we both had burger and chips. When we went back to check who had got the job, it was the white girl. Somehow she had coaxed the boss into being racist. Oh how I hate her! She ruined my big chance.

Zoe Scott (11)
Ballyclare High School, Ballyclare

A Day In The Life Of A Coke Bottle

My name is Mr Coke. I am being filled with dark brown stuff which humans call Coke. They think that this Coke is very tasty. At the minute I am sitting on a shelf, which is very cold. There is a girl standing in front of me looking at all my mates. Oh no, she is looking at me. I wonder if she likes me more than the rest. Ahh, she is looking at someone else. That someone else is my friend Timmy. She is lifting him now and she is walking away. I will really miss that boy, Timmy. He was very nice.

Why do they pick bottles that are my friends? Every day we Coke bottles get stared at by loads of people. It is very annoying really. If only they knew what it is like to be stared at by loads of people. I wonder how they would feel. They wouldn't be very happy would they?

Oh here comes another customer. I wonder which Coke bottle they will pick? They seem to be staring at me, they might be going to pick me. Yes they are! I am now sitting on a table and going through a red laser type thing. We are now going outside and my lid is coming off. Hey, stop that, you are making me fizz. Now they seem to be tipping me upside down and some of the Coke is going out into their mouth.

We are now driving somewhere. Oh no, they are going to have another drink of me. Don't they understand that it isn't very fair tipping me upside down? I wish I could tip them upside down and fizz them up and do all those horrible things they do to us. Now I am all done. I wonder where I will go next? I don't really care as long as they don't tip me upside down. Oh dear, I shouldn't have said that because I am now falling into something with a lot of rubbish in it. Argh!

Oh look, there's my friend Timmy Hill!

Rachael Bailie (11)
Ballyclare High School, Ballyclare

My Legend Story About The Loch Ness Monster

On a cold winter's morning in Scotland, fog eerily drifted over the loch's surface. Two local fishermen breached its deep waters, in the hope of bringing in an early morning catch. Little did they know that fish wouldn't be the only thing they'd be catching.

The morning started out fine until one fisherman looked over the side of the boat. What he saw made the colour drain from his face, he could barely shout to his friend to come and have a look.

They saw a great whale-like creature with fins and great big menacing jaws, swimming straight at them. Of course, being from the local area, they knew what this was.

Suddenly the small boat began to shake, until it was thrown five feet into the air. As the fishermen looked back, they saw the creature's long, narrow head and long snout rise out of the water. It began to propel itself towards the boat. The two fishermen were petrified, but sped away from the creature as fast as they could. The monster's superior fins gave it the advantage and it wasn't long before it was right alongside the small boat, completely dwarfing it.

The fishermen slowed their boat down and gazed at the creature in amazement. It craned its neck over the side of the boat and began to slowly eat the fish the men had caught, until there were none left. It then disappeared back over the side.

When they arrived back at port they let all of Scotland know their story.

Ryan Cooke (12)
Ballyclare High School, Ballyclare

The Headless Horseman

One cold winter's night, the same man who usually went out, went out with his horse and cart through the local village. It was pitch-black, wet and the thunderstorms were coming. The Horseman (as the villagers called him) was out cantering through the forest. Suddenly, lightning struck and the Horseman steered out of control! He couldn't see where he was going! Then when he finally got back on track, he looked up and then . . . *bam!* His neck and head hit a tree with the force of the horse's terror pulling the cart, completely ripped the Horseman's head off.

He was found early in the morning by a man walking his dog. The man quickly called the sheriff and reported the body discovery. The horseman had run off with the cart. All that was left was the body, the cloak and . . . the head.

The police took the body to the local undertaker. He sewed the head back on, put it in a coffin and buried it two days later.

Nowadays, no one believes in the story of the 'Headless Horseman'. But for those who do they say that every year, they hear a dog barking and then hear horses' hooves and the clanging of wheels of a cart going round and round on the rocky pavement. One person said, on that date he saw the spirit of the Headless Horseman (as they now call him) trotting along on his cart in the forest, then saw him steer out of control and his head then came straight off. That's what made him believe in the 'Headless Horseman'.

Laura Wilson (13)
Ballyclare High School, Ballyclare

He Had A Devil Of A Temper Did Young Mattie!

Mattie was no ordinary boy. He lived in a children's home since he was nine and he was abused as a child

Mattie ended up In a children's home because of his dad. When Mattie's mum died, his dad couldn't cope and turned to alcohol. Every night when Mattie's dad came home form work, he would be drunk. His dad would kick him, punch him, spit on him, and generally beat him up. Mattie couldn't stop him, he was too strong, so he blamed himself for his dad's condition. One night when it all got too much, Mattie was cutting himself and his dad walked in. It made it worse because his dad started beating him again. Only this time it was bad, his dad beat him unconscious.

When he was in hospital, he told someone what was happening and that was when something was done. Mattie's dad was charged with GBH and sent to prison and he was never allowed to see his son again. Meanwhile, Mattie was put into a home and given the best care he could have.

Because of Mattie's background, he had a very bad temper and the tiniest thing would set him off. Mattie's care-workers were finding it hard to cope with this, so they decided to send him to a psychiatrist to help him with his problem.

One day, Mattie was in a bad way. He was feeling very depressed with his life and was even thinking about suicide, but when he told his 'best friend' and closest care-worker, they talked him round and cheered him up.

The only thing Mattie wanted was a caring, loving family who would accept him as one of their own, but in reality this was extremely hard to find. Then all of a sudden a miracle happened for Mattie. His care-worker got a phone call to say that he would be fostered by a family of four who had a nice house, two children, both boys of Mattie's age, and a dog. Mattie was over the moon when he heard this. He couldn't believe his luck, he was finally going to get his family he wanted, who loved and cared for him.

When Mattie went to meet his family, he loved them. He got on very well with the two brothers and he enjoyed their company. Mattie soon got the papers through to say that the deal was done and he soon moved in with them.

Everything was fine for the first few months and Mattie was getting on very well with his new family, until one day his new foster 'dad', Robert, came home after his friend's stag night and was drunk. Mattie started getting flashbacks of what his dad did to him when he was younger, and this started off his temper. Mattie started hitting Robert very hard. Robert fell and banged his head. He was just lying there, not moving. Mattie phoned an ambulance and went to hospital with Robert.

A few hours later Robert woke up and Mattie apologised, Robert only had some minor cuts and bruises and was not kept in overnight. When the rest of the family arrived, Mattie thought he would have to go back into care. The family knew about Mattie's past and his temper, but still forgave him. Mattie learned that his temper got him nowhere and learned to control it, so for the rest of his life, with his foster family, he lived happily and temper free. Mattie's dad died some few years later and was buried beside his mother. Mattie did not care for his dad, but still looked after his grave as long as he lived.

Suzanne Weir (13)
Ballyclare High School, Ballyclare

A Day In The Life Of Homer Simpson

'Zzzzz, pheww, zzz, huh? Wha?'
   'Homey, get up or you'll be late for work.'
   'OK, Marge.'
   Five minutes later, *'Marge!* Where's my trousers?'
   'They are under the bed Homey, now hurry up!'
   Ten minutes later . . .
   'Bye Marge. Bye kids.'

Homer arrives in work late as usual . . . with Smithers waiting for him. They approach Mr Burns' office.
   'Mr Burns, this is Homer Simpson. You wanted to see him.'
   Mr Burns replies, 'OK Smithers, now shut up. So Simpson, you have caused seventeen meltdowns in my factory in the last year! So now I'm going to poke you with this stick for the next hour or so!'
   'Aow, aow, aowho, ho, stop it, boo, hoo, hoo.'
   Homer thinking, *mmm, now what to do when I get home, tickle Maggie, strangle Bart, annoy Lisa or watch TV?*

Homer pulls screeching into the driveway shouting, 'Marge! Where's the dinner?'
   'Be quiet Dad, you greedy pig!' says Bart.
   'It's coming now, Homey,' says Marge.
   'This is really nice, what is it?' says Homer.
   'It's roast chicken. I'm surprised that you didn't know what it was.'

Four hours later after watching television, Homer retires to bed. 'Night, Marge.'
   'Night Homey, see you in the morning.'
   Homer is already snoring blissfully and dreaming of doughnuts.

Next day when driving to work, Homer thinks, *mmmm, this is bad, it's my big test at work today.* 'Oh nooo!'
   As soon as Homer arrives, guess who he runs straight into? The dreaded Mr Burns.
   'Hello Simpson,' Mr Burns smirks to himself and thinks, *boy, I'm looking forward to humiliating that fool.* 'Time for your test, boy. Follow me.'
   They arrive in the control room with Lenny and Karl already waiting. They are taking part in the test too. Lenny says, 'Hey Homer, don't you think Burns is being a little good to you today?'
   Karl agrees, 'Yeah, Homer, Lenny's right, he is a little soft on you today!'

'Well, isn't that supposed to be a good thing, uh?' Homer says.

They all sit down and start the test.

Smithers asks Mr Burns, 'Did you put the trick questions in to catch them out? Hee, hee!'

'Yes, of course I did, you imbecile,' replies Mr Burns.

Homer thinks . . . *d'oh! This could be quite easy if you had the brains, d'oh! Which I don't have.'* Homer starts to panic but tries his best. The next thing he hears is Mr Burns saying, 'Time's up! Now give me the tests and go back to your ugly families.'

Homer leaves work with Lenny and Karl at his usual pace, then the race is on to get to Moe's for a drink.

'Hi, Moe. Hi, Barney. Hit me with a Duff, Moe,' says Homer.

An hour, and a lot of Duff later, Homer shares a joke with his mates. 'Shey fellas, and the pig says to the horse . . . hey fellas why the long face?'

They all laugh drunkenly and fall out of the pub and make their way home.

Alex Hagan (11)
Ballyclare High School, Ballyclare

A Day In The Life Of Tommy Pickles

Hi, I'm Tommy Pickles and I have two friends called Phil and Lil and they are twins. I have a little brother called Dil. I also have a very bossy cousin called Angelica. My best friend is Chuckie. Chuckie is a bit of a scaredy-cat though. I have a dog called Spike and he is the best dog ever in the world. I would like to tell you about one of the days in my thrilling life. I call it 'Twin Sister Act'.

It all started when me, Chuckie, Phil and Lil were playing with Reptar. Phil and Lil had just got these new Reptar Patrol badges from their mum, for not eating any worms for a whole week. Phil and Lil had a big row about who got the best worms to eat and Lil walked off on Phil and said, 'I don't want to be your twin no more.'

Phil shouted back, 'Fine!'

Lil was so mad that as she walked past Angelica, she shoved her out of the way, and Angelica asked, 'What's your problem?'

Lil replied, 'Phil and I aren't twins no more.'

Angelica had a plan and told Lil that she could be someone else's twin instead. Lil thought it was a great idea, so she went looking for someone. Lil thought about me as a twin, and Angelica said, 'No! He already has a brother.'

Lil said, 'What about Chuckie?'

Angelica thought that was perfect. Angelica dressed Lil up to look like Chuckie and took her badge off her and put it on herself instead. Angelica introduced Lil to everyone saying, 'I'd like you to meet Chuckie's new twin, Charlene.'

Chuckie was shocked at what he had just heard. Angelica thought that her plan was brilliant and should keep us occupied, and she loved her new, nifty Reptar Patrol badge. Phil wagged his finger at Lil and said to Lil, 'Take those clothes off Lil, stop messing around.'

Lil replied, 'Lil? Who's that? My name's Charlene.'

Phil disagreed and Lil insisted. Lil and Chuckie sat on the grass together and then Chuckie got bored, so he asked Lil, 'What do we do now?'

Lil said, 'All kinds of stuff!'

Phil interrupted and said, 'Yeah! Having a twin is great, you always have someone to be lookout when you're trying to get some cookies, there's always someone to play on the see-saw with, you always have someone to blame for breaking something, and best of all you have someone to share your worms with.'

Chuckie said, 'I definitely don't eat worms, *eeewww!* I don't think it will work.'

Lil said, 'If you don't want . . .'
'. . . a twin?' Phil finished.
Chuckie replied, '*No I don't!* 'Cause I do most of that stuff with Tommy. Well except for that blaming part, which isn't nice!'
Lil said, 'But now I don't have a twin no more.'
I said, 'You and Phil were already twins anyway, so why don't you go back to being his twin again?'
Lil said that she didn't want to be Phil's twin anymore because he hogged all the worms. But I reminded her that it was her who hogged all the worms. Lil apologised for hogging them and they were twins again. Angelica was raging and told her that she was supposed to be Charlene, Chuckie's twin. Lil snatched her Reptar Patrol badge off Angelica and walked off. Lil took all her dressing stuff off and then my mum came out and Angelica got the blame and got into more trouble for blaming us.
So that was a day in the life of Tommy Pickles.

Rachel Brown (12)
Ballyclare High School, Ballyclare

A Day In The Life Of John Frusciante

I woke up this morning because I couldn't really sleep right, we are now touring Australia. I think there is something strange in the air. I have to go now and get my breakfast, because I have a long day ahead of me. First of all, we have to go down to the studio and rehearse for the big concert we are holding in the Telstra Stadium. I am more nervous than usual, it is because all of our Australian fans are very loyal, so we don't want to disappoint them.

When we got to the studio, we had to battle our way through the crowds of fans. We go in and set up, but then I realise that I can't find my pluck for my guitar. It just doesn't feel right not having it to play with. It takes me 10 minutes looking for it. It was at the bottom of my guitar bag. After rehearsing with the rest of the band, we go back to the hotel and relax.

After a while, we go out around the city and see what Australia's like. We then go back to the hotel and have one last rehearsal before we go to the Telstra Stadium.

When we arrive at the concert, I always go out and see the stadium or venue with all the fans. It is huge. When the concert starts, everybody comes alive, all the fans are screaming and we are jumping around the stage. The concert goes amazingly.

Afterwards, we go back to the hotel and relax. I sit and think that we have another four concerts to do before we go back to America.

Scott Wylie (13)
Ballyclare High School, Ballyclare

My Favourite Possession

My favourite possession is my Man Utd television. It is the same as any other TV only it is red and it says Manchester United along the top and has the Man Utd symbol on the bottom left hand corner.

It was bought for me by my mum and dad about four Christmases ago, I was so surprised when I got it because I had never seen one before.

It was special because Manchester United is my favourite football team and I have supported them all of my life (or most of it anyway). It is also special, it is the first Christmas that I really remember properly.

I keep it in my room on my computer desk, pointing at my bed so I can lie in my bed and watch it if I am feeling tired and lazy, it also means when I wake up I can turn it on with the remote and sometimes I lie in bed at night and watch it.

I intend to keep it as long as I can or until it breaks.

Trevor McClintock (12)
Ballyclare High School, Ballyclare

A Day In The Life Of Bart Simpson

First of all the alarm rings and I wake up and race my sister downstairs to breakfast. Meanwhile my lazy dad is getting off the sofa to go and get more beer, but he trips over Santa's Little Helper and while trying to keep his balance trips over Snowball II, falls to the ground and as usual shouts 'D'oh!' After breakfast I get ready for school and since it's a nice beautiful day, I ride my skateboard to school. Riding by the Kwik-E-Mart I see a poster on the window, it reads: 'Soap box derby put your life on the line. Race down 'Death Mountain' in a soap box derby race'.

'Woooaah dude I've got to make a soap box racer.'

When I got to school I was late because I looked at the poster for so long. As usual the teacher kept me behind in school to do lines because I made funny noises that made everyone laugh. I had to write 100 lines and this is what they were: 'Funny noises are not funny . . . '

I couldn't wait to get home to build my soap box racer. When I got home I asked my dad to help me build my soap box racer and he said he would, so we went out to the garage to look for some junk that was lying about. The main part of it was made out of cardboard, the steering wheel was from Maggie's pram and the wheels from my go-kart.

We were all ready to test it, my friends were round and it looked amazing. 3, 2, 1 - bang, the wheels fell off and the whole thing fell apart. I should have known my dad, my dad is not mechanical.

Three weeks later, we had made a good one with some help from a professional, well at least he thought he was a pro. It was Groundskeeper Willie.

The day was here, it was the first race down Death Mountain, the first two people past the finish line were in the final.

'3, 2, 1, go!'

Halfway down Death Mountain Nelson threw spikes in front of me and flattened my wheels and the race was over for me. Martin and Nelson both passed the finish line at the same time but Martin crashed because his brakes failed and asked me to race Nelson in the final, his racer is great.

'3, 2, 1, go!'

Martin's car was so fast you wouldn't believe it. I zoomed by Nelson and won the race.

When I was getting the cup, Martin came and took it from me and said that he deserved it. Then I drove home in the car with my dad and we decided that we would get a really good pro to make the car next time.

Kyle Clarke (12)
Ballyclare High School, Ballyclare

A Day In The Life Of Patch

My name is Patch, I am a black and white dog and live with my owners in a bungalow in a place called Ballyclare. I really love my owners because they rescued me from an animal shelter where I lived a miserable life with lots of other poor, unfortunate dogs. I was mistreated before so I'm very happy now to be with people who love me.

A typical day for me starts at about 7am when I'm woken from my lovely, warm sleep by the person they call mum. She puts me in the garden where I have great fun chasing the birds. When I've finished this important job I go with my friend Eric, who is the other dog that lives with us to inspect the garden and sniff out any strange smells. Once we've dealt with this task we go into the house to grab any scraps of food that have fallen to the floor. Then I go back to my bed for a snooze until my master comes to take Eric and me for a walk through the fields. Next to eating and sleeping, galloping through the fields, chasing rabbits and sniffing wonderful smells, is my favourite hobby.

After this walk it's home again where I can enjoy sleeping until 4.30pm when the one they call Ryan comes home from school and plays with me until dinner time. Having scrounged all I can to eat, I'm ready again for another exciting trip through the fields where I can throw myself into a stream or muddy puddle. Then, when I get out, I love to chase the people with me so that I can shake all the wetness off myself and onto one of them, usually Ryan. It's such good fun!

Thought that you might like to see this picture of me, guarding my Bonio, following one of my garden patrols! I really think my name should be Lucky and not Patch because I love living where I do with people who think that Eric and I are both very special.

Ryan Mairs (12)
Ballyclare High School, Ballyclare

The Charleston Gazette

Children Checkout! Hunt is on for two missing children after plane crashes in Australian desert.

Yesterday a plane departed at 16.30 (American time) from South Carolina - bound for Adelaide, Australia. The plane was carrying 250 passengers and 20 flight crew.

The plane all of a sudden had engine failure and crashed in the barren desert of Northern Australia. Only 2 of the 270 people onboard are thought to be alive, a young boy and his older sister. The boy, named Peter, is 8 years old and his sister, Sally, is 13.

They have no knowledge of edible plants and if they are not found soon they are likely to die.

We interviewed the children's mother, who is now widowed, to try and understand what she is going through.

'Mrs Stevenson, do you think your children will survive this ordeal they are being put through?'

'I have every faith in my children but I cannot stop thinking what would happen if they didn't pull through. They are all that is left of my family now that my husband is dead'.

'Why were your children and husband travelling to Adelaide?'

'They were going to visit my husband's brother, Keith, who lives there and is celebrating his 40th birthday'.

The search continues for the children and rescue workers hope they stayed beside the wreckage of the plane or else there is only a very small possibility that they will be found alive.

Andrew Purdy (14)
Ballyclare High School, Ballyclare

Jennifer Lopez

Where did you get the clothes you are wearing today?
I got these clothes from Donnetella Versace. When she heard I had this premiere to attend, she contacted me to see if I would like something made up especially to suit the occasion. I am very pleased with the outcome, but I know that Versace's work will always be stunning.

Who are your favourite designers?
My favourite as I said before would have to be Versace. I think her work is just amazing. She provides for all occasions and everything she does will be stunning. I think one of the pros to working with Donnatella is that she knows me, and my body. She can design clothes that will suit me and she knows my different tastes.

How would you describe your style?
My style is not set, I like to experiment with different looks. When shooting the video 'Jenny from the Block' my clothes were more casual and not as dressy. But when I'm going to a premiere I will like to dress up in a beautifully made, elegant gown. I like to be up-to-date with fashion trends, but I also like to have my own style. I dress according to what suits me because I know how to make the best of my figure.

What was the most fashionable era?
I think the era we're in at the moment is very fashionable, because as well as new trends being about, there are styles from past decades eg. 60's and 80s style. There is also vintage clothing making a comeback. I really enjoy keeping up-to-date. Even if some of the clothes I wouldn't wear, I like to see what is on the catwalks each season.

What was the least fashionable era?
I wouldn't say that one era in particular was particularly bad, because there are usually so many styles going around you are likely to find something you will like. I think the neon colours and leg warmers of the 80s were a bit dodgy, but some people suit that look. It just wasn't for me.

What item can you not live without?
I can't think of one item that really stands out to me that I couldn't live without. I always like to have a good supply of evening dresses in case a premiere or party turns up at late notice. I usually would be quite prepared though. My favourite 'comfort clothes' are my velour tracksuits. They are so comfy and the velour is so soft on my skin, so I suppose I would hate to be without them for my comfy days in.

Are accessories important?
I love to accessorise, I think it can really finish off a look in an outfit. I love diamonds and can't get enough of them. What they say is true in my case, 'Diamonds are a Girl's Best Friend!' I love hats too, they can complete a look by giving it a certain edge. I think when accessorising you have to be careful, it is OK to personalise but not to go overboard with mis-matching colours.

Jayne Cluff (14)
Ballyclare High School, Ballyclare

A Day In The Life Of A £5 Note

It's 7.15am and I've just been handed over in Mace for someone buying bacon and eggs for their breakfast fry up. Now I'm sitting in the cash register beside £2 coins and £10 notes. Before long, I'm handed over to someone in their change who was buying a morning newspaper. I've been straightened out and have been slipped inside their pink purse. Now I'm being handed over for their bus fare to go to Belfast. Almost straight away someone with black, grubby hands has snatched me up and crumpled me in their back pocket. I'm squished as they sit down. 'My car's broken down; I'll be a bit late Rob.' I hear him say as he talks on the phone.

After what seems like a lifetime, the grubby hands pull me out of their back pocket after I'd just about got comfortable. The hands try effortlessly to shove me into a slot of a Mars bar machine. The man curses and shouts as he pulls me out again with a big rip in the middle. Instead he hands me over for a McDonald's. He's ordered a Big Mac Meal and a McFlurry. Now I'm being given to quite a large woman with a little boy. She's holding on her tray a Happy Meal and a burger. First she puts me into her big red purse but after she sits down I'm changing hands again. 'Here you go Jimmy, your monthly £5 pocket money. Remember to put it in your money box when we get home.'

The greasy hands put me into their Action Man wallet. When they get home Jimmy slots me into his piggy bank where I'll lie with other coins waiting to change hands again.

Sarah Tilbury (14)
Ballyclare High School, Ballyclare

A Day In The Life Of A Pair Of Trainers

Today's the big day. We've been practising for weeks now. We've been out in rain, snow, sun and hail; I have been dragged through the mud and had a big adventure in a machine afterwards.

I see the light as the wardrobe is opened, I am awakened and ready to go. I am placed onto a pair of feet, my master's whom I adore. I have overheard people saying that I am very comfortable but I must say it took me a while to get used to a pair of feet squeezed into me but now I have taken to them as a duck takes to water.

We are at the startling line for the big race. I believe it is the 1,500 metres. I crouch down and get ready to run like I've never run before, well my master is anyhow. I hear a bang and we're off. We're not in the lead. There is a stone but, too late, we have tripped. I feel the same depressed feeling as when my master trod me through a sticky mess and had to poke at me with a stick to get it off me.

We are shaken but not stirred. We're not out of the race yet but we've got a bit of catching up to do. This gives us more determination to win the gold medal. We run past the Hi-tech trainers, we're in third place now and it's only the last 100 metres left; we're still in with a chance. We come into second place so there's only one other person to pass. At the last second, we just take over but it is so close we will have to see a re-run to see who has won.

It's us, we've won! I feel so triumphant and have done my master proud.

Catherine Vennard (14)
Ballyclare High School, Ballyclare

An Irish Legend

CuChulain was an Irish version of the Incredible Hulk, terrifying, with rage; yet who returns, when the need for anger has passed, to a gentle and sensitive mortal. His name at birth was Setanta. Setanta was the nephew of King Conor of Ulster, son of his sister Dechtire, and it is said that his father was the sky god, Lugh.

King Conor was invited to a banquet at the house of Culain, a blacksmith and he asked Setanta to accompany him. Setanta was playing a game of hurling at the time and said he would follow his uncle shortly.

When the guests were seated at the feast, Culain asked the king if all the expected guests had arrived and King Conor replied that they had, forgetting about Setanta. Culain unchained his huge hound to guard the house. Unaware of the danger ahead, the young boy arrived at Culain's house. The vicious dog leapt at Setanta, who had only his hurling stick and ball with him. Undaunted by the ferocious beast the boy flung the ball down the animal's throat. The hound was forced back by the blow and Setanta was able to grab the hound by its legs and smash its head on the stone courtyard.

When Conor heard the hound howling he remembered Setanta and ran outside expecting to find him torn to pieces. He was amazed to see him unharmed, standing above the dead hound. The blacksmith, Culain was distraught on the sight of his fallen dog. Setanta, although without blame in the duel, vowed to take the place of the dog, protecting the pass into Ulster, and became the hound of Culain - CuCuhulain, pronounced 'Koo hoo lin'.

Philip Saunderson (14)
Ballyclare High School, Ballyclare

A Day In The Life Of An Astronaut

Dear Diary,

Today was a big day for me. It was going to be my first time in space and to prove that all that training has paid off. I was wired to the moon but excited. I could barely hold it in. I couldn't sleep the night before but I tried everything, including counting sheep. Eventually I got to sleep but I don't know how. I woke up early and went for a run. To try and let some steam off, I had breakfast and the rest of the day flew by until 1 o'clock when I was to get ready.

Take-off was scheduled for 1515 hours. I was staying on the site with the rest of the astronauts. The nerves were building up in everyone, especially me. I was ready and given a final call before I made my way to the shuttle. I was given a few minutes with my family before I went up. I couldn't bear it, it was so harsh. Then the rest of the astronauts and I made our way out to the bus which would take us up to the take-off pad.

It was like something out of the movies, walking out to the bus in a straight line beside each other. I felt so proud. My dream had come true. It felt like it took forever to get to the bus and going up to the take-off pad was even worse. I thought I would never get there. We got off the bus and made our way up to the shuttle. We were strapped in and ready to go.

'10, 9, 8, 7, 6, 5, 4, 3, 2, 1 - Houston we have lift-off.'

Those were the last words I heard before we took off. *Oh my God!* I was in space. I couldn't believe it, it was amazing. A sight every person on Earth should see. It was like a sea of black speckled with white snowflakes. I couldn't believe it, this was the best thing I had ever done in my life. Our destination is some space station; I can't remember the name of it because I was too excited.

Adam Sharratt (14)
Ballyclare High School, Ballyclare

The Legend Of The Cat Demons

The legend goes that every night when the moon can be seen through the dark clouds, a pack of man-beasts, half men, and half cats patrol the Antrim Hills looking for meat, mainly from sheep, but for an unlucky few, people as well. It is argued about how they actually came to exist, but it is said that a great warrior king attacked the fortress of a mighty wizard. He almost succeeded but in a last desperate attempt to save his own life, he cursed the warrior kings army to become a creature of the animal kingdom. Many became worms, some became sparrows but the warrior king and his 2 generals managed to dodge the magic spell and became cat demons. They ravaged the castle and left only rubble in the aftermath, but the only person who knew how to retract the spell, the wizard, was killed during the fighting.

So now they roam the hills, immortal due to the wizard's curse. They have built their numbers up by scratching unknowing victims. It is unknown how great their numbers are, but it is said that they have somehow spread across the world. There are many rumours on how to kill these demons, but the primary one is to cut off its heads with a black sword that has the magic spell that will cure the wizard's curse. There are a chosen few, know as the Black Templars, dedicated to banishing these cat demons back to Hell.

James Spence (14)
Ballyclare High School, Ballyclare

A Day In The Life Of Adolph Hitler

10th June 1944

I wake up to the sounds of gunfire. The English, American and French have started early in the morning. The time is 4.26am. Sometimes I just wish that I had never started this war. Time is marching on, have to go and meet Eva Braun to talk about future plans. Eva and I are getting married on the 29th April 1945.

I heard that the soldiers have battled strongly against our opponents. I remember myself fighting in the First World War. I always wake up scared thinking that this could be my final day ever living on the Earth. I hate those Jews. I want to start a new world, the master race.

I am now off to see Paul van Hindenburg. It will be interesting to hear what he has to say about the war. I just wish we could win. I am thinking about what I should do if we should be defeated. I think that I may kill myself since I have put so much work into this war. Germany has been against this war ever since the Americans joined in. They say that we will never win because their country is so much larger than ours. Sometimes I even doubt myself as well.

The commander of the infantry told me that about one third of them have died. The English have a good way of warning everyone about an aircraft from our side. It is called a siren. I might introduce this to our country but for now I will just concentrate on winning the war.
Herr Hitler.

Emma Gault (11)
Ballyclare High School, Ballyclare

A Day In The Life Of Sweep

Hi, this is Sweep Kennedy here! Bet you have heard about me. The postmen talk a lot about me. Well I'll tell you about my pets. Their names are Grace, Maurice and Elizabeth. Grace is nearly 13. She runs for 20 miles each day after me just cos I stole a few sweets. So what?

Grace is also a good victim of mine. I pretend I am a good pup. She pats me. Then I bite her. Usually she laughs but sometimes she gets *mad* like the time I bit her ages ago and she still has the scar.

Grace throws tennis balls for me (which I love chasing). Elizabeth (mum) is 21 + *VAT.* I have to be nice to her or she won't feed me. Maurice (dad) is nice all the time. He lets me do *anything* I want and just pretends he doesn't notice.

Well, enough of all that - let's get on to the story!

7.30   Time to get up. Dad takes me out at this time *or else!*

8.00   Grace gets on this thing (it's called a bus or something).

11.00 Mum takes me outside to play.

12.00 Now I play inside while Mum cleans all those things called chairs (which I would love to bite) with a cloth. Once I borrowed the cloth and Mum shouted, 'Give me my duster back!' So I guess that white thing is 'a duster'.

16.00 Grace comes in and plays with me. Then she does something called homework which is not a very nice thing and she complains a lot about having it. Once I helped by shredding it but she didn't like that.

18.30 Tea time. Best part of the day. Especially when the family are in a good mood.

21.30 Walkies. I'm dragged up from my lovely pup nap to go for a walk in the cold.

22.30 Phew! Bedtime. I love my bed a lot. I sleep well until morning . . .

Grace Kennedy (12)
Ballyclare High School, Ballyclare

Loch Ness Monster

I was out on a boat with my friend in the middle of Loch Ness. There was barely a ripple on the water's surface. Everything was so calm. We had heard the stories and were out now to see if we could spot anything for ourselves.

As I was looking out across to land I felt a nudge on my back. It was my friend. 'Turn around,' she managed to say in a whisper. As I turned I noticed why she was quiet, there looming above the water, disturbing the water, was a dark, huge shape. It was what we had come for. I knew what it was. A hump rose up and a long, thin neck appeared. The creature reminded me of a camel because of that hump. It was 100m away but it seemed like a mountain to me. It must have been about 25ft in length. My friend and I sat mesmerised by it. We hardly dared to breathe.

All too suddenly, it disappeared. It thrashed its tail and slowly began to sink underneath the murky, deep water. It was gone. We were silent and began to row back to shore so we could tell our tale. We had witnessed what many had done before us. There had been sightings of this and there had been many pictures. It had caught the public's imagination since those sightings and had caught ours too. What we had seen was the Loch Ness monster!

Julie McCormick (15)
Ballyclare High School, Ballyclare

The Chinese Dragon

Most of us have come to know and are familiar to the concept of dragons being 'fire-breathing' creatures. To the Chinese, dragons are water gods.

In Chinese mythology there are five types of dragon:-
1. Those which guard the gods and emperors,
2. Those which control the wind and rain,
3. Earthly dragons which deepened the rivers and seas,
4. Guardians of hidden treasure
5. The first dragon.

The first dragon appeared to the mythical emperor Fu-hsi, and filled the hole in the sky made by the monster Kung Kung. Its waking, sleeping and breathing was thought to determine day and night, the seasons and weather.

They are divine mythical creatures which grant humanity, prosperity and good fortune. This is the reason as to why the dragon has become the emblem of royalty the good emperor whose wisdom assured the well being of his subjects. Any sighting of a dragon during a particular ruler's reign boded well, for it meant that heaven was pleased with the job he was doing. The Chinese dragon has four claws as standard, but the Imperial dragon has five, this is to identify it above the lesser classes. Anyone other than the emperor using the 5 claw design was put to death.

Unlike their fearsome western cousins everything associated with the Chinese dragon is said to be blessed. To the Chinese those born under the Chinese zodiac of the dragon are thought to enjoy health, wealth and live a long life.

Emma Montgomery (15)
Ballyclare High School, Ballyclare

The Trojan Horse

There was a huge battle between the warriors of Greece and the people of Troy. Prince Paris from Troy had stolen away the Greek queen, Helen. The Greek warriors set sail for Troy to fight for their queen. To this day, Helen's face is said to be 'the face that launched a thousand ships'.

The battle outside Troy raged for ten years. Athene, goddess of war, gave Ulysses an idea for a plan to end the war. They built a big wooden horse which they put in the middle of their encampment. Next, they pretended to abandon their camp. In reality many soldiers hid inside the wooden horse.

Once they thought the camp had been abandoned the Trojans went out to check. They needed to know if the war was really over. They walked through the abandoned encampment and eventually found the wooden horse. They could not decide what it was. Some wanted to take it into the city, others thought that it was a gift to Zeus and feared touching or moving it in fear of upsetting Zeus.

In the end, they pulled it into the city.

A huge celebration started. The city was free from war for the first time in 10 years. Everybody feasted, drank and danced until eventually they all fell asleep.

This was the moment that the wooden horse opened and out crept Ulysses and all of his men. They killed the sleeping troops, rescued Queen Helen, met up with the rest of their army and set sail for home.

The story of the return journey is told in The Odyssey, a collection of poems piecing it together from the many different places where the events took place.

Emma Wilson (14)
Ballyclare High School, Ballyclare

Pippi Longstocking

Where did you get the outfit you are wearing today?

I got my boots from an army surplus store and my T-shirt from a charity shop. I made my pinafore from a bed sheet with a napkin for a pocket. My stockings are from two different pairs as my horse acquired a taste for stripes at one stage last year.

What are your favourite shops?

Army stores and charity shops. They sell stuff I love and are cheap too.

How would you describe your style?

I don't really follow fashion. I like to wear clothes that are comfortable when I practise my weight lifting. I would say my style could be all the rage next year.

What is your favourite fashion era?

The 60s are definitely my favourite fashion era. I love the loose, short dresses; I used to have a black and white one, which, after the 19th hole, had to be given to my monkey as a blanket.

What is your least favourite fashion era?

The era which had all the tight fitted dresses. They are much too feminine for me. The one with all the frilly bits and layered stuff. I think it was the Victorian era, I don't know how long it would have taken them to get dressed. They were probably lucky if they got to the table in time for the after dinner mints.

Who, in your view, are the best and worst dressed celebrities?

I quite like the way Björk dresses, very uniquely. My worst dressed celebrity is probably Victoria Beckham. I have never seen her in tops or clothes that are not fitted tightly around her chest.

Do you think accessories are necessary?

Apart from my horse and weight lifting equipment, no. Necklaces especially, are so awkward when tree climbing.

Amy Camlin (13)
Ballyclare High School, Ballyclare

Class Reunion

It was a cold night in September and the trees outside Walter Baylor's mansion were rustling up against the window of his bedroom. He awoke from his bed, turned around and looked at the clock.

'Oh damn it, another 16 hours rattling around in this huge house all on my own. Even the mice have left me because there's nothing to do. If only I was to be invited to something good.'

Just as he spoke he heard the post box shut. 'Oh goody, the mailman has arrived. Let's see what he's brought me. Bills, bills, bills, bills, oh hang on. This one has got a stamp from my old school on the front. I'll open it and see.

'Dear Walter Baylor of Miss Twirler's class. You are invited to a night of mirth and mayhem with some of the past pupils of Lizzie Borden High School. Friday 27th September at 7pm. Do not be late'.

'Hey wait a minute, that's tonight. I can't wait. I wonder if I should put on my groove shoes?'

Later that night he climbed into his Lamborghini and roared off up the road. Tammy Wynette was singing 'Stand By Your Man' on Country FM and he was singing along at the top of his voice when all of a sudden a tractor came out from nowhere. It was too late; he hadn't a chance against a tractor so he veered left into a field. Not looking in front of him he hit an oak tree, wrapping the car around it.

The next morning a passer-by was walking his dog up a country lane when he heard loud music coming from a field nearby. He ran over and saw the Lamborghini absolutely written off, wrapped around a tree. He rushed over to see if there was anybody inside. Walter's corpse was laying slumped back with blood on the leather seats.

The passer-by ran to the nearest phone box to call the police. When they got there, there was nothing but a trail of warm red blood over the grass. Walter has yet to be found.

Graeme Farquhar (12)
Ballyclare High School, Ballyclare

A Day In The Life Of My Pony Sammy

Hello! I am Sammy and I live in a field with my friend Henry, I am brown and Henry is white. Because we live in the field we are very mucky. Henry loves being mucky.

In the morning at about 7am my pet, called Alison, comes out to feed me and Henry. We love our food and Alison loves to feed us. When I get to the gate Alison is there waiting for me and then I look at her, as if to say thank you for another day of care, food, water and attention. After I give her this look Alison will give me the bucket of meal and she will let me eat it.

Alison will then go into the house and start to get ready for school, when it is time for her to leave for school and she starts to walk out the lane, I watch her walking, and I let out a neigh as if to say bye-bye.

During the day, when Alison is at school, I spend most of my time eating the grass in my field and sometimes I sleep and rest. I always think about Alison, where she is and what she is doing.

At 4.15 Alison comes home from school and of course I have to let out another neigh to welcome her home. Alison disappears for a while, because she has to go into the house to get changed. After she has got changed she comes outside to ride me, bringing my saddle and bridle with her, Alison comes to the gate and puts my tack on. Alison brings me out for an hour's ride and it is so much fun. We go on long walks and trots around the countryside and when we come back home again she will put me into my field and take my tack off. I love getting out for rides. Alison will then go and get my bucket of meal and give it to me, but before she gives it to me I give her a big lick right down the side of her face. Alison loves to get licked.

It's night-time now, so I have to say bye, I will see my loving pet Alison again tomorrow morning with my bucket of food.

Alison Crothers (12)
Ballyclare High School, Ballyclare

A Day In The Life Of My Pony Snowy

Hello, my name is Snowy and I am a very pretty pony. My mistress is called Rosie and I think she is very nice, in fact she spoils me terribly by giving me apples and Polo mints, which her dad said will teach me to nibble and bite, but I think he is just jealous because he wants to eat them himself.

Today is Saturday and I am going to a show. I get fed my oats and hay earlier than usual, which doesn't annoy me one little bit but afterwards the most terrible thing happens to me, I have to get my mane and tail plaited, argh. Just when I feel like having a nap I am put in the horsebox and driven all round the countryside to get to the show.

When I get there I am brushed for what seems like hours to make my beautiful coat gleam (as if it needs it). Next they put black oil on my hooves to make them look more attractive and finally I get my bridle and saddle put on. Rosie rides me round the field for a while to get me warmed up, as she calls it. I enjoy this as I hear parents and children exclaim, 'What a lovely little pony!' Next Rosie's class is called into the ring. We have to parade round the ring showing off our movements, which involve walk, trot, canter and figures of eight. Rosie likes to canter everywhere but I prefer walking, as it's not as energetic.

Oh I can't believe it, our number has been called in first. We receive a red rosette and a big silver cup (which is not much use to me).

At last it's time for home and Rosie gives me extra special pats and hugs and even a juicy red apple. Yippee!

Rosie Ramsey (12)
Ballyclare High School, Ballyclare

A Day In The Life Of An Abandoned Baby

Hello my name is Emma. I am a year old.

This morning, when I wake up I am not in my room or even my house! I am in the middle of the woods. I cry and cry but no one comes. It is cold. I am hungry and scared. I am stuck in my car seat and I can't get out. Eventually someone comes, a girl of about 20 and her husband.

They take me to a big, busy place, I think I've been here before. There are lots of sick people here. Some old guy is here, he keeps poking me, opening my mouth and shining a light in my eyes. They call him 'Doctor'.

They finally get me a bottle of milk, but it doesn't taste the same.

They have taken me somewhere now. The sign says *Orphanage*. There are lots of kids here, some big, some small and some my age. They leave me with this mean old lady and say goodbye.

And you know what - I couldn't be happier to say goodbye to them!

It's great here. Much better than my old house, they used to keep me locked up in a freezing room with a tatty old blanket and a bottle of milk.

I've got lots of toys and friends. Even brand new unbroken crayons and just an hour ago I was given a lovely, soft teddy bear.

Just a couple of minutes ago one of my new friends, Martha, was taken away by some family. I'm scared that will happen to me too because I love it here so much. I want to stay here forever.

Oh no! The worst possible thing ever has happened! I've been adopted by the people who found me in the woods. I have to say goodbye to all my friends now and we only met a couple of hours ago. *Oh* this is horrible!

Kate Aisling Jones (11)
Ballyclare High School, Ballyclare

A Day In The Life Of A Love-Struck Girl

I go downstairs in the morning and tell my dad that I'm in love with a boy who's seventeen and goes to my school. He smiles and tells me not to be so stupid, that a child of twelve cannot possibly even know what love is.

Mornings are the hardest times, so I'm not going to talk about them anymore.

I go out of the house, walk down to the bus stop, praying to God that he'll be there. Finally the bus comes and I get on.

On the bus it seems that I can't keep my eyes off him. It's only when my friends give me a nudge and tell me not to stare that I take my eyes off him.

When we get to school, I take one last look at this gorgeous young man. I then hurry to my form room to have a chat with my friends and to find out what they did over the weekend. Whilst in class I can't seem to concentrate, I drift into a daydream about him and me, which is interrupted, very rudely, may I add, by the school bell ringing for lunchtime. We race to the caféteria and that's when I see him again. All my friends start saying my name when they know that I can see him and I can feel myself going redder and redder.

At the end of the day I get on the bus and to my horror see him and his girlfriend sitting on the back seat. Sometimes, I feel like she's mocking me, which is stupid because neither he nor her know that I exist. I love that boy with all my heart but no matter what, no one will believe that. If only he felt the same. I pray that some day he will.

Ruth Young (12)
Ballyclare High School, Ballyclare

A Day In The Life Of A Snowman

Christmas Day was the day I was born. The snow had been falling the night before as the children had been sleeping, waiting for the arrival of a special bearded man.

Well anyway, the children who created me are called David and Anne. David is nine years old and Anne is seven. They seem lovely compared to last year's. Last year's children kicked me over and I fell onto the road. You can probably guess what happened next, horrible even thinking about it.

Let me introduce myself. I'm Jack and the children think I look 'cool', no pun intended! I have coal for eyes and stones for my mouth. I have a large carrot and this is my nose. The children gave me their grandfather's pipe and Anne gave me her blue and green scarf. I also have a huge light brown coat which I wear as well.

I'm different from other people because I'm born almost every year. There is only one thing that is a weakness, to be in sunlight. When the sun comes out after the snow goes away, I slowly, over a period of a day or two, disintegrate from snow to water. This isn't a sad process because I know that next year I'll be born again and I'll look different, live somewhere different and have a different name.

Well I'm beginning to sweat and the sun's coming out, so here's to next year.

Ryan Glass (14)
Ballyclare High School, Ballyclare

Florizal

'What did you buy in town?' asked Jennie's mum.

'Oh just a few things,' she shouted as she ran up to her room. She had just gone into town with Lisa and Sam, her two best friends. She left all her bags sitting on her desk and went back downstairs. 'What's for dinner?' she asked when she walked into the kitchen.

'Soup,' answered her mother. 'So, did you have fun?' she asked.

'Yip! It was brilliant,' Jennie replied, 'Oh I bought you something,' Jennie left the room and ran upstairs to grab the pink Lush bag on her desk. But it wasn't there! She went over to her wardrobe and there it was sitting inside neatly tucked away. She opened the bag and screamed.

'What is it?' shouted her mother from downstairs.

'Oh nothing! I just tripped!' fibbed Jennie, as she looked into the bag and then she saw it. Sitting on top of a small purple soap was a little fairy.

'What are doing here?' she asked.

'Help me, I can't get out!' the small creature said.

'I will help you if you grant me three wishes,' said Jennie.

'I can't grant three, I can only grant one,' replied the fairy. 'My name is Florizal.'

After Jennie helped the little fairy out of the bag, she asked, 'Can I have my wish now?'

'Oh!' said Florizal, 'I said I could grant one wish, but never said it was your wish! It's my wish! and I wish I was out of here.' And she disappeared like a bubble burst and all that was left of Florizal was a little fairy dust.

Becky Archbold (12)
Ballyclare High School, Ballyclare

A Day In The Life Of My Rabbit Dazzle
And Her Sister Razzle

I woke up to a beautiful sunny and warm morning. My sister Razzle was, as usual, all jumpy and over-excited. It was pretty obvious she wanted to get out into our run.

'Oh! Look it's Rebekah. I'll bet she will let us out into the run,' shouted Razzle with excitement.

Rebekah came over and sure enough she opened our door and let us out into our run. Razzle grabbed her toy and took it out with her. She carries that toy everywhere.

Later, whilst I was quietly eating grass, I was hit on the head with something hard. 'Ow Razzle! That hurt.'

It was Razzle's toy. Things like that often happen.

For example one day when I was having a nap in our run, and Razzle being her normal self, was running up and down the run and doing flips and jumps, next thing I knew I was awoken by a bang and a thump as my sister had run into my side. 'Sorry,' Razzle said.

'That's okay, just be more careful next time.'

After Rebekah had come home from school, she came out and fed us. That was my favourite time of the day because I love to eat. Oh it looked lovely, there was a mixture of pellets and ordinary rabbit food, topped with treats like Alfalfa and natural hay treats and a juicy chunk of carrot on top.

This is the life, a nice big run, lots of toys and all our treats. A cosy bed and getting plenty of grass to eat when we go out into our run.

Rebekah Buchanan (12)
Ballyclare High School, Ballyclare

A Day In The Life Of Orlando Bloom

Thursday 25th March 2004.

I'm so wrecked, I had to get up at five o'clock this morning. We're back in the Caribbean shooting the second 'Pirates Of The Caribbean' film. It's quite good. Johnny liked it here so much when we were filming the first one, that he bought a house which cost about £2 million!

I had to spend about an hour in make-up, I get off easy though because Johnny and Geoffrey spend at least two hours in there!

Johnny had to steer the Black Pearl today. It's so funny watching him because he has no idea what he's doing. He's great to be around, he's always in a happy, messing about sort of mood.

Geoffrey and I had a sword fight and I got cut on the arm again! It wasn't too bad.

On Saturday it's the pirates day off. So Johnny, Mackenzie and me might go and chill for the day. Gore has some things for the special effects team to work on which will take all day.

I really love it down here but that doesn't mean that I'm going to rush out and buy a £2 million house or anything!

I'm so tired, I'm going to go to bed now, it's another early wake-up call in the morning, unfortunately!

Rebecca Hamilton (13)
Ballyclare High School, Ballyclare

A Day In The Life Of Homer Simpson

'Oh I love those lazy Saturdays. D'oh! it's Wednesday.'

Homer is three hours late for work. He runs down the stairs and shouts, 'Marge, where's my breakfast?'

Marge is already in the kitchen, cooking breakfast. He eats his breakfast and quickly jumps into the car and drives to work thinking of an explanation to tell Mr Burns. When he arrives at the power plant, he goes to Mr Burn's office, he knocks on the door and he hears Mr Burn's fragile voice say, 'Come in!'

Mr Burns yells, 'Who are you and what do you want?'

Homer replies, 'I'm Homer Simpson from Section 7G.'

'Why are you late?' yells Mr Burns.

'I - I - was taking my kids to school!'

Mr Burns says, 'Excuses, excuses, get out!'

Homer walks out of his office and walks down to his own office sulking with a box of twelve doughnuts to comfort himself.

After a few hours sleep Homer is wakened to the sound of, 'Homer you've won!'

'I've won what?' he asks.

'You've won a trip to London.'

Homer jumps up out of his seat and *runs* home to tell Marge and the kids.

A few weeks later the Simpson's arrive in London. Homer spots Busted and they invite him to a gig to be a backing singer, but they don't know that when he sings it's worse than a cat being strangled!

They arrive at the gig around 7pm and they get up on the stage with about two hundred people watching them and 200,000 people watching them from around the world.

When they start singing everyone yells because of the screeching of the microphones and they all ran out. Busted tell Homer not to go into a singing career too soon without ten years practise.

The Simpsons go sight-seeing, they visit the London Eye, Blue Water and then they go to Buckingham Palace where they meet Tony Blair.

Homer says to Marge that it was a real privilege to meet Mr Bean.

The Simpsons spend four days in London but are glad to return to 742 Evergreen Terrace, apart from Homer who is down at Moe's having a drink.

Stuart Crawford (12)
Ballyclare High School, Ballyclare

The Man In The School

It was late one Friday evening and I was on my way home from school. I'd just got home when I realised I'd left something important that I needed for that weekend in my locker.

So I waited until my mum got home from work, which was about 6 o'clock. Then we drove to the school.

I got out of the car and went into the school by myself. I walked upstairs to my locker and I was about to open it up when I heard a noise. The school was empty when I looked round so I lifted out the gear I needed and started walking back to the car. But then I heard the same noise again. I started walking towards the place that I'd heard the noise coming from and saw a small shadow. I thought I must have been seeing things so I just started going back and got in the car. I didn't bother to say anything to my mum because I thought it was just stupid.

That weekend, all I could think about was what I had seen, so I made a plan that on Monday night, after school, I would go back by myself and see if there really was something there.

Monday night came pretty quickly and I left at the same time as before, six o'clock, and made my way to the bus stop.

When I got to the school, I went to the same place - my locker, and waited for about five minutes. Then surprisingly enough, I heard it again, the same noise. This time I followed it to where it was coming from and saw something run round the corner. I quickly followed it wondering what it was! Just then I saw it run into a classroom. It was trapped, I slowly and carefully made my way towards it, shaking a bit. I took one look at it and saw that it was a man, so I sprinted out as fast as my legs would take me, away from the school and to this day I've never spoken of it again.

Matthew McKnight (13)
Belfast High School, Newtownabbey

The Escape

They were there. They've finally caught up with me. I could see their shadows getting darker and bigger just around the bend of the tunnel. I was drenched in foul sewage and was smeared with dirt.

Kevin was my sole companion and my loyal friend who had always been like a brother to me. All of a sudden he grabbed my shoulders firmly and forced me to turn to face him. He said in a shaky, but calm voice, 'You escape. There's no way that we can both get out of this mess. I'll hold them back as long as I can. Now go, *go!'*

Warm tears drizzled down my cheeks and I couldn't move. Everything became blurry because of the tears. Kevin too was in tears. But he shook me violently to get my conscience back. The sound of the faint police radio amplified and footsteps and splashes of water run through the tunnel. 'Please man, will you just go!' I felt a sharp, distinctive pain on my face and that woke me up from my devastation.

Slowly I ran, looking back at my partner. As I saw Kevin's body getting smaller, I watched him in the distance pulling his pistol out of his back pocket and cocking it. Still weeping softly, I wiped the dried tears from beneath my eyes with the palm of my hand.

I fell flat in the muck when I heard loud gunshots, but the gunshots ended after a few moments. Then a loud thump and a splash in the water echoed. I heard a distressed shout followed by a few deafening shots and replying fire. Fear overwhelmed my body and I jumped on to my feet. The sound of dogs barking added to my fright and boosted my sprint towards escape.

Around the corner I could just see the spotlights of sunshine shining through the drain. This inspired me to give everything, all I'd got to get out of there and run free. When I arrived near the drain, I spotted a rusty ladder leading to it.

'Look! He's there!' a SWAT officer yelled pointing his index finger at me. 'Shoot to kill!' As soon as he gave the command, his force of armed men fired a quick burst of lead, even before I could understand what he was saying.

Suddenly I felt a deep impact in my chest and I began to lose the tight grip I had with my fingers on the ladder - to freedom. It wasn't too long before I was lying on the cold concrete with sewage trickling past me.

The SWAT team surrounded me immediately and shone their blinding torches into my eyes. My chest squeezed drastically, making a challenge for me to keep breathing.

Everything went blurry and I felt coldness wrapping around my body. I felt no pain despite the fact that I was bleeding to death.

Am I going to die? I can't die yet - I don't want to die yet! But my eyelids feel so heavy and I can't keep them from closing. I fear this is going to be the end of me . . . I'm really sorry Kevin - please forgive me!

Sehyeon Kim (12)
Belfast High School, Newtownabbey

A Day In The Life Of A Homeless Person

I woke up this morning with an icy cold breeze on my face. *Time to tackle another day,* I thought to myself.

The hunger I was feeling was unbelievable because I didn't get to eat yesterday. I feel so helpless now. The pain in my arms and legs is nearly killing me.

It looks like another bad day again because there are lots of dark grey clouds above. Today I really need to eat and I only have £1.36 left, so I really need to start begging early today.

I went along High Street and got £1.70, I find that when it's a really cold day, people don't give you as much money.

With this money I went round to McDonald's and got myself some chips. These cost me £1, but it was worth it. They were lovely and warm and they really filled me up. After this I had £1.56 left. It's now 3 o'clock and I will start to find myself somewhere to sleep for the night.

I had been walking for forty-five minutes when I came across some toilets. I went in and had a good wash. I felt so refreshed because I haven't been able to wash for a few days. It sounds really bad but I can't help it!

As I was saying, I was just washing when a middle-aged woman came in and told me to get out! Well, I told her that she didn't own these toilets and just to have a good day! I've found out that I just have to stick up for myself.

So on I went and found myself a good sheltered doorway. By then it was half-past nine, so I settled down for the night ready to face another day tomorrow.

Claire Rea (13)
Belfast High School, Newtownabbey

Jack-In-The-Box

Yesterday morning a baby boy was found on a police woman's doorstep. The police woman was leaving her house at around 8am to go to work when she came across a cardboard box and inside was a little something wrapped in a blanket. At first the police woman, PC Eleanor Wilson, thought it was just a parcel but when she picked it up and unravelled the blanket she was amazed to find a little baby boy with a note beside him saying 'Please look after my little baby, Jack'.

Eleanor told us that when she found the baby he was freezing and he must have been sitting there all night. The police have appealed for witnesses to come forward and one woman was quoted as saying, 'I saw a young woman at around midnight walking up Eleanor's drive with some kind of package in her hands and at the time I thought nothing of it. She was about 16 years old with blonde hair and medium height'.

The police are now asking for anyone who knows of someone answering this description that has just had a newborn baby to pass the name on to them. The police have said they will not be pressing charges as this woman has possibly got family troubles with her parents or has got postnatal depression or some other illness.

The baby is staying at a foster home temporarily and if no one comes forward to the police the baby will be put up for adoption.

The police have had some cases like this in the past and nearly every time someone has come forward. So the police are hoping for the best in this case.

Hannah Scott (13)
Belfast High School, Newtownabbey

A Day In The Life Of A Cat

Ah . . . another day. Oh yum, chicken and milk for breakfast, brilliant! Umm, this milk is refreshing. That's me ready to go. My first journey every day is to next-door's huge flowerpot. It makes a great loo! The neighbours don't like it so I must be careful they're not around.

I feel like a walk. I know, I'll go to the building site. It's been great fun coming here since they started building because all the mice and shrews come out. I don't like to eat them. I just love to tease and play with them. Oh dear, here comes a fat man in a yellow coat. He doesn't look happy.

'Gerr off!' he grunts. I'd better scarper off home.

I feel like a sleep. The car bonnet looks comfy and warm, and will do nicely for a snooze.

'Hello puss.'

I would know that voice anywhere. It's the 'The Ginger Intruder' known as Marmalade. 'Hiss, get out of *my* garden.'

'I was just passing and I thought I'd drop in because you always have such good grub,' he smirks.

'Not for you, now back off or I'll pounce!'

'I've got other business but I'll be back puss!' he snarls.

I'm glad he's gone. Good, here comes that friendly little girl. I could do with cheering up. 'Miaow, miaow.'

'Hello little kitty,' she says as she strokes me.

'Purr, purr, that's so nice!'

'See you tomorrow,' she cheers.

Look, there's Snowflake my sister in the garden.

'Hey Snowflake.'

'Hi bro,' she replies, 'I just love lying in the afternoon sunshine. Wait, what's that? Oh how lovely, pigeons.'

'Let's play with them!'

Snowflake and I chase the birds out of our garden. She hits one with her paw and bites it.

'Stop Snowflake!' I cry.

Feathers are flying everywhere. Suddenly all is quiet. All I can see are a few bones and a bit of corn, which must have been in the bird's stomach. Snowflake looks satisfied with herself. Suddenly I hear a gruff voice from across the hedge. I hear him. Someone is missing! Oh no, it must be Mr Adams counting his pigeons. Oh heck, we'd better make ourselves scarce before he looks over and sees that it was us.

'Run Snowflake!'

I charge back to my doorstep and sprawl out. My owners will be home soon. It's been a long day and I'm ready to get into the house for some tuna fish and a long drink of cool milk. Then I can sleep beside the lovely warm burner of the heating system in the utility room. I think I'll just pull one of these towels off the washing line to lie on - at least until the adults get home from work! Then all that will change - no more sleeping inside for us. The lady will soon have us back outside again. Later we'll have supper and go to bed in the garage. Another day over. I wonder what tomorrow will bring? I think I'll visit the school around the corner for some lunch.

Lynsey Pritchard (12)
Belfast High School, Newtownabbey

Final Result

I woke up very early as I was so excited, but nervous at the same time. I jumped out of bed and walked swiftly down the hallway. Suddenly, right in front of my eyes I saw a letter addressed, *Michael McCullough.* I carefully tore away the paper and took the enclosed letter out. My eyes glanced towards the top right hand side and it said *Grade: B1.* I started jumping about and ran straight back upstairs to wake my mum. When I told her the news, her face lit up and she was so pleased with me.

After all that was over I picked up the phone and dialled the numbers of my friends and family and told them all my grades and what school I had been accepted into. Most of my friends had got As and that made me even happier because that meant that I wasn't going to be stuck in a school with none of my old friends.

All my family came over to my house later that day and gave me presents. In total I had made £105 which meant that I could buy the new bike I had always wanted. We then had a huge party with my favourite music playing and lots of sweets and sandwiches.

Later on that day my friends from primary school phoned me and asked me if I was willing to go out to the cinema. Of course I said yes and I set out on my way to their houses with £30 in my pocket, just in case I needed to buy anything.

Michael McCullough (13)
Belfast High School, Newtownabbey

A Day In The Life Of The Richest Man In The World (Bill Gates)

Have you ever wondered what it would be like to be the richest man in the world? I have, so today I am going to tell you what a typical day would be like for Bill Gates who started Microsoft (you know that programme on every single computer!)

It is 10am on Tuesday 23rd June 2004 and Bill's surround sound hi-fi starts to play Andrea Bocelli's classical music, as it does every morning to wake him (it is set every night by his butler).

He slowly climbs out of his four-poster bed at about 10.30am and gets into the silver lift at the other end of his room. He enters the dining room and one of his maids already has breakfast served for him (grapefruit followed by a fry-up). He then goes back upstairs in the lift and goes into his en-suite to have a shower in his gold and silver bathroom. Following that he chooses an outfit from his clothes room on the third floor. Today he picks a black suit, white shirt, red tie and black shoes because he has to attend a meeting at 3pm.

He is dressed by 12.30pm and he then goes out onto his private golf course with his wife to have a quiet, peaceful game of golf. After that he has lunch at 1.30pm which sometimes consists of fish or prawn salad and then pavlova for dessert.

He then plays a quick game of digital draughts. Then he gets into his white limousine and makes his way to his board meeting with the finance directors of Microsoft. His meeting lasts two hours so he is out by 5pm. At 5.30pm he has dinner, which can be anything from lobster to caviar.

For the rest of the night he usually relaxes by getting a massage, sitting in the jacuzzi or reading. He usually goes to bed after playing a digital game of chess on his computer and checking the closing price of Microsoft shares on Wall Street at 10pm.

Rebecca Neill (13)
Belfast High School, Newtownabbey

The Tribe That Triumphed

The tribe woke at dawn. Each morning they bathed at the river and then the men went to work. They would hunt until 10am and then come home for their first meal.

The women stayed at home with the children. This was not the easiest life to live, but the tribe liked it this way. There was only one thing that was making their life harder. White men were taking away their land. So, they had only one choice. To fight back.

At 11am, the men began to make their way down to the boundary of their once beautiful forest. They carried with them, spears and weapons. The white men had already begun.

'No,' the tribe chief shouted, 'stop white man!'

The white men just laughed from their machines.

'No,' he bellowed, 'white men not destroy Indian homes. We will fight white men.'

'You won't fight us.'

'Then white men go away.'

'No, what good is one person against all of us?' they laughed.

'My people are here and will help me,' he hollered. The white men laughed. 'Come my people,' shouted Kawi.

The white men watched in awe as hundreds upon hundreds of Indian men approached them carrying large spears.

'White men go now, or my people fight.'

Kawi smiled inside as the white men started up their machines and reversed away. He was proud of his tribe and his land was safe, at least for now. He knew eventually white men would take over, but he wasn't going to give up his land without a fight.

Amanda Ritchie (13)
Belfast High School, Newtownabbey

Dancing

Dancing, it's what I do; it's what I love. Every day I wake up, it's the first thing I think about. I am a student at the Royal Cambridge School of Dance. It's a boarding school and I love being here with all the other people as interested as me. We're taught many different styles of dance but I am majoring in three very different techniques: ballet, salsa and modern. Different forms of dance, yet they all have one thing in common, rhythm.

You have to have a smooth rhythm for ballet. You have to be in perfect timing which is hard when you have just woken up. Then there's salsa. My teacher and my dance partner say I have good rhythm for this type of dance. You also have to have a good partner that can move with you. You both need to reach each other's thoughts instead of their actions.

Now my favourite type of dance is modern, you can do so many different moves but it still looks good. Full turn and cat leap is my favourite move, bringing your feet up to your knees while you spin. We have modern last thing so I can practise it straight after.

If you'll excuse me I have to go to salsa. Mr Thatwit will kill me if I'm late again. I hope I have to do an example. I love performing!

Victoria Patton (13)
Belfast High School, Newtownabbey

The Day I Died

I woke up on Saturday morning; it was just like any other morning. Mum came in to my room and woke me up gently like she usually does. I looked out the window at the street below, Mr Marley from number two was cutting his grass as this was the first dry day we had had in a week. I jumped with joy as I realised what day it was. My best friend Nicola was having a birthday party today and I was invited. We were planning on going to the cinema and Pizza Hut then we were going to head back to her house and have a disco.

I ran downstairs to have my breakfast. Mum had already set it out. I was having bacon on toast. I gobbled my breakfast down as fast as I could. I ran back upstairs and began to get ready, the outfit I had chosen was really funky. I was wearing a black mini skirt and a white strap top. Mum put my hair up for me. I was all set to go, so I got Mum to drive me to the cinema.

When I arrived Nicola was already waiting with my other friends Gemma and Megan. We all walked into the cinema and decided to see 'Along Came Polly' a comedy film we had heard about. The film was really cool and I enjoyed it. We walked out of the cinema and decided to go for a walk before going to the Pizza Hut.

We walked down along the shore. The cool breeze off the sea was lovely. The sun was peeking through two large white clouds and was shining down on the sea making it glisten. We walked a little further then Megan's stomach started to rumble so we began to walk back towards Pizza Hut.

We walked back along a narrow path because it was a short cut back to the main road. I was walking behind everyone else. Then all of a sudden Megan (who had taken led file) shouted three and they all darted off in different directions. I decided to follow Gemma as she was heading towards the main road.

Gemma stood still and looked left and then right but I couldn't figure out why. I caught up with her and tapped her on the shoulder. Then she started to run again. By this point I was exhausted so I waited for a couple of minutes then started to run after her.

All of a sudden there was a screech of brakes and then I was thrown across the ground and landed with a large *thump.* At that split second I realised why Gemma had stopped. There was a small dirt track which only farmers used.

The next thing I remember was the smell of disinfectant and someone shouting in my ear, 'Shona, can you hear me?'

I tried to reply but I couldn't move my lips. I tried to move my arm but nothing happened. I suddenly realised I couldn't do anything.

My body was lying on a hospital bed, but I was kind of hovering above it. I looked down on myself and there was a large man who I didn't recognise shouting in my ear. My mum was sitting beside my bed crying and my dad was talking to the man saying, 'Doctor what has happened? Is she OK?'

The doctor answered, 'I'm afraid she's gone.' My mum cried some more and then I floated away. I wasn't heading to Heaven but I wasn't on Earth anymore. I was just lingering in a large, white open space filled with people but nobody spoke. I didn't know what to do. I didn't exist on Earth anymore and I didn't fit in here. That was when I decided to float back down to Earth and watch over my friends and family and that is exactly what I did. I am still just floating but at least I will be with my family.

Shona Mulholland (13)
Belfast High School, Newtownabbey

The Chase

I was sprinting as fast as I could, dodging trees, jumping over logs and ducking under branches. The footsteps were gaining on me, pounding through my head like loud beats on a drum. They created a sharp pain that pierced through my skull like a knife. My heart was beating faster and faster and I thought that any second now it would pop right out of my chest. My fists were clenched as though I was holding on the side of a cliff about to fall into a bottomless pit. The sweat on my forehead was dripping into my eyes. It started to get harder and harder to run. The wind was howling and holding me back. It was as if there was a wall in front of me preventing me from where I wanted to go.

I could see, in the distance, a light. I knew that if I could just get there I would be safe. I don't know how, but I knew I would be safe, away from the forest and free.

My legs were starting to get sore and I didn't know if I could go any further. I could hear loud panting in my ear. Suddenly without warning I felt my whole body launch forward. I had fallen. I must have tripped.

I rolled over and bending over me I saw a large, hairy figure baring its teeth. I was surrounded. Within an instant I was being handcuffed, manhandled and dragged away for a crime that I didn't commit.

Emma Murphy (13)
Belfast High School, Newtownabbey

Terrified

Hi, I'm Jane McCusker. It's exactly 7.59 now and any minute my alarm is going to go off, telling me it's Monday, telling me to get up, signalling another day of fear . . .

Ring, ring! No! It's Monday. I can't stand Mondays. I can't stand any day of the week, apart from Saturdays and Sundays. It's because of them, Sharon, Imelda and Sarah, the school bullies. No matter what day of the week it is, they're always there, standing right outside the school gate, waiting for me. Waiting to get me . . .

I drag myself out of bed, as slowly as possible, clutching every single bit of quilt I can reach, not letting go until it reaches the very end of my fingers. This is the part of every day which I hate. Morning. It means I'm going to have to face *them* again. It's awful. Really awful.

By the time I'm ready for school and walking down our garden path, surrounded by grass scattered with tiny daffodils and daisies since it's spring, I'm already ten minutes late for school but I don't care. Maybe they won't be there, maybe they'll have gone on into class, but my tiny bubble of hope is suddenly burst, *pang,* just like that. They *are* there, waiting for me. They're going to get me.

My stomach ties into lots and lots of tiny wee knots, my heart pumps faster and faster. I feel sick, like I'm about to vomit. I think to myself, *turn back Jane, turn back,* but my thoughts are suddenly interrupted by Sharon saying, 'Oh look, it's Jane the pain!' Her two accomplices, Sarah and Imelda, splutter with laughter. Those horrible, evil, cackly, witch-like laughs. What am I on about?

They already *are* witches! Anyway, I can't take it any more. My stomach bubbles with rage, my face turns bright red with fury. I march toward them, my flat rubber school shoes making a horrible *thwack* sound on the pavement. I stop. Right in front of them, face-to-face with Sharon. They look at me weirdly, as if they can tell I'm angry. I'm sure there's steam coming out of my ears. They're smirking, all three of them.

All of a sudden, my brain seems to be taking over my actions, because before I know it, I'm raising my trembling hand higher and higher and then I slap her. *Smack!* I've hit Sharon. The toughest, bravest, most courageous one of them all. The smirk vanishes from her face. The smirk vanishes from Imelda and Sarah's face too. They look at me, their expressions becoming fiercer and fiercer, angrier and angrier. Uh-oh! I'm for it now . . .

Emma O'Neill (13)
Belfast High School, Newtownabbey

The Jockeys

In the USA not such a long time ago, there was a man called Bob. Bob was a poor man. He looked after horses for a rich farmer who travelled a lot. He didn't make a lot of money from this, so he sold horse manure to gardeners and farmers.

One day the rich farmer came to Bob and told him he was going to emigrate to Jamaica. When Bob heard this, he didn't know what to do. He was scared, sad and also angry at the rich farmer. Then the rich farmer told Bob that horses were illegal in the part of Jamaica he was moving to and he wondered if Bob would like a horse. Bob chose his favourite horse Betty. Betty was a strong horse and her dung was full of minerals for growing plants.

The rich farmer moved to Jamaica and Bob was left with Betty. When Bob saw Betty run, he was shocked at how fast she was. He thought that maybe he could race her, so he bought a saddle and all the other gear (which I don't know the name of) and he entered her in a race.

Betty didn't win her first race, probably because she never left the starting gate! Bob had wasted a lot of money getting her trained so he entered Betty in another race. Bob knew Betty was nervous so he gave her a new hard look and spray painted her red with 'Betty' written in black.

When they turned up at the racecourse, everybody was looking at Bob and Betty. Bob didn't care, he knew she would win the race and he would be laughing at them. Then when Betty won the race by miles, Bob pointed and laughed at the little five-feet men.

Bob became very rich as Betty won race after race. Then she soon qualified to compete in the State Championship. The prize was $50,000 so if Betty won this, all Bob's financial problems would go away, and he could buy what he'd always wanted, a smoothie maker.

Bob and Betty went into the gate and waited for the race to start. All the other jockeys were smaller than him; some of them could only be four-feet high.

The race started and Betty was winning but another jockey was close. Then suddenly Betty had a sudden burst of speed for the home straight and they won the race. Bob went to the podium to receive a trophy and cheque for $50,000. Bob left Betty in the stables and tried to get away from the people trying to ask him questions. Then a jockey invited him into the jockey's lounge. He followed him and when he opened the door, he wasn't there! A hand came out of a hole in the wall and pulled him into the small hole. It was a slide which went on for ten minutes and it ended up in an underground forest of weird-shaped trees, with doors and windows in them.

There were lots of little people walking about with pointed ears and with green Santa hats on. They looked a lot like Leprechauns. Bob asked, 'Who are you people?' Then they sang, 'We're the Jockeys, Jockeys are we and we live underground in a fibreglass tree.'

Bob asked them what they wanted; then they moved out of the way to reveal the head Jockey. He was scary-looking. His ears were bigger than his head, his lips were so big he could barely talk and his fringe was about a metre long and stuck out straight ahead of him - it looked like it was metal because it was so straight.

Then a Jockey brought him a stand for his hair and the head Jockey said to Bob, 'Your horse must lose the next championship or we will eat your brain.'

Bob agreed only because he wanted to get out of there. So they threw him out of the hole which ended right outside the stables.

When the next championship race came around, the rich farmer came back and wanted to see Bob race Betty. If he didn't win the race then the rich farmer would take back Betty, but if he did win the race, the murderous trolls aka Jockeys, would eat his brain.

When the race started, the Jockeys were whipping him instead of their horses. Then Betty ran faster than she'd ever run before and after he finished, he got off the horse and kept running until he got away.

He tied a rope across the street and waited for the Jockeys to come. When they did, they didn't see the rope so they ran into it and fell off their horses. Bob put them all into a plastic bag and threw them into the river and watched them float away downstream, into the sea.

Then he went back into the Jockey's forest to find the big-eyed Jockey. When he got there he hid behind a fibreglass tree. Bob saw them arming themselves to get back at him. Bob could not run from all the Jockeys, there were too many of them. A new day had arrived. The war between Jockeys and men.

Peter Mackey (13)
Belfast High School, Newtownabbey

Return Of The Jockeys

(A sequel to 'The Jockeys' by Peter Mackey)

It was a hot summer's day and Bob was out in the fields, working for the rich farmer. His horse, Betty, was galloping around the field in her leather jacket, enjoying the fresh air. Bob used to be a poor man, working to buy food and decent clothes. But now he was very well off, and had a lot of money. He had won the money in a horse racing tournament the previous year, with Betty, in which he won fifty thousand dollars. He had since retired from horse riding to begin a quiet life.

He was packing up to go home when he heard something very familiar, that made him freeze.

'We are the Jockeys, the Jockeys are we . . .'

He suddenly remembered the time last year, when he had ended up in an underground land and told that he must lose the race. Little people called Jockeys, with big pointed ears and green hats had taken him there. They sang their Jockey song, then let him go. He had then put all of the Jockeys in a plastic bag and left them in the river to float away.

'. . . We live underground in a fibreglass tree.'

He could hear the Jockeys calling out their song in the distance. He called Betty over and they both ran as fast as they could. He heard a whistling sound behind him. He looked up and saw something fall out of the air and land in front of them. It was a large stick of dynamite. They turned and ran in the opposite direction. They suddenly saw that an army of little Jockeys were coming in that direction. They turned again. More Jockeys. They were surrounded.

'Leave us alone, you midgets!' shouted Bob.

'We are the Jockeys, the Jockeys are we. We live underground in a fibreglass tree,' sang the Jockeys, as they all pulled out massive shiny guns. They pointed the guns at Bob and Betty. Bob pulled out his mobile phone. The Jockeys thought that it was a weapon, so they all fired their plasma guns at Bob and Betty. They ran as fast as they could, back to the farmer's house.

Bob was calling the human jockeys to come and help. He put the phone back in his pocket and ran into the farmer's house. The farmer told them that the human jockeys were on their way.

Soon the human jockeys were marching through the fields towards them. They took out their jockey whips and began to chase the Jockeys away. The farmer picked up his pitchfork and chased as well. The Jockeys all ran for their lives. But the head Jockey was still standing there. Bob remembered him from last year. His ears were bigger than his head and very spiky. His lips were so big that Bob was sure he could not talk. His hair stuck out three or more metres from his head, in a giant flick. He pulled out a giant hair comb and waved it at them threateningly. They ran at them with their jockey whips and he ran, like his Jockey friends, into the forest.

We people have all different stories of what happened next. Some say they just disappeared, never to be seen again. Some say they were horribly massacred and their bodies fed to the animals. But one thing is sure. The Jockeys were never seen again . . .

. . . at least, not yet.

Aaron Keys (13)
Belfast High School, Newtownabbey

A Day In The Life Of An Athlete

Ring, ring, ring, ring. I'm awoken from my peaceful weekend dreams to the dreaded sound of my alarm clock. I groan and switch it off. Turning over in bed I think to myself, *this is it.* The day I've been building up to for months has finally arrived. Getting out of bed I breathe a sigh of relief. Thank goodness I don't have sore muscles. I walk down the stairs slowly thinking about the day ahead. I go through the race in my mind as I force myself to eat a breakfast of Weetabix. Before I know it I'm in the car on my way to the running track.

The journey there is always the worst. A swarm of butterflies seem to have moved into my stomach but I'm trying to think positive thoughts. *You can win this,* I tell myself, *you're better than all the others. Yeah right,* I think again, *why are you even bothering to run? You could be warm in bed right now.* But I know I have to run, to prove something to myself.

Things get better when I arrive at the track. I spot loads of familiar faces all smiling and saying hello. I watch the other athletes participating in their events, but the butterflies seem to be turning into elephants. About half an hour before the race I go for a slow jog, then I go through my routine warm-ups - stretches, strides, high knees, flicks. I put on my running spikes, making sure they're tied up tightly. If one fell off it would be fatal!

Our race has been called and I line up at the starting line along with the other competitors. The gun sounds and we're off! After the first bend I'm in second place, the leader is a good bit in front of me but my coach is shouting at me to keep steady. We're into the final lap now, I'm in the lead but can I keep it up? *Come on,* I tell myself, *you're nearly there.* I go round the final bend and hear a massive cheer. I look up to my right and see all the other athletes from my school. I can hear my mum's encouraging cheers. I sprint into the finish. I've won! The rest of the day is great. I keep getting congratulated. But the major race is next Saturday. I've got to do it all over again. Well, I suppose that's just another day in the life of an athlete!

Rachel Ramsey (13)
Belfast High School, Newtownabbey

Day In The Life Of . . .

5.30am

Getting up this early has to be the worst bit about working as a doctor, also the mild hangover from last night doesn't help the situation much either. My breakfast was quick and tasteless, basic toast. A quick shower and shave wakes me up and gets me ready for work, I hope the traffic isn't too heavy.

5.45am

I'm on the way to work and there's some idiot in front of me that doesn't seem to have discovered the accelerator yet. I'll never to the Ulster hospital in time. I'm already walking on thin ice!

6.30am

I couldn't help myself and decided to stop off at McDonald's for a quick snack. *Why, why* can't I fight temptation? Only arriving now, I have two seconds approximately to get to the top floor for an operation in the theatre.

6.45am

I'm dead, I'm dead, I think to myself, *I'll never get there in time.*

6.47am

Boom! I busted down the doors of the theatre, I hear the sound of *deeeeeee* 'Good Lord, I've put the patient into shock!' I say aloud.
'He's got a severe lung blockage, we need to get him out of shock!' the head nurse informs me.
'Quick get the defibrillator!' I shout. The nurse gets me it, my heart is pumping. 'Come on, live, live!' I scream. I was on the verge of tears, it was all my fault! I got ready to give the patient another shock . . .

Karl Ewart (13)
Campbell College, Belfast

A Day In The Life Of My Grandad

Yet another Sunday morning and I am awoken by the radio at 7.30am. I lie in my bed listening to Radio 4 and especially to my favourite reporters John Humphreys and James Naughty. I have been working for fifty years and I'm very much used to waking up to the same routine every morning.

As the programme ends I make my decision to get out of bed for another day ahead. Every morning I find it harder to get up. I am beginning to ask myself a few questions. 'How is my hip today? Is the pain still there?' The operation hasn't been as successful as I had hoped for?'

On getting up I immediately put on my gardening clothes and go out to inspect the garden. I love the sight of flowers starting to bloom in the summer season. While I'm in the greenhouse I pick some ripe tomatoes and courgettes, next I water the plants and finally I feed the fish in the pond.

After a snack lunch I drive the car and go to visit my daughter Jayne and her family for tea. I am greeted with a warm reception from my daughter, son-in-law and grandchildren. After a delicious meal I decide that I better leave and get back to the house.

As I get back to the house I realise that it's very late so I decide to get washed and get ready for bed. What another fantastic day, can't wait until tomorrow.

Mark McLean (14)
Campbell College, Belfast

A Day In The Life Of Lance Armstrong

Lance Armstrong is one of the world's best cyclists and most famous for holding the record for winning the Tour de France six times in a row. He is also famous for his heroic battle against cancer, as statistics would prove him dead and yet he still made a full recovery and has gone on to win the Tour de France as well as other major World Cup races.

His daily routine starts around 6am, as he needs to be up before the rush hour traffic can interfere with his training. He states in his books he brings his own stitches with him, as he is knocked off so many times. As the Tour de France is his main event he focuses his whole year around it. Therefore he lives in Nice, close to many mountains that he will race up later in the year, although he's an American as he was born in Texas. The training can last up to five hours whether it's continuous repeats of climbing mountains at a gradient of up to fifteen percent or it can be a long 300 miles long cycle at fast speed.

Lance usually comes home around 11.00-11.30 in which he will have lunch and rest up for a few hours before he will go to the gym where he will train with the rest of his teammates, (United States Postal Service) this includes weight lifting using the spin bikes or going running.

Then at 4 o'clock, a tired and weary cyclist returns home to relax. Lance enjoys long afternoons enjoying the hot French sun or playing with his twin daughters and son.

For tea he will have a large carbohydrate dinner (like rice, pasta etc.) and then it is early to bed around 8 pm. He will get up the next day and do it all again.

The opening line of his book telling the story of his battle with cancer states, 'I want to die at one hundred years old with the American flag on my back and the star of Texas on my helmet'.

Stuart Brown (14)
Campbell College, Belfast

A Day In The Life Of . . .

Each day is the same for me. All I do is stand around, idly, watching the rest of the world go gradually by but I have no interest in what is happening around me, unless it somehow affects my way of life. In my universe, it is me that is the sun. All the other animals beside me; the lions, the giraffes and even the monkeys (oh I hate them so much) are just insignificant space matter which orbit around me. Everything revolves around me, *me, me!*

Today was just as boring as before. No, actually . . . to be perfectly honest . . . it was one of the most boring days of my long, meaningless life at the zoo (when I was free I always had something to do). During the early hours of the morning, I imagined my life prior to the prison. I saw the red sunlight on the horizon, the yellow evening sky and the dry, desert ground cracked around me. I saw my fellow pachyderms alongside. There would (I thought) be a future for me here, but that was not to be. It was a tragic tale, and I felt like I could cry.

Later, at about noon, came one of the only times at the zoo when I actually had to do anything at all which required staying conscious. Every animal used his or her 'acting experience' to entertain the onlookers. This is why I hate monkeys. They always steal the show in such a way that I'd have to walk on a tightrope to attract any attention.

When the day was over, the gates of the POW camp were bolted and the moon glistened overhead. My subconscious mind took me back to my African paradise, until the morning came once again.

Philip Erskine (14)
Campbell College, Belfast

Climbing

He climbed the mountain with a look of terror in his eyes, as it was a long way down and he could not see the bottom. He was alone; his 'friends' had already turned back telling him that it was impossible to climb, he refused to turn back. He was going to reach the summit against all odds. With every step upwards the fear was growing inside him. The ice-cold wind was nipping at the bare flesh of his face. The air was becoming thin and it was becoming increasingly difficult to breathe. With every breath he felt like turning back, but he was too far now to go back down, the summit was still a long way off but closer than the bottom. He had however nearly reached the ridge above him where he could rest.

He was able to conquer his fears, only by thinking about when he would finally reach the top. He ignored his nerves and the terrible pain of his exhausted body. He was so close now, about to reach the ridge above.

Suddenly he slipped, he feared for his life. Then he felt a sudden jolt, his safety rope had stopped him and he had fallen about ten metres and had been bashed against the rock an excruciating pain shot through his body. He recovered his footing and began to climb once again, his morale was broken but still he dragged his limp body upwards. On he went climbing, he had never felt a pain like this before and was convinced nobody else had.

Grant Montgomery (14)
Campbell College, Belfast

In The Forest

The innumerable branches whipped against my face, causing my eyes to flicker open and closed. I cautioned a look behind me and felt a shudder of pain sprint through my body. I stumbled and started to fall, my arms flailing madly behind me in an attempt to cushion the impact. They failed, and I lay there motionless, panting and bleeding slightly from the head.

I lay there for a moment, touching the wound gingerly in a vain attempt to stop the bleeding. I looked up at a massive trunk sticking out of an ancient looking oak. Ouch. My head was still spinning and the intense pain at the back of my head had still not subsided.

With a wince, I pushed myself to my elbows and looked around. I was in a massive clearing in the woods, closed in by a wall of leaves that almost no light could get through. I saw a massive tube about thirty metres away, gleaming in the small amount of light that did make it through. In the fall I had completely lost my bearings, and I scrambled to my feet and faced the object in question.

I stood there for a minute, but curiosity got the better of me, and I stumbled over to it.

It was long, cylindrical and divided into sections. The texture was slimy and scaly, and it spanned the entire clearing, at least fifty feet. Then, with dawning terror I realised what it was.

It was a snakeskin!

Conor Campbell (14)
Campbell College, Belfast

A Day In The Life Of A WWII Soldier

The boat was silent. The cold chill and the dark grey sky fitted the grim mood. The cold water was a deep grey and the cliffs above the beach, also grey. Ahead loomed the dreaded beach with the dark cliffs at the back. All that separated Captain Millar from these cliffs was the sea, the wooden obstructions known as hedgehogs and the place of death, the beach. Soon they would be dumped in the icy water. The time was upon them.

The door dropped open and the men ran out. The chill killed many but the guns killed more before they saw the beach. The sea turned red and the surf was orange. Men were drowning all around and shells dropped like wildfire. Men became shell-shocked and sank beneath the waves. The men struggled feverishly to rid themselves of their heavy packs. This was all in vain. Most men who succeeded in ridding themselves of the pack were shot to pieces.

It was like rain to the survivors. The hedgehogs splintered, the steel on the boats splintered and flew everywhere and the concrete blocks made a mist.

Disorientated, Millar climbed out of the icy deep and tried to hide behind a hedgehog. His friends were a blur and he heard nothing. That was when it happened. He sank beneath the waves like many before him. He saw nothing, he heard nothing, he died with nothing. The only consolation was that he died a hero on the field of heroes.

Patrick Gouk (14)
Campbell College, Belfast

A Day In The Life Of My Dog!

Just a bit more, squeeze and I am free! Stupid people think I need to go to the toilet and it's easy to get that itchy, horrible collar thing off.

OK! Freedom. Where to go! What to do! Oh! Birds, I love birds! Let's chase 'em! 'Bark! Bark!' Oh this is fun!

'Tess, Tess!' I can hear someone yelling. Silly people, I'm not going home till lunchtime. Now where did those birds go? Aw I lost them, hey, a river, I need a drink. 'Slurp . . . slurp . . .' Much better, I've been running for ages.

'Sniff, sniff,' I smell sheep! Or cows, I don't know but let's chase them anyway!

(20 minutes later) OK time to go home. What's that smell? Another dog! There it is and it's at *my* house. But wait, we can play! The other dog leapt forward onto my ball! *My ball*! I jumped on it and bit down hard, then I pulled on my ball, and pulled, and pulled, but the other dog wouldn't let go. She was really strong, just like me.

So we played some other games, chasing each other's tails until we were really, really dizzy, then wrestling and ball. We were just about to race when someone came out and said, 'Doogles, time to go!' So the other dog got into the car, it started and then pulled out of the drive. Oh no, I'm all on my own, Doogles, that's a nice name. OK, nothing to do, boring, oh birds, let's chase 'em!'

Jonathan McRoberts
Campbell College, Belfast

A Day In The Life Of Herman Maier

The season had gone well, I had raced faster than ever and came first in almost every competition. Stefan is still getting faster and my title as the best ski racer in the world could be under threat.

I was travelling down Acne Road on my motorcycle. *Beautiful trees,* I said to myself, glancing at the trees on my left, I turned my head round and suddenly slammed into a car at 50mph. The force of it sent me flying into the back of the car, legs first. The front wheel on my bike flew off, the handlebars and engine had been twisted and mangled. My leg stung to the bone and it wouldn't move, 'Help!'

It was a man in the car, he got out his mobile and it looked like he was ringing someone. A few men from the other cars behind me, tried to lift my bike, but it was too heavy.

'Are you alright?' one man said. What a stupid question.

'Can I have your autograph? said a boy who came running up to me.

'Hey, get back here!' yelled his father.

I couldn't believe it; my skiing career is probably over. All because of looking at the trees, all those races I've won, for nothing. I'm so angry and bitterly disappointed. My mum had said a long time ago, not to buy a bike, they are dangerous, I hate it when she's right!

Nico Butler (14)
Campbell College, Belfast

My Day In The Life Of Tony Blair

Dear Diary,

We are now officially at war with Iraq and have been for over a week. I have no regrets about going to war and sending British troops to the Gulf. I know I made the right decision and the Iraqi people will thank the United Kingdom and America when the war is over and Saddam will have been overthrown.

I feel awful about the innocent Iraqi civilians being killed by the falling bombs and I hope we can get aid to them as soon as possible. I also feel so sorry for the families of the heroic soldiers that have been killed in the fighting so far. Not many have died yet and I hope it stays this way.

I am getting extremely annoyed by the press. They are telling lies of why we went to war and a lot of people believe it. Saddam has killed many thousands of innocent people during his dictatorship and this must stop. His own people want him out of power so why should he not? He is an evil man. It is bad for the soldiers' morale when they see the British public are angry about being at war whilst they put their lives at risk. It makes the soldiers think why they do this.

Another reason why we are at war is because Saddam possesses weapons of mass destruction and he will not be afraid to use them in acts of terrorism against the world. We cannot let another atrocity such as September 11th happen again, it would devastate too many people's lives.

Nicky Watt (14)
Campbell College, Belfast

A Day In The Life Of A Siberian Tiger

I start the day striding through the snow, it's everywhere. It is quiet now, peaceful to the outsider. There were days when you would see many animals roaming the forest; those were the good days, the hills were teeming, alive with fun and laughter. That has changed now; there is much danger for all the animals of the forest, there are not many animals now anyway. The reason for this is the standing bears; they look like them but are much more deadly. They set deadly traps and have dart-firing sticks that make so much noise. They are so loud but they create total quiet, if you meet them you are sure to be dead, you can't outrun the darts they fire, only dodge them.

Once you're dead they take your fur. They are pure evil, their sole purpose in life is that total destruction of animals with value. I know they will come for us all some day it is not a question of if but when?

'Oh no!' They have seen me run faster than the wind, I run for dear sweet life. *Bang*! I have no chance now, I tumble and fall. I notice the all too well deadly quiet. Before I go I will tell you this. We are not theirs to kill, we are ourselves, you cannot tame us, we must be free; we will always be wild no matter what you do.

This is my final breath and with it I say goodbye dear, cruel world.

Chris Larmour (14)
Campbell College, Belfast

A Day In The Life Of A Dog

Most mornings when I wake up I go straight outside and mark my territory. But then the sun is just appearing, so I decide to scratch and bark at the door to wake the pack up. This is now always met with a good response - 'my man' comes down most mornings and starts yelling at me. 'The lady man' comes down, sprints around a lot and then leaves; I'm a bit confused by this. Then everyone else comes down but they all pay me little attention. Finally 'my man' feeds me but by the time I come back they have all gone.

After what seems like minutes the 'two little ones' come back and they play with me for a while which is great. Then 'boy' comes in and he runs around with me for ages, he cleans out my fortress and he gives some of his biscuits. The door slams shut, it's 'big girl' she doesn't like me, every time I go to greet her she screams and starts kicking me.

'The lady man' comes home shortly after the cubs but she sits in one seat for ages looking at pieces of paper, not paying me much attention.

Much later 'my man' comes home, I'm ecstatic and I start jumping up on him, he starts laughing and he then feeds me. Later on he puts on his trainers and we go for a great run. I love it because I get the chance to smell different things and mark my territory.

Chris Scott (14)
Campbell College, Belfast

Campbell College

On a normal school day, George Caley was able to glance through his mail at break. His mail consisted of the usual junk and the gas bill. Then he spotted something odd, a letter from his distant uncle, Sir Robert Caley. Robert was extremely rich from inventing the solar powered cell that the Earth will be so dependant on it the not so distant future.

'Dear George,

I am about to tell you something I have never told another living soul. When I was doing my research into the cell, I had a competitor, my once dear friend, Henry Martin. I couldn't let him do it, I had spent my life in this glorious crusade to find the answer. I was going to save the human race from their own destruction. It was going to be me, all me, no one else but me.

Henry had to be eliminated. I killed him. You must understand it had to be, it was the only way.

So I give you a choice, an awful choice, that I wish I had never made to happen. You can inherit the money and live a lie keeping my secret or you can do the honourable thing and die unrecognised and poor giving the invention to whom it really belongs. It is up to you now, dear nephew. Goodbye.

> Sir Robert Caley'.

George sat silently, almost mourning. He folded the letter into his pocket and cried.

Alexander Leitch (13)
Campbell College, Belfast

A Day In The Life Of Alex Ferguson

When people say it must be easy to manage a football team I have to disagree. I, Sir Alex Ferguson, probably the most successful manager in England, have been through everything possible to happen. I've had a heart scare, a pacemaker fitted, I made national headlines when I kicked a boot at David Beckham's head and I've just been fighting for a horse.

Today it wasn't made any easier for me. I arrived for training this morning and I found that some odd-looking boy had got in and was staring in awe at the players. He looked like a street child due to his bony body, his torn clothes and his dirty appearance.

I walked up to him and asked, 'How can we help you?'

He looked like he would explode with joy. After five minutes he announced, 'I am your number one fan and I will get your autographs!'

I was quite shocked and refused but then he proceeded to chain himself to the goalpost and announced he had no key.

'What are you doing?' I yelled. 'This won't help you.' As if things couldn't get any worse, he announced that if he didn't get what he wanted he'd kill himself.

At first I didn't believe him but he was clearly a nut so I couldn't take chances. I went in to ring the police while the lads calmed him down. When the police arrived and cut the chain he shouted abuse.

I don't really understand what happened today but I guess it's just another day in the life of Sir Alex Ferguson.

Mark Wilson (14)
Campbell College, Belfast

A Boy In Africa - 1866

It was the beginning of another day in Zambia, Africa. The sun was high in the sky and the birds were singing happily. However for Nambi, a young African boy, it was the beginning of yet another hard day of labour. His parents had both died when he was very young and so he was sold as a slave.

'Boy! Get up now,' boomed the voice of Chiumbo, the leader of the slave trade in Zambia. He was a small, round man with snow-white hair and bloodshot, droopy eyes. Chiumbo strongly resembled the look of a basset hound. Nambi was in a deep sleep dreaming about one day being free . . . *crack, crack* went Chimbo's long, dark, black whip across the thin back of Nambi. Immediately the boy shot up off the floor.

In tears Nambi said, 'Some day . . . I will be free!'

Chiumbo took no notice as he grabbed the skeleton-like Nambi by his hair and threw him outside. 'Now boy, get to work!'

Nambi struggled to pick up the spade, as he was weak. Nambi had a friend, Kamala, who was a year or two older than he. Kamala had suffered the same background as Nambi. Together they picked up their spades and started digging.

It was now the afternoon and the sun shone down on their backs. Every day was a survival.

All of a sudden in a confident voice Kamala said, 'Nambi, tonight we escape!'

Christopher Hill (13)
Campbell College, Belfast

The Cheetah

I'm Ka, a cheetah, and I live in Kenya with my two kids, Timon and Pumba. I'm three years old now and these two are my first litter, they are both about twelve weeks old and today they're going to eat their first bit of meat.

It is now about 2pm, time for lunch. I'm in the mood for hog today but I think that would be too tough for the kids, so it's going to have to be gazelle. At the moment Timon is trying to catch flies and Pumba is just lying around. 'Get up, it's lunchtime,' I tell them.

'Good, I'm really thirsty,' says Timon.

'You don't remember do you?' asks Pumba. 'We're having meat today.'

'Well remembered Pumba. Now follow me,' I say as I jog off into the grass.

A bit later I find the perfect place to approach from. The wind is blowing towards me and the herd is straight ahead. It takes fifteen minutes before I come within pouncing distance, there is a foal right in front of me. I bolt. It sees me coming but I catch it.

I call the kids over and at first they are reluctant but soon they are stuck in. Then I see some hyenas, so we just let them have it.

'That was a brilliant meal!' they both shout.

Michael Kinahan (13)
Campbell College, Belfast

The Battle Of The Planets

The Apollo 900 was lifting off at Houston, USA to launch a satellite. Meanwhile down on Mars the Orgbons were having a typical day. Then the Apollo 900 broke down and crashed on their houses. Their president was angry and blamed it on their arch rivals Venus. The Mars council got together and decided to invade Venus. The Orbon army marched off to their star ships.

Down on Venus the Venusians were partying. They were celebrating Queen Venus' 1025 years at the throne. Then there was a sudden cry of panic as Orgbon star ships started to land. The doors opened and out came the Orgbon soldiers. It was total chaos.

Meanwhile down on Earth Ryan Woods had just joined the army. He was sitting in his room when all of a sudden the general came in and said, 'Venus has called for help and we must answer!' Ryan marched out and saw everybody getting into a mini ship. A mini ship was small and could only hold one person. They flew to Venus and as soon as they got in range the Orgbons started firing. Ryan saw a hole, which the guards were guarding.

'Ryan,' said the general, 'get down that hole, we'll cover you.'

Ryan sped off. The firing distracted the guards and Ryan slipped in. He found lots of prisoners caged up. He found the keys and let them out. They ran out and got some weapons off the dead and started firing at the Orgbons. Then the mini ships stormed a castle and killed all the guards, then they rescued the queen.

Stephen Browne (12)
Campbell College, Belfast

The Legend Of Thor

The legend of Thor goes like this. Thor was a mightygod, he was immensely strong, strong enough to crush a boulder and as tall as a giant. He had long black hair in a ponytail and had a deep, booming voice like an ogre. Thor was known to wield a mighty hammer of lightning and he rode his lightning chariot with his mightyhorses, Storm and Thunder. They were meant to be the fastest horses in the Norse lands and Azgard.

His father was called Odin, Lord of Azgard. Azgard is the land of the Norse gods. There were about five minor gods, including Thor and about six major gods. There were rumours that Thor went into a den of giants and killed all of them in one monstrous blow. Thor soon went from a minor god to a major god and soon became popular amongst the other gods and humans and all species of animals in Azgard and in the Norse lands.

Soon, when Thor's father stepped down as Lord of Azgard, Thor took his place as the Lord of Azgard and he was the most powerful god in all of the Norse lands. Thor was even stronger than his father and all other gods. His horses Storm and Thunder, were even faster than before. Thor must have felt like he was on top of the world, bigger than every mountain in the world. He must have felt wild.

Lewis Howell (12)
Campbell College, Belfast

The Terrible Town

(In the style of Lemony Snicket)

If you are sitting in a comfy chair at the moment, ready to start a happy and fun story, then you'd better put this page down right away. This story starts nastily and finishes worse. So I'm afraid if you want to hear about fairies riding ponies then this isn't the story for you.

One day Flora, Bob and Sarah were going to town with their Uncle Monty. Apparently he wanted to buy wooden clothes hangers, which the Bombadair children thought was a bit unnecessary because Uncle Monty only had one outfit and he always wore it.

As they went into the shop they stared at all the odd items it sold. There was a thing that cut the top off eggs and then squirted the yolk out and there was an electronic vacuum cleaner. All of these items were completely unnecessary and their job could be done without a machine if people weren't so lazy.

So the Bombadair children decided to go and look at the unnecessary kitchen appliances while Uncle Monty got his hangers. As they looked, the Bombadairs found themselves daydreaming. Daydreaming, meaning to dream in the day, it's pretty self-explanatory really.

Anyway as they daydreamed they started to sort of drift towards the busy street outside and in a couple of seconds they were in the street and had no idea where they were.

As they searched, Flora tried to invent something that would fly them back to Uncle Monty and Bob tried to think of books that could help.

Sadly they never found Uncle Monty, but they did find a guitar and were made to busk for the rest of their lives, singing songs like, 'The Birdie Song' and 'YMCA' . . . I would rather die!

Josh Mackey (12)
Campbell College, Belfast

A Day In The Life Of A Lion

Today I was hunting with the pride when we came across an elephant, it had to be twenty times the size of me so we all tried to surround it without being seen. I was convinced we would be seen but we weren't until we attacked. It was hitting us all round with its massive tusks, fighting for its life until someone bit it right on the neck. The blood rushed out as the elephant lay down dying painfully. It was not until it was done that it hit me that it had friends and family as well. But you have to do it or you would die of starvation.

Once we had eaten we heard a loud bang from the trees and all of a sudden these humans started chasing us with sticks that made lots of noise. They chased us until we got tired. Why are they always after us, trying to kill us and our children? They killed three of the cubs today, luckily they didn't get any of mine but they still make me so angry. I just feel like going up to them and chopping them up into tiny little pieces. Why can't they pick on something their own size instead of our cubs? They are too weak to fight us without using those weird stick things and anyway, we had this land first so they should go back to where they came from.

Aaron Ferguson (11)
Campbell College, Belfast

My Trip To Anfield

As I walked up the stairs to the Kop with my dad, we heard many supporters talking about whom they thought would win and nearly everyone said Liverpool. When I saw the light to the pitch I didn't think it was real. The atmosphere was outstanding! The supporters cheered even though no one was actually on the pitch. I didn't think anything, my mouth was dry and my hands were shaking. The pitch was way bigger than on TV and I heard chants, roars and cheers. I felt like I was in a weird dream and it was just dramatic.

The first half was a scrappy, dull half with the ball mainly in the centre of the pitch. There was no real action or excitement as neither team went close. We played rubbish and if we kept it up we could lose.

The second half was pretty much the same as the first, scrappy and rubbish. Suddenly Liverpool hit Charlton Athletic on the counter-attack with ten seconds remaining. Steven Gerrard cleared the ball and left Michael Owen and Dean Kiely one on one. They got closer but Michael Owen somehow beat him and scored an open net. The crowd went insane as Owen scored. As soon as the referee blew the whistle we all ran onto the pitch. We were delighted as Liverpool won and got into the Champions League. We all cheered in delight. We sang songs until our voices were dead, it was a match to remember.

Richard Simpson (12)
Campbell College, Belfast

Belfast Telegraph

On Saturday 20th, a few boulders were knocked out of England's fortress, Twickenham, by the Irish, resulting in their most famous victory of all time.

As soon as the ball was kicked off, Ireland were up at England. The English team just couldn't stop the tide of green shirts washing over them. England then gave away a penalty, which was immediately kicked by O'Gara through the uprights for an early lead, 3-0 to Ireland, thanks to superb kicking by O'Gara.

As soon as England kicked off, Ireland were at them again harder than ever and moving towards the try line slowly. Then coming up to half-time Ireland scored again through O'Gara with another penalty.

At half-time the commentators were amazed with Ireland's performance, especially their line out.

The start of the second half looked to be exciting, with England scoring first with a converted try and then a penalty, but Ireland snatched it back with two penalties by O'Gara and then a try by Dempsey, converted again by O'Gara to make it 19-10 to Ireland. The last play of the game was when England got a penalty, which did not help much so the final score - Ireland 19 - England 13.

At the end of the match the Ireland players were ecstatic, along with the fans. According to the commentators, Ireland were the stronger side, with only one Ulster man on the pitch.

Adam Patton (12)
Campbell College, Belfast

A Day In The Life Of A Dog

Yesterday I was playing with Bob. Bob is my owner. He loves to play with me and I love to play with him.

Last night there was a storm. The storm was really bad and I was cold because I had no shelter because it had blown away in the wind and it was raining. I decided to run away to get shelter. I ran out to the road. As I was running I turned off the road and ran into the country. I kept running until I realised that I was lost. I felt sad because I thought that I would never see Bob again.

I kept running in all directions not knowing where I was going. But then I saw an opening, so I ran towards it and then I fell. I fell down a very steep slope, it seemed like it was never going to end until *thud!* I hit the ground. I hurt and cut my leg on a sharp stone. I felt sore when I started to walk. I had a limp and it really hurt. I walked until I got to a road. I lay down and slept until a car stopped. The person driving the car got out, he lifted me, wrapped me in a blanket and took me to the vet. The vet fixed my leg and then the man took me home after reading what was on my collar. When I saw Bob I felt really happy. Then the man told Bob all about my leg.

Alexander Hamilton (11)
Campbell College, Belfast

The Report
(In the style of Lemony Snicket)

Today there was a tragic accident in a small village in the capital of Northern Ireland, Belfast. The village was called Cherry Valley. Near the village there was a zoo for animals but this zoo was not for any old animals, this was a zoo for freak animals.

It was called 'The Zoo of Extraordinary Animals'. It was either the biggest or the smallest of an animal, or the heaviest or one of the lightest. It was like Noah's Ark. There were two animals in each cage. But yesterday something tragic happened.

One of the kids in the park started to pull faces at one of the giant gorillas. The giant gorilla went into a rage and started thumping his chest and yelling violently. By fluke one of the bars fell off. He jumped out of the steel cage and some of the animals were getting fed so they jumped out too. All of a sudden everybody in the park started running and screaming at the tops of their voices.

You heard people screaming, snakes hissing, gorillas shouting, elephants stomping and foxes and dogs howling, It was horrendous, there was non-stop yelling and screaming. Everybody was in so much shock that it was a while before anyone phoned the police. Sadly it was too late. By the time the ambulance got there it was tragic. Two people were dead and six were injured. All the animals were rounded up and the village almost lived happily ever after.

Conor Winning (12)
Campbell College, Belfast

2004 Renault Schools' Cup Final

This year's Renault Schools' Cup Final brought together Belfast school, Campbell College and country school, Royal School Armagh. Campbell College, outright winners 22 times, looked to extend that tally today with captain David Cobain, once a winner already. Royal School Armagh, last winners in 1977 beating MCB, look to regain the cup, coming behind captain John McCall, a current member of the U19s' Ireland squad. Campbell coach, Brian Robinson, capped 25 times for Ireland, looked optimistic to challenge Armagh's unbeaten run and to leave with the cup judging on his side's performances in the competition this year.

Kick-off began with Greer Winnington kicking into the physical pack of Armagh. Armagh played with pride and enthusiasm as the scoreboard told at half-time with two tries from Armagh centre, Allen Ethan and winger Jonathan Ruddock.

Gillespie kicked two superb conversions to give Armagh a lead of 14-0. The second half began very well for Campbell, putting continuous pressure on the Armagh back line. The breakthrough came for Campbell when winger Blair Clements produced a blinding break to put the first points on the scoreboard for Campbell. RS Armagh's head coach, David Eakin, has coached his side extremely well this year. Armagh's pack is extremely physical and well experienced, with six playing for Ulster's U17s and upwards, and two playing for Ireland schools.

The final whistle blew when breaking Campbell hearts and inflaming RS Armagh's pride regaining the cup for the first time in 27 years. Armagh supporters ran on to the field to congratulate their team for their achievements, before being awarded with the school's cup.

Jonathan Philpott (12)
Campbell College, Belfast

The Deadly Fall

I was beginning my preparation for my training in the RAF when I was called up to do a parachute jump. My name is Patrick. I have nearly completed my training and hope that I can become a full-on parachute jumping extraordinaire.

It was Friday 15th of February and it was a sunny, humid day at our ground in West Yorkshire. I was getting kitted out with all my necessary equipment and with my teammates I walked nervously over to our little jet plane. I was shaking and sweating frantically as I reached up to the plane. I then sat quietly in back bit of the plane and thought about what I was going to do. I looked out of the plane every so often to see how high we were and I noticed that all my teammates were nervous and scared.

We sat until the plane slowed in one place. I was about to jump out at 3,000 feet. I jumped and fell into the sky. I saw loads of clouds and all the distant fields and buildings. I got pulled by the force of the wind and flew right off course. I neared the end of my fall but I was in a lot of trouble. I heard the whoosh of the wind flying through my ears. I was about 600 feet from the ground. I then calmly pulled my cord. Nothing happened. I was 150 feet from the ground. I then knew that I was going to die in the most painful way!

Ben Craig (12)
Campbell College, Belfast

Ireland Vs Italy 6 Nations

Today there was a very exciting game at Lansdowne Road. After Ireland beat the world champions, England, this should have been an easy game against Italy. There were gale-force winds blowing across the pitch which made it difficult for both teams' kickers.

As the players came out of the changing rooms, the looks on their faces showed the determination that they wanted to win.

Ireland played well in the first half after a scrappy lineout by Italy, which went straight to Malcolm O'Kelly who scored Ireland's first try. Ronan O'Gara had a tricky conversion and he missed it. Italy were starting to fall behind after the famous O'Driscoll one-two to get Ireland's second try. The crowd went wild, I was nearly deaf. That made O'Driscoll Ireland's top scorer with 24 tries. Ronan O'Gara converted and he was happy. 12-0 to Ireland in the first half.

Ireland didn't play as well in the second half but they still fought on. Italy could have scored their first try but they just knocked it on and the crowd jumped on their seats. After the counter-attack by Italy, O'Gara made an excellent pass to Shane Horgan who got Ireland's third try. About 10 minutes from time, Brian O'Driscoll made a high tackle on Italy's scrum half, Fredrick Mechalck and he went to the sin bin. Italy finally scored a-plenty and the Italian crowd were really happy. That wiped the smile off the Irish. Final score Ireland 19-Italy 3. The Italian Job.

Paul Hunter (12)
Campbell College, Belfast

The Battle For Helm's Deep

(Based on 'The Lord of the Rings' by JRR Tolkien)

The sun rises over the eastern hills turning the sky blood-red. Banners flutter in the morning breeze, the white stag flying high above them all. Both men and horse alike are tense, they know they fight an unknown evil. Witches, goblins and trolls cackle mercilessly, thinking victory is surely theirs. The drum beats, the horses shiver and twitch nervously, the men draw their swords, they are all brave and willing to fight to the end.

One lone rider comes to the front of the line, a crown upon his head. He remembers what an old friend once said, 'Look to the west on the third day.' These words echoed across his mind, this was the third day and still nothing had come. He must give his men the courage to fight. 'My brothers, we have survived thus far, now we must fight and fight we shall.' His men let out a loud cheer as their king galloped down the line, 'On to battle and to victory!' he yelled.

The trumpet sounded. The men surged forward and metal clashed against metal. They fought late into the day until few remained, the field was soaked in blood. The king heard a horn blow and looked to the west. There he saw the white stag and upon it a rider, shining, clothed in white. The stag reared and surged forward, thousands more like it streamed down the hill. What ensued was chaos and then, silence. The battle for Helm's Deep was won. Victory was theirs.

Naomi Deering (13)
Carrickfergus Grammar School, Carrickfergus

Emily

She was called Emily and she was 12 years old. She was a poor child and had no parents. Emily lived with her grandparents. She had never been to school and didn't know much.

One day Emily woke up and found her granny had died in her sleep.

'Why did she die?' Emily asked.

'She died because she was ill and God wanted her back in Heaven,' her granda replied.

So that night Emily got all her possessions and put them in a bag with food and water.

'Goodnight!' Emily's granda shouted.

'Goodnight!' she replied.

When he finally went to sleep Emily left home to look for Heaven. After a couple of hours it got dark and Emily got very tired. Not long after she found an old cottage where she thought she could stay. Emily walked into the cottage and slept in an old, musty bed. While Emily was asleep she had a dream. In her dream she saw a church and down the aisle was a figure. Emily's granny.

Emily then woke up. It was morning. Emily set out for the church. After a day's travelling she found the church and saw the figure at the bottom of the aisle.

'Granny!' Emily screamed.

'Emily, I must tell you. I know you are looking for Heaven. It is in the sky and you are at home in your bed,' Emily's granny replied.

Emily woke up in her bed at home. She saw her granny sleeping. Emily smiled and went back to sleep.

Jessica Black (12)
Carrickfergus Grammar School, Carrickfergus

A Light In The Sky

It was a cloudy night, Tom couldn't sleep, so he got up. He gazed up at the moon which was staring back at him. Since he could remember it had been his dream to be an astronaut.

The next day he woke up from three hours sleep and walked downstairs to get his breakfast. At half-ten the phone rang. He answered it and a voice said, 'Hello Tom, I know that you have always wanted to come to space, so tonight at ten wait in your back garden for us.'

'Hello, hello, is anyone there?' Tom asked. He just ignored the phone call for the rest of the day.

When ten came Tom remembered about the call, he thought he might as well see what the call was about. So he walked outside. Suddenly a light started to shine. He looked up and saw two little purple men with three red eyes.

'Come with us now!' cried the alien.

'What! Who are you?' screamed Tom as the aliens dragged him off into the light which was a spaceship.

Tom was so scared that he fainted, but when he woke up he was in a silver room with the two aliens.

'Let me go home!' yelled Tom.

'Don't worry we just want to eat your brains!' explained the alien.

'Aarrgghh! Let me go home!' begged Tom.

Then the aliens started to chase him and . . .

'Tom, wake up it's half nine!' shouted Tom's mum.

Tom wondered, had it all just been a dream?

Leigh McClurg (12)
Carrickfergus Grammar School, Carrickfergus

The Hoard Of The Rings: How Much Is This Gold Thing Worth?

(Inspired by J R R Tolkien)

J R R Tolkien is not telling the truth, his books lie about the Hobbits and their names and houses, oh and the ignorance to even call all the creatures of the Shire Hobbits! First of all these creatures are called Bobbits and their homes don't have circular doors and square windows, they have circular windows and triangular doors. The reason or should I say 'real reason' for everyone to be fighting over a ring is simple, you can cash it in for a good million pounds or so. The reason that no one has ever done this is because they get killed on the way to the pawnbroker.

The current holder of this ring is Dado Goggins, who knows nothing, he received the ring from his uncle Bingo, who is too old to walk to the pawnbroker. Assisting Dado is his really stupid friend Ham-Dum-Gumgee and the great and powerful, Deep Wizard Gandeap, oh and I forgot Hairy and Dipin.

Astonishingly they are actually walking down the road that leads to the pawnbroker and are only a mile away. The bad thing is that the Dark Lord Salman is watching them but he is only an eye. Oh and I bet you are wondering where Gimli, Aragorn and Legolas are? They don't exist. Where was I, oh yes, they are walking down the road . . . when all of a sudden Holem, the skinny, bony, pink thing, attacked but he was too late and watched in horror as Dado held a million billion pounds in his hands!

David Stockard (12)
Carrickfergus Grammar School, Carrickfergus

Night Fright

'Bye,' said Amy leaving her aunt's house. She was making her way home through a murky forest when . . . *bang!* the car came to a halt, it was lifeless. Amy got out of the car and walked through the thick smoke to the engine. It was wrecked. Amy heard menacing noises around her. This made Amy feel uneasy. She looked round thinking someone was watching her. She gazed into the thick darkness trying to make sense of the unfamiliar shapes around her. Amy could see the skeleton trees laughing at her misfortune. Confused she rushed into her car to get her phone. Amy called help. 'Hello, my car has just broken down,' mumbled Amy, 'could you help?'

The woman on the phone replied, 'Of course, where are . . .' The phone went dead. What was Amy going to do now? She got out of her car and started walking along the road, which had worn away over the years. Amy turned round wondering whether she'd heard someone behind her. 'Hello . . . is anybody there?' whispered Amy into the darkness.

There was no reply.

The night was getting colder and Amy could only see a couple of feet in front of her. Tired, Amy sat down by a tree. She didn't have enough energy.

'Argh!' screamed Amy at the top of her lungs. These two big hands grabbed her not letting her go. 'Get off me!' yelled Amy.

Amy kicked it, which made it let go. Amy ran and ran not looking back!

Jessica Moore (12)
Carrickfergus Grammar School, Carrickfergus

A Day In The Life Of Tayter

Chapter 1 'The Harvest'

Hello, my name is Tayter and I live on a farm, but I don't exactly do anything, not that I'm lazy! It's just this, well, you wouldn't exactly call it a problem, it's just, I'm a potato.

Today started normally but the air seemed to be more chilly than usual and Mr Jackson the farmer seems very excited about something. After that I didn't see him for a while, but when I did, he was coming out of shed number 3. (Lightning crash). Suddenly it hit me, *Harvest Day!* Well that thought wasn't all that hit me, a dirty great big rake ripped me out of the ground. I felt Mr Jackson's hand, (which was colder than usual when he comes to inspect us), probably because the winter's coming. He wrapped his hand around my leaves and pulled them off.

Chapter 2 'The Processing'

After all that happened, I was taken to the market and put on a shelf. Another creature, that looked the same as Mr Jackson, lifted me and I was taken with lots of other potatoes to what I overheard was, a *factory*.

'We've heard rumours of what goes on in there,' some of the potatoes said. It was driving me mental (which is saying something for a being with no brain), all the screaming and moaning, and one of the guys was playing a harmonica made of dried grass.

Inside there were shapers and grillers and smashers and mashers and all sorts of torturing devices. We were split up and I went first into *El Splice and Slice* machine.

It was horrible, too disgusting to describe, and some of you readers could be eating while reading this, and I don't want you to see what you swallowed last again. When I came out I was 12 thin, neatly cut little pieces. And then came *the frying*.

It was a wonderful sensation, floating in half a gallon of oil, burning oil. After that I was put into a box with this sign on it, 'McDonald's'.

Chapter 3 'The Eating'

It was disgusting. Only 3 words could describe it.
Snarf!
Gobble!
Grunt!

David McClenaghan (11)
Carrickfergus Grammar School, Carrickfergus

Disaster Strikes Again!

Early this morning, disaster struck in the form of what is said to be the biggest earthquake ever to hit the Earth. It started in the streets of Detroit around 7.30am this morning and is said to have killed hundreds of people with many more still trapped under the rubble.

Firefighters have had to deal with a wild fire caused by the earthquake while it rumbled round the city wrecking dozens of family homes and public buildings. The police and emergency crews are still working away to free the remaining survivors from the wreckage and tend to the wounded who were lucky to escape with only a few cuts and bruises.

I was speaking to the mayor of the city, Mr Belding, who told me that the earthquake has traumatised the city. He also remarked on the excellent co-operation of the emergency crews and the police.

The city is in a terrible state, there is wreckage lying all over the roads causing problems for the emergency crews getting to the injured.

There is hope of finding many of the people, who are still trapped beneath the rubble, alive! It has been recently reported that 20 people are recovering in hospital after the bus they were travelling on was damaged by a falling chimney from a nearby house. Two people were killed and another was critically injured. Mr Belding hopes to restore the city soon and wants to tell all the citizens that he is thinking of them all.

Nicola Ford (12)
Carrickfergus Grammar School, Carrickfergus

The Monk's Footsteps

Way back in 1930 there was a lighthouse keeper named JK. JK worked on an island called the Skelligs with two other keepers called Sean and Danny. They each took their turn keeping watch over the light, listening to radio broadcasts and searching the horizon for passing ships.

The lighthouse was at one end of the island and the accommodation was at the other. A long, winding stone path joined the two buildings.

One dark, wintry night JK finished his watch at the lighthouse and began his long walk across the path to his bed. JK had not travelled far when he heard the sound of footsteps and some sort of robe trailing along the small stone path behind him. JK just couldn't turn around, no matter how much he wanted to, he just couldn't, as he knew there could be no one there. He had left Danny in the lighthouse and Sean was fast asleep in his bed.

He had heard stories from other lighthouse keepers about strange goings on involving the monks that lived on the island in the 6th century.

One story involved another lighthouse keeper who found an old chalice buried inside one of the monk's ancient, beehive, stone hut-type dwellings. After the keeper cleaned the chalice he discovered it was solid gold.

Ignoring the advice of the other keepers he told them that he intended to sell it on his next trip to the mainland. When the other keepers awoke the following morning they found him sitting in the corner, his head in his hands. When they asked him where the chalice was all he would say was, 'It is where it belongs'. He never talked about it again!

By now JK was very scared and not looking back he hurried along the path to the safety of his bed.

Robbie Coburn (12)
Carrickfergus Grammar School, Carrickfergus

Time Splitters: Time Crystals Of War

When evil aliens plan to destroy Earth only three things can save it, a man, a machine and . . . a monkey!

You think it may only be a legend but who knows? A tale that is out of this world literally . . .

Chapter 1: Monkey Business

The night was clear and calm, a perfect night for monkeys and Jo-Jo the monkey was swinging on the branches of Aztec admiring the nice warm night without a cloud in the sky. Jo-Jo lay down and stared at the stars, then all of a sudden a shooting star whooshed by. Jo-Jo made a wish, a wish that he wanted more than anything in the entire universe. Then the shooting star rushed towards Jo-Jo and landed with a crash beside Jo-Jo knocking him out cold.

The sun shone on Jo-Jo. 'Ugh!' Jo-Jo had awoken. 'What happened? Uh! I can talk, part of my wish came true,' exclaimed Jo-Jo and he started to dance.

Jo-Jo didn't know and didn't care how he could talk all he cared about was that he could talk. Jo-Jo was dancing around unaware that the shooting star was still there. 'I'll have to go tell Captain Ash and RO19.' So off he trudged but the shooting star, which Jo-Jo still hadn't remembered about was glowing and doing something very mysterious.

To be continued . . .

Christopher Campbell (12)
Carrickfergus Grammar School, Carrickfergus

Through Malfoy's Eyes

One radiant day at Hogwarts Castle Harry Potter and his best friend, Ron Weasley, were walking along the edge of the lake while the sun smiled down on them. They were being watched very carefully by Draco Malfoy and his gang (Crabbe and Goyle).

'Look at Potter, he is strutting around here like he owns the place,' sneered Malfoy hatefully. 'Look at me, I'm Harry Potter and this is my boyfriend Ron Weasley.'

By this point Crabbe and Goyle were on the ground, rolling round in fits of laughter. 'I'm going to get that Potter and finish the job that my dad and Voldemort didn't and couldn't finish,' Malfoy said maliciously.

By now Crabbe and Goyle were on their feet, scared of what Malfoy was thinking, and what he was going to do. Malfoy was smiling very strangely and looked mad. Evil thoughts were swirling round in Malfoy's head. Things were going to get very interesting.

It started to rain and Harry and Ron decided it was for the best to go in and keep dry instead of getting soaked. They had just got in on time for dinner and were just going to take a seat when Hermione burst in. She looked very distressed and her hair was soaked because she was looking for Ron and Harry outside. 'Harry word is going round that Malfoy is plotting to get you,' she said very anxiously.

'So, that's nothing new Hermione,' Harry said coolly.

'Yeah Hermione we all know that Malfoy has been plotting against Harry from the first year,' Ron added.

'You don't understand! This time he is serious, dead serious,' Hermione said defiantly.

To be continued . . .

Matthew Surgenor (12)
Carrickfergus Grammar School, Carrickfergus

The Rescue

'Mum, can I go away with Tom, Katie and Ben next week?' Sophie pleaded to her mum after school. Earlier on that day Katie had asked her three friends to go to Italy on a skiing trip with her big sister and her friends.

'OK,' said her mum laughing at Sophie on her hands and knees on the floor begging.

Next week they were in Italy in the hotel. 'Wow this is amazing!' exclaimed Katie and Sophie in unison as they walked into their room.

'Look at the beds,' said Sophie.

'Look at the slopes!' exclaimed Katie jumping up and down.

When they went out skiing the next day Tom and Ben decided to have a race against the girls. When they got halfway through the race the boys were ahead so the girls took a short cut. It was starting to get dark so they didn't see a turn in the track and went off the track and into the trees.

'Argh, my leg!' screamed Katie crying. 'Sophie are you OK?'

'No, I think I have broken my arm,' replied Sophie crying.

They sat there for hours, it was now dark and cold and the trees looked as if they were reaching over to grab them and gobble them up any minute. Then they heard very distant voices. Finally they found them and got them home safe and sound. The girls did go back to Italy but decided never to take the short cut again.

Sarah Nelson (12)
Carrickfergus Grammar School, Carrickfergus

Parry Hotter And The Teacher's Phone

In a class in Oakfield Primary School there was a boy called Parry Hotter. Parry was 11 years old and was in Mr Sheppard's class. Mr Sheppard was the VP and taught P7.

One day at break time Parry was punched in the playground and was brought back into the classroom. When he got in he saw the teacher's phone sitting on the desk. Parry was a very nosy child so of course he went to look. The phone was a Nokia 6100 and the camera was attached to the bottom of it. The teacher had been taking pictures with it. The pictures were of the class and below them the teacher had written things about each pupil. Parry looked for his picture and found it. He read the writing and it said . . .

'Parry loves school and likes his work especially maths and science. He is always a good child, does well in physical education and religious education, and has lots of friends in the class. He is always friendly with me and the rest of the teachers especially his mum, Mrs Hotter. He is easily my favourite pupil'.

Parry had no idea that the teacher favoured him above the rest of the pupils, he did not even think teachers were supposed to have favourites. Just then he heard Mr Sheppard coming up the corridor so he put the phone on to keypad lock, put the phone on the table and went and sat down like a good boy.

Craig Edwards (12)
Carrickfergus Grammar School, Carrickfergus

The Stolen Phone

One day a boy called Craig was out playing rugby. He had left his coat down on the pavement while he was playing.

After an hour Craig went back to phone his mum to ask if he could stay longer, he lifted up his coat and noticed that his pocket was open. He reached inside to get his Nokia 6100 and all that was there was a note, which read:

'Dear Craig,

Now you've noticed your phone's missing, you can say hello to Max-Mouse! I have your Nokia 6100 and you're not getting it back. Ha, ha, ha!'

So Craig borrowed his friend's phone and called the police, they sent a unit straight over. The officer took full details of the phone's make, model and IMEI number.

Make: Nokia

Model: 6100

IMEI: 3525849/00/627983/0

Then he remembered his friend called Jim had wanted a Nokia 6100 and his parents wouldn't get him one, so the cop went right over to Jim's house and searched it and found the phone with exactly the same IMEI number.

He had also remembered he had been talking to Jim on MSN® Messenger® and his chat name was Max-Mouse! So this was it, it all pieced together.

Jim had to pay damages and for a new N-Gage. The best bit was that Craig got an N-Gage instead of a Nokia 6100.

David McCammond (12)
Carrickfergus Grammar School, Carrickfergus

The Fight For Life

In Los Angeles at 9.30pm there were strange happenings like some sort of electrical surge. Then all of a sudden it appeared, it was like a human but it wasn't! Its mission to protect the world from the attack.

James was preparing for the attack as he had suspected it for a long time, he knew he had to stop it but he couldn't do it alone. He needed the help of the thing that had arrived earlier that night, he tracked it down and brought it to his house.

He knew he couldn't take it out unless it had a name so he called it David. James got the plans of how to get into the Delappino factory, he knew how to stop the attack but when could he do it? The building was always full of people and not very nice people at all.

He planned to go in with David under darkness as there would be less chance of anyone seeing them.

The next night at about 10 o'clock James and David left for the building, they arrived 10 minutes later and got on top of the roof and were about to enter when the men started to attack. David stopped them while James went inside to stop them taking over the world. Trying hard not to be seen James went through room after room trying to find the computer to stop the attack. Suddenly James found the computer, he shut it down, but what happened next . . . ?

Jamie Crates (12)
Carrickfergus Grammar School, Carrickfergus

Undead Conquest

In the World of Azeroth, in the county of Lordaeron, in the village of Strohnbead, the sentries of the southern defences spotted a mob of undead ghouls approaching from out of the forest. There was at least 30 ghouls.

'Sound the alarm,' shouted one of the sentries.

The alarm quickly sounded and 8 human archers went up onto the southern wall. Then another mob of ghouls appeared but this mob had 2 ladders and a battering ram. The 2 mobs of ghouls charged towards the wall. The human archers shot their arrows and 4 ghouls fell, but then the ghouls got the ladders into range of the wall and up went the ladders and ghouls started climbing up them, but before any ghouls got onto the wall the humans knocked them down.

However this distracted the humans long enough for the ghouls to bring up the battering ram and after 3 hits with the battering ram the gate fell, but after that more mobs of ghouls came out of the forest and ghouls came pouring through the gate. By nightfall Strohnbead had been captured.

Meanwhile in the freezing country of Northrend in the fortress of Ner'zhule the Lich King.

'Excellent,' said Ner'zhule.

'As you can see our forces have captured Strohnbead,' said the Dread Lord Tichondrius.

'Now Tichondrius,' said Ner'zhule, 'I want you to send the undead armada to land in North Lordaeron and the undead conquest begin.'

Scott McCrudden (12)
Carrickfergus Grammar School, Carrickfergus

Carrick Castle

She walks alone down the dark entrance that is Carrickfergus castle, or so the gossips used to say. Seen as a monster to society, some say she's an optical illusion or myth.

Granny used to be a cleaner there, told me the real story. Back in the eighteen hundreds, a grand and popular queen who was loved by all of her people drowned.

Some cleaners stumbled upon a secret door only opened by pulling the head of a statue in the main drawing room. Inside was a written letter to his father in detail. Only the king knew of these quarters and kept all his personal belongings there.

He had become jealous of the love his people had for their queen. He took his wife on a walk telling her he had to speak to her immediately. It was a rough sea and when he got her on the edge of the pier, he told her she could no longer be and at that very moment pushed her.

He returned to the castle to tell of how she tripped to her death. As the town went into mourning strange things started happening. Sights of a ghost said to be the queen, looking for her husband at her time of death every day deserted the town. She is said to haunt the castle corridors scaring those who see her to this day still.

Carolyn Creighton (13)
Carrickfergus Grammar School, Carrickfergus

The Two Mythical Horses

There once was a horse with huge wings, which gave him the ability to fly. This horse was called Pegasus, he had a brilliant coat of white. Pegasus was a strong and mighty horse. He was a proud horse and he could hold his head high up with the Greek gods.

This horse could walk on and above the clouds. Pegasus could fly higher than an aeroplane and higher than you could see. Although he was strong and mighty he was also a very kind and caring beast, he looked after wounded humans and animals he found on the mountains. He would let the humans ride him without having to be tamed. This horse was almost perfect except for its brother horse, which was called Ixion. He was nothing like Pegasus as he could not fly nor was he white, he was black but knowing this he was still strong and mighty but there was not a lot of love or care in him. Instead of being able to fly he could wield the power of thunder and lightning and he could concentrate the bolts to hit a certain target. He was very evil and envied Pegasus with his heart and soul.

Ixion tried to hold his head high and become proud like Pegasus but he could not as he was far too self-centred deep down. Both creatures were extremely powerful beasts but Ixion could never be half the horse Pegasus was.

Kurtis Moffatt (13)
Carrickfergus Grammar School, Carrickfergus

Hotel Out Of This World

It was reported this week that astronaut James Rocket, also known as Rocky, discovered a hotel on the moon. Rocky was sent to the moon to bring back moon rock for scientists at NASA to study but little did he know what he would find.

'I was moon walking when before my eyes I saw this large building with a sign that said *Moon Beams Inn*. I could not believe it!'

Rocky informed us that the hotel was like any other hotel except it was completely deserted! 'It was empty! No human, animal or creature in sight. I had a look around and there was only what you would expect to find in a hotel. I kept getting the feeling I was being watched so I did not stay for too long!'

So after we interviewed Rocky we spoke to some scientists at NASA Space Centre where they read out this statement, 'Although we do not know who or what built this hotel we do know that there is life out of this world!'

Denise Boyd (13)
Carrickfergus Grammar School, Carrickfergus

A Day In The Life Of A Tiny Salmon

I'm swimming in the stream, all day every day; I know my way quite well. I know the ducks, the owl, the little miner bird, and the great big frog that sits nearby at the second bend. I have come to know this stream quite well, as I am always chasing that impossible dream of reaching the top. I have only climbed to around halfway, where the rough water starts, and then time after time I run out of puff and get washed back to the stills.

Today I plan to reach the top. The friendly owl agreed to help and he said that he has some sort of plan but I cannot possibly think of what it is.

I have been waiting at the stills for over two hours now and there's no sign of the owl. It's getting dark and I'm not particularly fond of the upper stream whenever I can't see what is coming up ahead, so I guess my plan was not the best if I can't even do it on my own. I just don't know what could possibly have happened to owl that he couldn't get here.

This is what happens, every day; that's all it is, trial, *error,* trial, *error.* I hate it! But that's what it's all about, I just wish that one day, I would finally reach the top. Oh well, there's always tomorrow.

Stephen Hackworth (13)
Carrickfergus Grammar School, Carrickfergus

The Legend Of Seamus O'Driscoll

One day in Ulster a giant was sitting in his house when his friend Bob popped in. 'Donald McRonald was saying that you can't fight, can you believe that?'

'No way! He won't be saying that when he is lying on the floor unconscious!'

Furious, Seamus tore down the rocks from the cliffs at the coast and threw them across the Irish Sea creating a causeway. Donald could feel the vibrations and went out to see the commotion. There was a huge path straight to Ireland, he thought of this as a challenge. 'Ha, ha,' he laughed, 'this will be too easy!' as he ambled across the sea.

At this time Seamus was getting worried. As he looked out the window at a vague silhouette of Donald McRonald approaching.

'Ermmm . . .' Seamus said anxiously,' Sinead could you help me dear?'

'OK I'm coming love.' He quickly explained everything and they devised a plan.

There was a knock at the door. 'Yes?'

'Ermmm . . . hello is the master of the house in?'

'No, sorry, he'll be home soon, come on in and wait.'

She sat him by the baby's cradle, what he didn't know was that Seamus was hiding inside. 'Wow, your baby is massive! How old is he?'

'Only eight months, he's a real fighter, just like his father!'

'I'd hate to see the size of his dad!'

'Yeah I know, I'd hate to get in a fight with him! I'll make some tea!'

Sinead left and Donald started playing with the baby, suddenly Seamus bit Donald's thumb off! In agony, he ran off screaming to Scotland. That was the last Seamus ever saw of Donald McRonald!

Rebecca Irwin (13)
Carrickfergus Grammar School, Carrickfergus

A Day In The Life Of My Mum!

My mum is called Maxine Renton and is 37 years old. She is training to be an English teacher. She is always working! Here is an insight into one of her normal days . . .

My mum usually wakes up at 6.30am and takes a bath while listening to the radio. This is her quiet time because no one is awake. Once she finishes getting dressed she gets a lift up to Larne Grammar with another teacher friend. She teaches English to classes ranging from Year 8 to Year 11. She finds it really enjoyable but a lot of hard work.

When she gets home she sits down and reads the paper with a cup of coffee. Then we all have our dinner together and chat. My mum goes to bed at around about the same time as me as she needs to get lots of sleep so she can wake up bright and early.

Emma-Kate Renton (12)
Carrickfergus Grammar School, Carrickfergus

The Old Woman

She walked about with a smile on her face, just recovering from all the grieving she did when her husband died. Mrs Dorothy McLeash is her name and she is 76 now. She has not had a very busy life because she has always seemed to be extremely rich but she does not work, the truth of the matter is that she gets it all from her dead, rich husbands. Everyone would say 'poor Mrs McLeash losing her darling Rodney', but I would see her face sometimes, that sneaky grin, staring right into my face.

One day my friend Sam and I thought we would sneak into her house while she was doing some gardening. We went up the creaking stairs and into the master bedroom then Sam said, 'Wait somebody's coming.' It was Mrs McLeash and out of sheer panic we jumped into the huge closet.

There was this horrendous smell and shakily I said, 'Sam, are you touching me?'

'No,' he replied, and then I remembered I had some matches in my pocket, I took them out, struck one and what I saw was unreal! There were about five dead bodies.

We burst out of the closet and standing there was Mrs McLeash.

'I've seen them,' I said.

'What?' she replied.

I said, 'The dead bodies in your closet, you murderer!'

Sam and I sprinted out of the house, of course nobody believed us. We phoned the police, they went in and we showed them the closet, there was nothing, not even a trace and to this day Mrs McLeash walks about with a smile on her face.

Jonathan Goodfellow (12)
Carrickfergus Grammar School, Carrickfergus

A Pirate's Life

I always wished to have the life of a pirate. When I was six, I wanted to be a pirate; I wanted to feel the wind; survive risky storms; steer my ship to places no one has ever been before. I wanted to find buried treasure; fight Peter Pan with my sword. I wanted to say 'hoist the main sail' and 'full speed ahead'. I wished to fly the pirate's flag high; fire my cannons. I wanted my ship 'Miles Ahead' to be the fastest ship on the sea; I wanted her to cut through the waves not ride over them. I would have a parrot on my shoulder called Bobby who would give orders to the crew, not me.

I don't know where my fascination came from but I suspect it came from my dad because he has had me sailing all my life. He got me my first boat for my seventh birthday and I called it 'Miles Ahead' as my name is Miles. I always remember saying to my dad every time a big boat went past I would say, 'Dad is that a pirate ship?'

As I grow older now I realise that my childhood adventure, whilst just a dream then, is really life personified.

Miles Canning (13)
Carrickfergus Grammar School, Carrickfergus

Myths And Legends: The Minotaur

In Greek mythology a Minotaur is a monster with a head of a bull and a body of a man which dwelt in the labyrinth of Minos. A Minotaur in Greek means 'bull of Minos'.

I will now tell you a story/tale of a Minotaur.

The Minotaur was the offspring of Pasiphae, wife of Minos, and a snow-white bull that god Poseidon had sent to the king. So handsome was the bull that Minos refused to sacrifice it, as Poseidon had wished; angered, he decided to take revenge on Minos, and used his divine powers to make Pasiphae fall in love with the bull.

After Pasiphae gave birth to the Minotaur, Minos ordered the architect and inventor Daedalus to build a labyrinth so intricate that escape from it would be impossible without assistance.

Confined to the labyrinth, the Minotaur was fed up with seven young girls and seven young boys whom, every year, Minos exacted from Athens as a tribute.

Theseus reached Crete with the intention of killing the Minotaur, having Minos' daughter Ariadne fell in love with him, in secret gave him a ball of thread, which he fastened to the door of the maze and unwound as he made his way through it. When he came upon the Minotaur, he beat the monster to death and then led the other sacrificial youths and maidens to safety by following the thread back to the entrance.

Stuart Mckee (12)
Carrickfergus Grammar School, Carrickfergus

A Day In The Life Of Bam Margera

I lifted my skateboard and walked out of the door and started to skate down my driveway as I suddenly realised I had forgotten the keys to my Ferrari and my house and then I realised I locked the door.

I would've had to wait for five hours until my dad came home but I didn't want to wait that long for him to open the door, so I decided to look for an open window so that I could climb through it. I decided to climb through an open window in my living room. I started to climb through the window then I suddenly realised that I was stuck and I couldn't move back or forwards. And guess what, my mates came up the driveway and started to laugh at me. They decided it was so funny that they decided to start to film me trying to get out of the window.

Four hours and fifty-five minutes later, I was still stuck in the window and finally my dad came up the driveway. My dad didn't realise I was there and he went in to sit on the couch and then he suddenly saw me. He said, 'Bam, why are you stuck in that window?'

I replied, 'Because I locked myself out and I forgot my keys and I couldn't get back in!'

He answered, 'Well when I came in, the door was already open!'

I guessed that this was the most humiliating thing I did in my life!

Mark Dunn (13)
Carrickfergus Grammar School, Carrickfergus

White Stones

As I stood among the white stones I wondered what it had been like on that July morning. My mind started to imagine that it would have been cold and damp as the mist and fog slowly cleared. At that moment the continuous noise of the night would have stopped. Would fear and anxiety have been the emotions felt as the sun started to rise?

The young faces all around would not have been much older than me. How would I have felt at that moment before the whistle blew? Would my mind have thought of home and family and those I loved? I really struggled to understand the whole idea of what would have taken place. How far would they have got before being shot? I looked closely at the rows of white stones, with the names of so many young men engraved, from Larne, Belfast, Enniskillen and Armagh, buried in France so far from home and loved ones.

I wandered along the endless rows of white stones, all seemed to be the same and yet they all represented very different people with one cause. It was meant to be the war to end all wars!

Just then I heard the sound of a car horn, it was time to go and drive to Calais to get the bumpy hovercraft to travel towards home. We had stopped for only a moment yet it had felt like an age staring at the white stones.

Geneviève Cathcart (13)
Carrickfergus Grammar School, Carrickfergus

A Day In The Life Of My Dairy 11.09.01

We were just back at school after summer. I'd just started P7 so we were preparing for our 11+ in a few months. Little did I know, when I woke up that morning, that something was going to happen that would make me forget all about school and my exams.

We got through all of school without hearing there was major chaos halfway across the world. When I was picked up after school I heard on the radio the Twin Towers had collapsed. My first thought was that someone was reading out a fiction story or an 'imagine if . . .' but when we got back to my minder's house and we switched on the TV, no matter how many different channels we checked every one said the same thing 'Twin Towers collapsed'.

At first I didn't believe it, even though I was looking at these pictures of the two buildings in flames. I sat on the sofa in the conservatory staring at the TV in disbelief. Every time I read the writing at the bottom of the screen I read something new.

I remember I tossed and turned for ages that night. The terrible events of the day haunted my thoughts as I still imagined things in my head. the thought that so many lives changed or ended in a few hours scared me. People today are still affected by that day. I know it changed my perspective. I never minded flying but now there'll always be a little doubt in the back of my mind every time I get on a plane. I don't think I'll ever fly on September 11th.

Louise Davey (13)
Carrickfergus Grammar School, Carrickfergus

Aliens Are Coming

Last night the Hubble space telescope sent clear images of a giant spacecraft and many other small spacecrafts. Unfortunately 30 minutes later the Hubble telescope was destroyed. Hubble had sent one last message saying 'There is a high speed object flying straight towards us. The main ship is now heading for the ISS. I am not sure we'll make it'.

The Ministry of Defence secretary then stated, 'They were sighted at 21.38 yesterday. We are trying to communicate with them but have not yet been successful'. The Ministry of Defence secretary James T Kirk states that, 'For the last 50 years in conjunction with NASA we have been tracking some alien activity who were hiding behind the moon's orbit since we started the Apollo missions. In the late sixties and early seventies unsuccessful attempts to make contact with the aliens from the lunar surface have been made. We tried a different approach using the cover of probes to other planets in the solar system in an attempt to contact the aliens from the supposed home planets from within the system, these too were unsuccessful. It has been apparent over the months that the aliens would become visible through a normal telescope. We have now decided to inform the public to dispel any panic as to the aliens' intentions. We have the capability from the ISS to protect Earth using hitherto secret laser weapons to confront any aggression towards the people of this planet'.

Joshua Whitall (13)
Carrickfergus Grammar School, Carrickfergus

Why They Call Me Chicken

The day I had been dreading for four weeks, Hallowe'en. You see recently I had been playing dares! I had been dared to go into the old, spooky, damp haunted house at 27 Avenue Drive and to stay there for at least an hour.

The day was miserable and the clouds were spitting down. The day flew in fast and before I knew it it was nine o'clock. I crept out of the house as silent as a mouse and started heading down the back alleys towards the haunted house.

I met my friends at the haunted house. It was very dark and windy. As I pushed open the half-broken gate, one of its rusty old hinges fell off. There was an ancient, crooked, gnarled tree and house windows were boarded up or else smashed. On the roof the slates were chipped and broken. The chimney was coughing out smoke rings that were floating up into the dark red sky above. As I tiptoed, trembling up the path overgrown with weeds one of the cracked slabs snapped and I nearly jumped out of my skin.

I crept up to the porch, fought my way through a curtain of cobwebs and nervously grabbed the door handle which felt ice-cold. At once the handle came away in my hand, I dropped it like it was burning my skin. I turned on my heels and sprinted as fast as my little legs would go, heart pounding in my chest as if it were ready to burst.

As I reached the corner of my street I saw my mates huddled in the alley waiting for my return. When they saw me they all started to laugh and call me chicken. They danced about flapping their arms and making chicken noises. My excuse was the door handle had fallen off but they knew by my fear that I would not have stayed in the house for five minutes let alone for an hour.

Aaron McBurney (11)
Carrickfergus Grammar School, Carrickfergus

The Untitled Piece

Remember the stories when you were young of Alice in Wonderland, Snow White and Sleeping Beauty? In these stories, everyone hated the 'wicked witch' and adored the beautiful heroes. (Don't feel bad or guilty, everyone does it.) You're probably wondering what this has to do with my story. Well now I'm going to explain it, but first think about those stories (already mentioned above) how the good people are *always* beautiful and wonderfully talented and skilful, but the bad people are ugly, stupid and clumsy, which is a complete and utter lie. (Imagine an author lying to children hmm, hmm) Now ugly people aren't that mean (most of the time).

We managed to track down the 'wicked witch' in Snow White. Now no laughing, she's been in a bad way since she played in the Snow White movie.

The Interview

Me: Hello, make yourself comfortable Miss . . .

Witch: Miss Blanche

Me: OK now we know your name Blanche.

Blanche: Yeah sure.

Me: Great! I've heard you lost everything you had, when Snow White came out on video and DVD?

Blanche: (In tears) Yes it's true, I lost Dopey my boyfriend, my friends and my job as an actor, they said I was mean to Snow White.

Me: And were you?

Blanche: No, I just wanted to kill her because she was a hateful cow to me and taunted me by saying she was *hiccup* better looking than me (faints).

Me: What a drama queen!

Victoria Cummings (12)
Carrickfergus Grammar School, Carrickfergus

Santa Claus - St Nicholas The Myth

St Nicholas was born in 271 AD and died around December 6th, 342 AD or 343 AD near the Asia Minor (Turkey) town of Myra, where he later became Bishop. St Nicholas performed many good actions and was a friend to the poor and helpless. When he died myths spread about him around the Mediterranean Sea. It was rumoured that he was able to calm raging seas, rescue sailors, help the poor and save children. He was named the patron saint of sailors and when Myra was overthrown, his bones were transported by sailors to Bari, a port in Italy, where a tomb was built over the grave and became the centre of honour for St Nicholas. The legend spread on around the Atlantic coast of Europe and the North Sea to become a European holiday tradition regardless of region.

Several children in European countries put their shoes in front of the fireplace at his nightly visits. They sing songs and leave a carrot or hay for the horse. At night Black Pete puts gifts and candy in the shoes.

In the Netherlands people celebrate St Nicholas' birthday the night before his feast (December 6th). During the evening, a loud knock will announce the arrival of 'SinterKlaas' (Santa Claus) and at the same time candy will be thrown from upstairs. A bag of gifts will be on the doorstep.

Wrapping the presents up and planting a trail of clues is part of the general fun and can sometimes be tricky to find.

Today all around the world the myth about St Nicholas or Santa Claus is still believed and loved by all young children.

Lauren Poots (12)
Carrickfergus Grammar School, Carrickfergus

First Monkey On The Moon

The Daily Monkey has gathered news that a monkey called JoJo has blasted to the moon in a rocket shaped like a banana. NASA are running the expedition and had this to say, 'We are very happy for JoJo'.

He is looking for his mother as when he was very young an evil monkey robber kidnapped her. His name is Jamimah and is an alien monkey who is now living on the moon. A half alien, half monkey called Jimmy will accompany JoJo.

What lies ahead for this brave monkey we do not know. But we all wish him the best of luck. Jimmy has been to the moon several times so he knows his way round it.

It will take JoJo one week to get to the moon and he will only have two months of supplies to last both him and Jimmy. JoJo and Jimmy have been armed with very dangerous weapons such as banana guns and banana peel shooters - anything to finish Jamimah off. Most of the foods they have been supplied with are bananas which don't really suit Jimmy.

The Monkeys Union have got Jamimah as their number one target.

Jamimah has assassinated many former leaders such as Silas the Great and *I Smell*. So it is up to JoJo and Jimmy to save the world and most importantly of all JoJo's mum, ZaZa.

Jonathon Greenaway (12)
Carrickfergus Grammar School, Carrickfergus

Abandoned

There once was a family living up in the hills, Andrew's friends. One day Andrew called for the twins, but no one answered, he told his mum Catherine but found that they had moved to Edinburgh. So the country hills were deserted again.

Andrew decided to look around the house with his dog Patch later that week and found it quite a mess. Bricks had fallen down everywhere and you could hear leaks.

He got bored after a while then went home. He woke up the next morning and found someone had broken in and rummaged through the fridge, or, it was more like someone had broken out.

After school the next day Mum said that Patch had been found up in the old house with food on his face.

That night Patch snuck out of the bedroom and outside. Andrew was amazed at how quiet he was. The next night Andrew followed him up to the old house and followed him through it.

All of a sudden Andrew heard a noise, it seemed to be like a squeaky giggle. He went into the room and there he saw Patch lying on top of a blanket. He crept closer and lying by Patch was a baby smiling and gurgling, playing with Patch's hair!

Andrew ran over and picked him up and applauded his dog, his Patch, his rescue dog! He ran home with the baby in his arms and showed Mum, she called the police to say that the McShannons had moved and abandoned their baby. They were tracked down and arrested and Andrew's family adopted the baby calling him Ben!

Nicole Orr (12)
Carrickfergus Grammar School, Carrickfergus

A Day In The Life Of Homer Simpson

I'm going to Moe's today before I go to work. Unfortunately I take a nap at work and I am fired. D'oh!

I'm going to go to the Kwik-E-Mart to talk to Apu about the Buzz Cola.

I go home to rest in peace, but to my shock Lisa is playing her sax!

I'll get my job back on Monday and try to help Mr Burns save his money.

I love Springfield!

Leo Gallagher (11)
Foyle View Special School, Derry

The Ugliest Person That I Have Ever Met

He had coarse, mucky hair, black with bits of dirt and grass through it, which gave me the impression that it hadn't been washed before. His forehead was enormous, and looked as if it had been painted with dirty, brown paint.

His eyebrows were huge and husky as if they had been stuffed with straw, as they closed over the top of his eyes; they looked so evil and full of rage. His huge, bulky nose appeared to have been broken before in the past. His skin was so weathered it was like brown leather and he had a dirty, bristly beard. His ears were cauliflowered, so chewed and smashed up that they were just fat, chubby skin. He had huge, fat lips, and, when he spoke, there were barely any gaps between them. With muscle built on top of his shoulders and his arms padded too, he held a rugby ball under his arms as if he had someone in a headlock.

His legs were tree trunks with black tape and bandage wrapped around them, his belly was made of bricks, and he was about six feet tall. His thumbs had been bound in tape too, looking at them it was then when I realised the size of his huge hands.

As a person, I would call him a monstrosity. Someone that definitely belonged on a rugby field; this was his home.

Christopher McNaghten (15)
Larne High School, Larne

The Trolley Man

His home life was that of a stray dog. A helpless and defenceless dingy cardboard 'house' was where he had his dreams. A small grey pillow rested his head. A musty scent and strong whiskey could be tracked five minutes before you saw him, and when you did, you knew it belonged to him.

A mop of sandy brown hair flopped over his ears, the fringe, raggedly cut, disappeared above his eyes. A bald patch on the back of his head bore a crimson, crooked scar. His forehead seemed to bury his eyes, frown lines bulging down, they sunk deep into his face. Piercing emerald-green eyes were a wonder. His face, ageing fast, looked withdrawn and withered. Scraggy lips that never bore a smile were just visible. A strong, square jaw faded beneath creases in his once-tanned complexion.

Broad, square shoulders, always hunched forward, were buried under layers of charity clothes. His neck was invisible, a grey knitted scarf hung down his chest, trying desperately to cover the patched holes on his long overcoat which disappeared at the ankles. The overcoat was his only belonging that he seemed to care for. Year after year the coat turned to a deeper shade of fading brown, but remained his prized possession. The stench of his never-washed overcoat made him a home nest to fleas. Tinted sea-blue jeans were ruined with mud stains on his knees. He never wore shoes, but only socks, scarlet socks, with his toes visible. His toenails had become ingrown and yellow.

Rudeness was his trademark. He viewed life of an empty space. He didn't seem to care about anyone or anything.

My impression of him didn't bother him and that described his mental state. The way he looked and talked matched his personality, unpleasant. Isn't every trolley man?

Traci Hunter (15)
Larne High School, Larne

Mysterious Place

As I walked through this mysterious place, I felt the moist grass flatten beneath my shoes. Each step I took was followed by the familiar squeak of my shoes as I moved onwards. Birds flew, startled, from somewhere above me. Craning my neck I saw their shadows swoop and soar in the pale moonlight.

Trees towered over and surrounded me, making me feel insecure, like they were looking down upon me. I leant against the trunk of a tree. Its dark trunk was damp from recent rain. It seeped through my shirt, making it stick to my back as if some magnetic force was drawing it close to my skin. Turning round, I ran my hands along the bark, taking in its cool, rough exterior.

My ears pricked up at the sound of movement behind me. I spun around and listened to noises of bushes rustling and the crackle of crunchy, dry leaves on the ground. I stared intently at the area from where the sound was coming - and staring out from the darkness were two, almond-shaped eyes which narrowed when they focused on me. They were fiery-yellow in colour and burned into my soul.

From the shadows emerged a grey wolf whose smooth fur appeared to be blue in the twilight. His head tilted to one side and revealed rows of razor-sharp teeth when he sneered. He pointed his long grey nose skywards. I followed his gaze which was stuck like glue to the moon. A low moan escaped his mouth which turned into an ear-splitting howl. I looked down at him but he faded away into the blackness of the shadows. All that remained was the mist that had settled onto the forest floor, surrounding my ankles like a swirling fog.

The forest floor was murky but there was some colour in the darkness. Vibrant wild flowers were growing amongst the undergrowth. The tall, passionate pink foxglove and the small, but equally beautiful snowdrops bloomed beside the dark blue colour of the bluebells. The fragrance was heavenly because the scent from every flower was mixing perfectly in the air. Raindrops had settled on the plants giving them an elegant, glittering effect.

Stephanie Logan (15)
Larne High School, Larne

The Man

This man looked as if he could knock you out with one punch, but instead chose to casually and level-headedly walk away. He had a bouncer's look about him, always calm and collected. He had a very distinctive walk; he strolled around like an ape with deliberate slow and steady movement, swinging his arms and shoulders freely. His hands and his face were as black as the midnight sky on a cold winter's night and the creased lines that crossed his face could tell a thousand stories or paint a marvellous masterpiece. His large pearly eyes took up most of his face and could sweep away the darkness from any room. Just below these sat a small stubby nose which was almost overshadowed by the magnitude of his eyes. His lips looked like furrows in a field - as tough as leather. The curly hair on his head, stuck together with sweat, resembled tangled, knotted string with straw mangled through it. His skin was like cracked mud on a hot summer's day with dirt and grime worn into it, almost as if he had been exposed to the weather.

I almost felt sorry for him because he looked empty, unfulfilled, deserted - like a bird with no song, or a tree with no roots, or the sky without the sun. The last time I saw this man he was lying in the same gutter in which I had first seen him. It was as if he had never moved.

Paul Magill (15)
Larne High School, Larne

The Courtroom

It was a cold, wet and windy January morning as we approached the courthouse in Stranraer. It was a rather imposing building made of brown sandstone with lots of windows. They all seemed to be staring at me, watching, waiting, what for I had no idea. I had a feeling in the pit of my stomach that would not go away. I felt as though I was going through the fast spin cycle of a washing machine. I had tried to eat some breakfast earlier on that morning but the cereal had stuck in my throat as I tried to swallow it, and the toast had been worse; it had been like trying to swallow sandpaper.

We reached the door and it opened automatically. I felt as though I was walking into a gaping mouth that was going to swallow me whole. My heart was racing like a runaway train and I felt my breaths escaping my body like little puffs of fire.

'Stop worrying,' my mother told me. 'Everything will be alright.'

That was alright for her to say, she wasn't the one going to be standing in front of the Sheriff. Suddenly I felt almost like a lamb must feel when it is going to the slaughter, frightened, alone, scared and unloved.

We walked through the large, cavernous hall. There was a door to the left with a plaque on it, it said *Procurator Fiscal's Office*. I wondered who that was and so I asked my mum and she explained that it was the prosecutor who told the court about the bad things that people were alleged to have done, when they ended up in court.

I gulped, I really didn't want to go in there. On the right of the hall were two doors, one sign said *Toilets* and the other said *Secretary's Office*. I did not like this strange and unfamiliar territory so I edged closer to my mum. As we walked to the end of the hall I saw a large imposing staircase. I'm sure that it was so wide, that at least five people, could walk up it side by side. We climbed the stairs together and as we did so, the heels of our shoes tapped out an unfamiliar rhythm on the cold concrete. I really did not like this place and felt like I wanted to escape from it there and then.

The top of the courthouse was a little different from the hall. For a start, it was a lot warmer and it was painted a nice pale blue colour, unlike the hall downstairs (it had been an unhealthy and sickly yellow colour) and it was carpeted. There were several doors leading from the top hallway. As I looked around nervously, I saw that they were all different courtrooms. I counted three in total. Once again my nerves started to get the better of me. As we reached the top of the stairs, I saw a group of people standing there. My heart was in my mouth as we walked across to meet them.

As we reached the group waiting at the end of the corridor, I heard a few hushed, whispered snatches of conversation. This did nothing for my waning confidence.

Just with that, I heard my mother say, 'Sorry we are late but the dentist took longer than we anticipated.'

'That's alright,' said Mrs Allison, 'the tour of the courthouse is not due to start for another five minutes, we've plenty of time. Now class, please make sure that you have you note pads and pencils at the ready and if you have any questions at any time, please raise your hand and wait until you are acknowledged. OK? Everyone ready? Good, then let's form an orderly line in pairs, please!'

Then, with that the whole class followed the teacher as we were given a guided tour of the courthouse. In a way I was glad that it was only a school trip and that my mum was with us helping out. I really wouldn't have liked to have been there for any other reason than a primary school trip.

Amanda Davidson (15)
Larne High School, Larne

Final Draft

I was sitting waiting for my bus to arrive at the bus stop. I looked at my watch, 3.11pm (11 minutes past 3), not long to wait now. I was feeling pleasant and happy. It felt like nothing could ruin this happiness which was flowing through me. Then, he arrived at the stop and suddenly all the happiness in me seemed to disintegrate into nothing. He was the ugliest, most unpleasant creature I had ever seen in my entire life.

His nose was pointy and thin, his ears were like cauliflowers and his eyes were bulgy and green. His head was more square than round and he had a neck like a giraffe. He moved about quite sluggishly when he walked. He had two big humps coming from his back - like a camel or Quasimodo. When he spoke, it was like listening to a bad singer sing a beastly, high-pitched note. It made the hairs on the back of my neck stand on end. It looked as if his face had been smashed off a wall, again and again. He could do with plastic surgery. His hair was scruffy and brown and resembled a dead animal lying on top of his head. He wore a black T-shirt with stains of spaghetti all over it - I doubt he owned a washing machine. His baggy trousers looked ancient and were torn to bits. His skin was pure white and resembled a corpse. He wore ragged, old trainers which had large rips in them around the sides. A revolting stench drifted from him and it could be smelt for miles around, like a scruffy dog which hadn't been washed. Only fifteen, the abundance of facial hair made him look to be more in his twenties. He was sickening. I noticed he had bushy eyebrows planted above his eyes. He looked like a survivor from a train crash with a deformed face. The longer you looked at him the more hideous he became.

Finally my bus arrived and luckily he didn't want the same bus as me. I hurriedly got on it and drove away into the distance.

Kyle McNeill (15)
Larne High School, Larne

The Beach

Walking over the sizzling, scorching hot sand, my feet melted like an ice cream cone on a hot summer's day. My forehead dripped with scalding sweat. I could hear the sea's waves smash against the rocks and gurgle with the movement of the green, stringy seaweed that slept on the seabed. The waves were as blue as the sky on this warm, baking day.

I spied the horizon over the sea and could see the wavy, lingering heat waves as they scattered across the baby-blue ocean. As men skimmed by on their jet skis, the water shot up into the air like an erupting volcano. Birds hovered about swooping and swerving and wasps and bees buzzed by, striking fear through children, as they ran swinging their arms like a pack of wild monkeys. People were frying like eggs with red-hot steaming skin which was peeling like potatoes.

I scanned the sandy beach, checking out the vast blue sky. I heard the roar of an aeroplane which crossed the sky, leaving a white line of fluff-like cloud in its wake. Tremendously huge palm trees stretched into the air, swaying like big fans, jolting a breezy, calm wind across the endless yellow, scorching sand.

Now the sun stretched across the sky, leaving an intensely gleaming, shiny spell of light and warmth which sat still in the air. The sun started to go down. It was time. My eyes unlocked, wide open and I sat there pondering. *What an imagination!*

Karl Irwin (14)
Larne High School, Larne

Sally

(This is a description of a girl called Sally, who I used to know when I lived in Birmingham.)

As she walks towards you, the first thing you notice is her bright smile, with teeth as white as snow and big bold lips with rose-red lipstick. Her eyes are blue and there is always a twinkle in them when she looks at me. She has a small, pointed nose with a stud on the left side and her ears are usually covered by her hair. Sally's hair is long, brunette and has streaks of blue at the ends. As she shakes her head she looks like a girl out of Baywatch!

She is tall with long legs - as tall as flagpoles - and just as thin. Her arms are also long and thin and her hands are long, but soft and elegant and she has a silver ring on her left hand. Sally is thin around the waist but is also top heavy, if you know what I mean! She is wearing a dark red polo neck, black mini skirt and red high heels.

When you walk anywhere near Sally you always smell strawberries and flowers. When I look at her I feel like lightning, and it's just me and her in the whole world.

Thomas Parry (14)
Larne High School, Larne

The Place I Live On A Wet But Sunny Day

The place where I live is on a street with two sets of terraced houses on either side, and mine is the very first one. Antiville School gate lies just across the road from my house. My mum and dad's car sits in my driveway as it always does. The street is quiet. All that can be heard are the birds singing merry tunes.

It's wet outside but still bright, as the sun has just come out from behind the dark, dull clouds. On the road the steam rises from the ground like in a hot bath. The sky is clearing as slowly as a snail. It's not very windy, just a gentle, cool breeze blowing like a fan when turned on. The weather now is turning into a warm day.

The grass isn't as green as it usually is and it must have been waiting for a drink of water before that last shower, because it hasn't rained that much in the past while. The leaves of the tree in my garden are now greener than the grass. Birds come to it often for food - shiny red berries - which grow on it at this time of the year. This tree in my garden is a rowan tree. My granny once told me that, according to folklore, it is bad luck to cut one down. Anyone who does is supposed to be cursed. Some people think rowan trees are fairy trees.

My front garden has a strong, titchy, red-bricked wall around it. Plants grow beside the wall in a perfect row.

Cars are parked haphazardly on the street, as if people have just abandoned them. Beside Antiville School gate, the light blue generator which powers the school, can be heard making a funny humming noise when running, if you are close enough to it. My uncle David lives next door to me and my granny lives three doors down. To the left of my house, straight across the road is my other granny and grandad's house. I must be lucky to have these people who are all so important, live so close to me.

The road on my street has no white or yellow lines and you can clearly see where workmen have put pipes down as it is a slightly different colour there. A footpath runs along either side. Bits of it are cracked and look as if a fork of lighting has struck them.

At the bottom of my road is a green that runs the whole way down to the Linn Road Garage. When I was young I used to play football there all the time. I remember those days dearly but since then trees have been planted to stop children playing football there.

Jonathan Cooke (15)
Larne High School, Larne

A Winter's Day

The uneven, cobbled road slept under a blanket of snow. The trees stood like cauliflowers, under a canopy of blue sky. As I walked down the fluffy, desolate street, the sunlight ricocheted off the ice-white paths sparkling like diamonds. Snow crunched under my feet like broken glass. Icicles gripped drains and window sills as the blinding sun melted their tips. The street was silent. Ice-cold wind cut through my ears, so cold that they froze.

Towards me came a man, trudging through the snowy earth, his white coat and trousers almost making him invisible to the naked eye. As I passed him, he looked tired, breathing out smoke like a fireless dragon. His hood covered any features but his hands shone blood-red.

Now the street was a white sheet of paper. Cars were half buried, sleeping in their drives. Hedges were topped with snow like caves with icing and lamp posts had been camouflaged by the white flakes, lightly sticking to the cold metal.

As the street got steeper, it became a battle with the weather. Stone-cold, frozen ground lay beneath five-inch thick snow. Ruffled robins stood on the branch of a tree, rummaging for food, trying to keep warm. Spiderwebs shimmered in the breeze like strings of silver. The last of the leaves floated about as the winter wind whistled and the sky flickered as darkness fell. Street lights brightened the road but left frightening shadows. Silently, softly to the ground, fluffy snowflakes tumbled down, glistening in the starry night.

Shane Martin (14)
Larne High School, Larne

Silent Story

I walked in via the decaying doorway. The smell of musty old men and mouldy cheese greeted me in the hall. Their stench hugged my body with delight. I waddled up the corroded stairway and entered the hovel. The floorboards were damp and rotten. Old, mouldy food lay in a murky crevice. Located in the corner were three dead mice, which by the assistance of a few mousetraps, looked to be hanging their heads in shame.

I shivered, then noticed the walls; all four stood, crunching under their own weight. They were old, they were dying, and each one had more cracks than dried mud. Old, decrepit paintings hung loosely on the walls, all of them draped with dust and cobwebs. Cracks shot through the canvas, paint discoloured and worn by ageing figures. Sadness spilled out of the damp walls, each crying in desperate pain and hopelessness of being happy. Bright pink flakes of paint speckled the window frames with colour.

I turned my back. Out of the room, on the floor was the most incredible sight; my footprints in a blanket of dust, they warmed the floor with their presence. Old, tired furniture lay in one corner, a battered wardrobe, a crushed chair, highlighted with a sea of miserable, drab cobwebs. Down the dark damp hall I dragged my aching feet, each footstep creating an ungodly amount of dust and dirt. In the master bedroom stood a full-length mirror covered in faded memories of its once very colourful life. A dead spider could be seen swaying in the chilling breeze.

The gate hung on rusted dead hinges, the garden savaged by animals and the weather. Each weathering shrub had a silent story to tell to small insects that visited its decaying body once in a while. I left this old, living building with a sense of humbleness about me.

Andrea McNally (14)
Larne High School, Larne

The Accident

The chlorine smell still fills my nostrils as I try to put the memories of that terrible day into the back of my mind. The muffled and splashing sounds all come back into my head and I have to relive the monstrous events of that day.

Like every other warm day of that summer, my friends and I had agreed to meet at the new and exciting water park that had recently moved into our town. It was the newest attraction. Everyone gathered at it and people who were not even from our town came to it to try it out. When I got there I quickly changed and decided to go for a swim before the rest of the gang came.

The water was freezing, but a relief to me as I was already sweating from the sun. The place was starting to get crowded and I could barely move. I was on my second lap when I saw my friends walking towards me. 'Great to have you here. This place is packed today,' I exclaimed to them.

'Yeah ano,' replied Dani. 'But there is no queue at the water flume.'

'Last one there is a rotten egg!' Jamie shouted as he zoomed past us.

Me, being the competitively challenged person I am, was definitely not going to be the rotten egg!

I got there second, but I knew I would have to get my bag before I went back down the slide as my asthma was very bad at this time of the year.

I climbed up the steps as Jamie went flying down the slide. I took my place, but I knew I wasn't completely ready. Suddenly I felt this pain in the centre of my back and I was suddenly whizzing down the dark tunnel.

My chest tightened and I gasped for my breath. I could feel my heart racing and my head pounding as slowly the dark tunnel walls caved in around me.

When I woke up, I was in hospital. Everyone was around me. All Joni could do was say she was sorry, before explaining that she had tripped forward and hit me by accident.

I still find it hard to go into water without becoming frightened and I definitely cannot go down big slides at all.

Some people think it's fun to mess around in water parks but very rarely do they stop to think of the consequences.

Julieann Houston (15)
Larne High School, Larne

How The Daffodil Came To Be

One day Zeus decided to give all the gods a job. Hermes was the god of weather, Nicarrus was given the job of looking after all the gardens of the Earth and so on until all the jobs were taken up, but there was still one god left, Daffodil. Zeus tried to think of a job for Daffodil but he could think of none. Finally he remembered one job he had missed. 'Daffodil,' he said, 'you will be the god of sleep.'

'Oh what a boring job,' she moaned. 'Can't I be the god of music?' she begged. But Zeus had heard her playing her trumpet and she was terrible. No matter how much she begged, Zeus would not change his mind.

From then on Daffodil followed Zeus everywhere he went, playing her trumpet. It was terrible. Many complaints were made to Zeus about the noise. He warned her stop. Daffodil defiantly disobeyed and Zeus became extremely angry.

One day as she was following him Zeus turned around and said, 'I warned you but you didn't listen, now you will pay!' With a zap of his lightning bolt, he said, 'You will follow me no more!'

He banished Daffodil to the Earth into Nicarrus' garden. Her long slender body became a long green stem, her arms were leaves blowing in the wind, her legs became rooted to the ground and her proud head took the shape of a trumpet. The trumpet-like flower was called a daffodil, after her. Now we can see daffodils with their proud heads pointing to the sky begging Zeus to change them back.

Sinead Corr (12)
Limavady Grammar School, Limavady

The Sunflower

Sunflower was a tall, beautiful young girl with long dark hair and a gloomy face but in her beauty she was dark and grouchy. Sunflower, despite her name, hated the sun and sulked about in the shadows. The sun did not appreciate this at all in fact, the more he watched her, the more it infuriated him.

One day the sun confronted Sunflower. 'I have watched you now for half a year, sulking about and I do not appreciate it at all, you had better cheer up or there will be consequences.'

One year on and Sunflower had paid no attention to the sun's words so the sun brought all his power together and all of a sudden, Sunflower was rooted to the ground. Her long, slender body became a stem, her feet roots, her arms leaves, her face seeds and her long hair became petals. The sun looked down on Sunflower and said, 'Now you shall pay.'

Over the years, Sunflower's hair became bleached by the sun, her pale face became tanned and now every day Sunflower stretches to the sun as if begging him to turn her back.

Niamh McCann (12)
Limavady Grammar School, Limavady

Thunder And Lightning

This is the story of how thunder and lightning came to be.

Once upon a time the god, Thunder, was ruler of the skies and controlled it all. The one thing that annoyed Thunder the most, in all the heavens and Earth was Lord Lightning. They were always fighting and bickering together.

One day Lightning decided to annoy Thunder more by running in and out of the sky in a flash. Thunder was so angry that he chased Lightning but couldn't catch him. Lightning was just too fast. In fact he was so fast, that Thunder could barely see him as he ran in and out of the sky.

Thunder is still chasing Lightning wherever he goes to this day. Thunder is so angry that he still hasn't caught Lightning that he comes with a roaring and a crackling sound.

That is why every time there is lightning, thunder follows.

Hannah Jack (12)
Limavady Grammar School, Limavady

Rainbow

Once upon a time up on Mount Olympus there was a god called Bow. Bow was the god of colours.

Bow liked to help the people to get places but this made Ace, the god of places, really angry. Ace never liked Bow. Bow helped the people by getting down on his hands and knees like a bridge.

One day Bow was helping the Scottish people get to Ireland, then all of a sudden Ace came and pushed him and he killed about 90 people.

'When will you learn that you have to stick to the colours?' said Ace angrily.

'Well I do a better job than you ever have,' said Bow as he turned to walk away.

'Stop.'

'No I have to go help the Australian people get to China,' said Bow trying to be funny.

'I will make you stay like your silly bridges, although you will be all the colours you make, nobody will be able to get to you. You will only be seen really clearly in the rain when nobody goes out,' said Ace.

Bow was a friend of Sarah, the goddess of rain.

'Bow I will look after you and I will try not to . . . '

Two men came close enough to see Bow.

'What is it?' asked one of them.

'. . . Rain Bow . . .'

The two men ran to tell people what they had seen.

' . . . So that you can watch over the people,' said Sarah.

Chelcey Douglas (12)
Limavady Grammar School, Limavady

Pollo And The Volcano

This is the story of how volcanoes came about.

Once upon a time, there was a man called Pollo. Pollo had a very bad temper, he would yell at anyone for the slightest bad thing done. Zeus, the almighty God, was aware of Pollo's temper.

One sunny August day everybody was lazing about outside and not doing any work, this was of course approved by Zeus. But Pollo was not happy; he needed his corn to be picked from his field except there was no one to do it. He went thundering down the path towards the lake to a boy called Pluto. Pluto was an especially lazy boy, but that's another story.

Pollo began, 'You will come to my field at once and pull out my corn.'

'But I am not one of your workers, go get someone else.'

Pluto loosened Pollo's grip around his neck. 'You dare to disobey me,' Pollo roared.

'He should not listen to you,' roared back Zeus. Zeus had been watching everything from a distance. 'You will be punished Pollo.' With that Zeus turned Pollo into a volcano.

So every time a volcano erupts Pollo is angry. The volcano also represents Pollo in his appearance. His hair was auburn-red like the molten lava, and his skin was berry-brown like the trunk of the volcano.

Joanne Reay (12)
Limavady Grammar School, Limavady

Limas And Rose

The story of the rose came about like this.

One day a girl called Rose was walking in the woods and every god that passed her admired her because she smelt lovely and was very pretty. There was one god especially who liked her called Limas, but Rose was very vain and every time Limas told her that she was pretty, Rose told Limas that he was ugly, then she ran away.

One day Rose died, when Limas heard this he went to her body and brought her back to his house and buried her in his garden.

One day Limas thought that he could smell Rose and the smell was coming from the garden. Limas went out and saw these lovely pink flowers growing and called them roses. They smelt lovely and looked lovely but were very prickly because Rose was vain.

Hannah Neilly (12)
Limavady Grammar School, Limavady

The Rainbow

Did you know that a rainbow is actually, when viewed from above, a circle? That is why you cannot get to the end. This is how they came to be:

In the beginning, people were just as clever as us, but on a smaller scale. Instead of inventing cars, they invented bikes and instead of inventing planes, they made boats. One inventor designed a coat that was very colourful. It had red, orange, yellow, green, blue, indigo and violet stripes.

Hermes saw this coat and became jealous. He begged Zeus to make one for him, but Zeus decided to test him. He sent him on an errand to tell the local people of Jerusalem that there was a new god. Hermes would have to pass the coat on the way. Zeus knew that if he took the coat, he was not fit to be a god and would have to be punished.

So, Hermes went on his way as fast as he could. On the way, he saw the coat, and became so jealous that he took it. When he flew fast, you could see only a long line of different colours. He was called to Zeus at once, who said to him, 'You are not fit to be our messenger, you will be only able to fly in circles. You will be invisible until the rain comes, and you will make people happy when it does, so you will still be doing a good job forever.'

That is why rainbows appear.

James McCaffrey (12)
Limavady Grammar School, Limavady

Thunder And Lightning

This is how the story of thunder and lightning came to be.

One day on sunny Mount Olympus, where all the gods lived, the fairies were flittering about. They were mainly annoying one god called Thunder. Thunder had big muscles and dressed in grey all the time.

Usually Thunder was quite happy but today he was starting to get angry. Then one of the fairies came up and started to make faces at him. By this time, Thunder was so angry that he chased after the fairies. With every step he made a big boom.

All the fairies that stayed down low got stepped on which made a wicked flash of light. This light hit the Earth's surface and scared all the people.

That is how thunder and lightning came to be, so when you see it again, you will know that Thunder is chasing the fairies and sometimes stepping on them.

Pamela Nicholl (12)
Limavady Grammar School, Limavady

Heather

One day when gods ruled the Earth, the goddesses were getting dressed to go to the annual ball. Heather was fiddling with her hair, deciding what way she would style it. 'What way should I put up my lovely straight blonde hair?' Heather asked Hanna, her sister.

'Your hair is lovely, no matter what way you have it. I like you just the way you are!' replied Hanna.

'I don't,' said a voice. It was Ellen. Ellen was an ugly, unliked goddess. Some even called her a witch. Ellen had not been invited to the ball and was jealous of those who had, especially the pretty ones like Heather.

'I'll show you what it's like not to be pretty.'

At that, Ellen pointed a finger at Heather and she shrank into a small delicate flower. It had purple curly petals that stood straight on end. Ellen was shocked. The flower was still very beautiful. Ellen remembered the god of all gods, Zeus, saying that beauty would never change despite how powerful the spell may be. Ellen stormed off embarrassed at her failure.

Hanna took the small flower outside and planted it in the soil. To this day, we still call the flower heather and it is still very pretty.

Clare Henderson (12)
Limavady Grammar School, Limavady

My Time-Travelling Experience

My name is Stephen and I have invented a high voltage time machine that's faster than the speed of light. Going back 10 years will take 10 seconds. Going 10 years to the future would take about 10 minutes.

Now I will attempt to go back when the designers at Austin were toying with the idea of making a car named the 'Mini'.

I quickly got into my machine which was painted as blue as the sky, well, actually, it was just a Ford Anglia with some modifications, but she was still my big blue beast!

I slammed my foot on the accelerator, flew through the garage door, bringing them off their hinges. I went over the coast, then right off the Earth, into space, around Mars twice, then flew back to Earth and parked outside the Austin Design Centre. I jumped out of my Anglia and walked over to the door. I found myself inside the centre. There were no computers for designing. All was done skilfully by hand.

There I was in the 1950s with the Austin Mini design team. That was last year and I can't even remember the designers' names.

Now the Mini I know and love is often called 'the Classic Mini'. BMW have made a new Mini called the 'Mini One', but I still prefer the Classic Mini. I know any time I want to go and see the first few Minis, I just get into my Anglia and fly across space faster than lightning!

Stephen Nelson (12)
Newtownhamilton High School, Newry

Spell Disaster

Alone, I sat in the dark room as I spoke the larken to give my potion the extra lift. As I stood there like a scarecrow, my pink skirt, suspended in mid-air did the salsa with my brother's Sunday trousers. It was like a dance competition they moved with such elegance. It was like they were possessed, then it was like the evil gene just kicked in. There were vases on the floor smashed into tiny little pieces, as I ran over the floor it sounded like bubble wrap. As I tried to remember the spell to stop this poppycock, my body was like jelly and my mind went blank and I fell to the floor, luckily I did too as a vase went flying over me. As I stood up I had a 'don't mess with me' look on my face.

As I said the words that would stop this destruction 'luma gayga' they just got worse, they were like propellers spinning round. As I thought like a professor of psychology, I felt like my brain as about to explode and I'd seen it in front of me and I'd faint and wake up from this futuristic vision. As I spoke some gibberish my skirt hit me like a cold wind.

As I spoke some magic words they just fell on the floor it was like someone had just cut their string. I felt such relief. Then suddenly I saw a twinge in the skirt and it suddenly became a showdown and I pointed my finger at it and said 'zip' and then that was the end.

Lynsey Dodds (13)
Newtownhamilton High School, Newry

The Lost Soul

As I lay silently in my bed I watched the candle flicker and dance like a dead ghost brought back to life by the spirit of night. As the tiny, fragile, snowflakes fell from the starry sky onto the rock hard ground, all I could hear was the footsteps of homeless children tapping away like a hammer trying to keep warm and huddling together like lost souls wandering the seven seas. Nowhere to go, no one to love and care for them. All they had was each other.

I hopped like a kangaroo out of my warm bed and over to the window. Outside snow settled onto the ground and melted like butter, in the ground, its funeral over in seconds. A little girl as small as a mouse and as thin as a stick, stood at the corner of my huge, red brick house. She looked about twelve or so and was like a statue. She glared into the sky; gazing at the stars her face was full of warmth and joy, like a newborn baby.

I tiptoed as quietly as a church mouse down the long, cold stairs and into the sweet-smelling kitchen. I opened the fridge and as quick as a flash of lightning I picked out some ham, bread and a drink of ice-cold milk. The cold November air hit my face, like a thousand sharp knives as I walked outside into the small, shabby street. Inch by inch I walked up to her and realised just how beautiful she was. She had bright, warm eyes like the sun. Her body was like a porcelain doll and it seemed that if she fell her body would be shattered into millions of pieces of precious gold.

When she saw me striding up to her she backed away like a nervous puppy but I reassured her not to be frightened. She gratefully took the food and gulped it down as if she had not eaten for years. We started to chat and she told me she was an orphan. Her mother and father were killed in a car crash, a few years back. Her eyes filled with liquid like a dry riverbed filling with water. She had been living on the streets ever since. The night went on and we talked for hours upon hours, like clucking hens gobbling on about nonsense.

I suddenly realised how late it was and out of my pocket I took a little piece of paper, saying the address of a children's association. This would help her to get her life in full motion again. She disappeared into the night like a bird flying into the sky.

I have never forgotten her and she still lies in the back of my mind, her delicate face glowing with warmth.

Lauren Henry (12)
Newtownhamilton High School, Newry

Shipwrecked

It's been a long day on this island like a small ant in the middle of the Sahara desert. I've been building a shelter out of the ship for my crewmates and myself, it is hard work, though it's worth it. We used the sail as blankets to keep us warm. As we had nothing for mattresses we all had to lie on the ground which was solid as rock.

Next day I'd had a sore back, no wonder, all of us had, except Hammar and Zelda were fit and well to work, Hammar started building mattresses while Zelda went and picked leaves and fruit. Hammar had already made our mattresses in five hours, while he was building them Zelda had come back with over thousands of leaves and fruit. So Zelda came up with an idea that she and Hammar would put leaves on the top of the mattresses but Hammar had already thought that up and that's why she was sent for leaves.

Three weeks later

I've just discovered a new fruit called alpingpine and you can make alpingpine juice out of it. We have just finished our house and are just starting on the other people's houses, which are very hard to build. There are many weird creatures about this place they are very weird indeed. I wonder, I wonder if they are a good source of food? *Yuck!* It wouldn't be very nice at all, I don't want to think about it but it won't come off my mind. Oh well! Time to go to bed, it's getting late, see you later, *I hope.*

Lesley-Ann Hanna (10)
Newtownhamilton High School, Newry

The Day I Thought My Life Changed

I woke up one morning and I couldn't feel my feet but instead fur!

I opened my eyes I looked down at my feet but I couldn't walk but instead I could fly! I had marvellous wings. I flew over to the mirror but I could not see myself but instead I saw . . . a beautiful butterfly with lovely wings that fluttered in the wind. My wings were pink, baby-pink, blue and violet. I couldn't believe it, how could I have changed from a stunning girl with flowing blonde hair into a butterfly?

I flew down to Mum but I didn't know what to say, but I never got to that point became Mum got a jam jar and she started swaying it around then a lovely strawberry smell came flowing up my nose. I started flying very fast to see where it was coming from. Then I realised it was the jam pot. She kept me in it for a long time I thought I would never get out and I was going to die. But thankfully she let me go. I flew up into my bedroom, and I woke up the next morning and realised it was just a dream, but then I saw a jam pot with a butterfly sitting on the window sill. I asked Mum when did she catch it. She replied yesterday, but that is when I had my dream. (Strange or what!)

Jennifer Stoops (12)
Newtownhamilton High School, Newry

The Orphan

Hello. My name is Emma. I am 11 years old. I wear clothes like any other homeless person. Ragged, old, dirty trousers that smell like rats and a grotty old T-shirt. I have no shoes and no money. I look like a big, ugly pig. I love the sweet smell of the bread, but I never eat bread, but as I pass the grand and rather posh houses I watch the women roll out the dough and then the smell pours out of the window like a river as the bread cooks.

I am at the minute sitting in an alley, thinking back to all the years I have spent on the streets. It's mid-summer now and the temperatures are high.

I wonder what life would be like if I went to the workhouse. Maybe it would be better to stay out here begging for my food. Life isn't so bad I suppose. I have my little box and my warm blanket to keep me warm and dry. I like the summers they're like being in an oven with the bread. I love the summers when I lie out at night and look at the stars as they twinkle like diamonds.

Oh how I loved the smell of Mum's perfume and the laugh of my dear sister.

I will probably never get enough money for a bed. My life will just go on living on the streets of London and begging for my food.

Laura Nesbitt (12)
Newtownhamilton High School, Newry

Heartache

The ambulance with its blue roaring siren raced up the road like a flash of lightning followed by the cops.

'What's up with them?' I questioned my loyal friend.

'Who knows?' was the reply.

Just hours later my next-door neighbour arrived and I was taken out of the boring French lesson. I returned, eyes red as roses from crying and fighting to keep the tears from streaming down my face. I remained silent! Spoke to no one! The shock never sunk in. I believed I was dreaming! I wished I was dreaming! I kept nipping myself.

'Why me?'

A police officer approached and confirmed that two people had been shot by evil, heartless intruders, one dead the other severely injured. Reluctantly I entered the house. I will forever regret it. Bloodstained walls! Forensics everywhere! Worse of all - how do I explain to my four-year-old sister that her dad is in Heaven and Mum is seriously hurt? She'll never understand.

I had to go to the hospital, identify the body but while I was there I received more shocking news. Mum had died from internal bleeding! I broke down. I don't remember much of what happened next but I do remember the next morning, my little sister comforting me. Bless her! She knew no different, just wanted her 14-year-old sister to be happy. Everyone was great but I'll remain positive that those horrible monsters will be brought to justice. Then I'll live in peace.

Jenna Smyth (13)
Newtownhamilton High School, Newry

Our Exciting But Scary Day Through The Forest

One beautiful Saturday morning, the sun was shining brightly in the sky. I decided to walk over to John's house, he was my friend. When I went over his mother made John and I breakfast, and we talked a good part of the morning. Then we decided to go for a walk through the forest, down by the old river.

So we set off heading towards the forest down by the old river. We were thinking about the summer holiday, which was coming up soon, and what we would do throughout the glorious and wonderful summer. We were walking through the forest as happy as Larry talking about what we would do through the summer, when all of a sudden we heard a very quiet noise coming from the tree, it sounded very scary! We ran straight home to fetch both of our parents and we all ran as fast as we had ever run before.

Then eventually we arrived as scared as if we were being tortured. We were walking about through the forest for about two hours to find the same spot when we heard the noise. When we got there we heard the noise again but none of us had a clue what it was. We decided to call up to Uncle Joe's to get a ladder to see what it was.

When we came back to the forest John's dad David went up the ladder to see what it was. As he moved slowly but surely up the ladder it was getting louder and louder! When he got to the top he realised that it was just a baby squirrel. Then we all laughed and laughed the whole way home at how stupid we had been.

Gareth Scroggie (13)
Newtownhamilton High School, Newry

A Final Farewell

As she lay there the pale walls surrounded her and a screen kept bleeping. The sound of people no longer concerned her, not knowing the details, there she was, torn apart. Health was no longer hers. Her companion from the car, where was he? She remembered his cheery face and how they had laughed together. That was history. She gave a hopeless sigh. The door behind her opened, who was it? She did not have the strength to turn.

Her mother walked over to her side, her eyes red and tears streaming down her cheeks. 'Katie,' she said and then began to cry. 'There's no hope for you, the doctor said 24 hours.'

She did not move, she was expecting it, but not just as soon. Why did Jeff have to drive so fast? Was it even his fault? What would his parents think of her?

'Where's Jeff?' she spluttered.

'He's in intensive care, but he's going to pull through,' her mother croaked.

Well at least that was a burden off her heart.

'What must his parents think of me?' she groaned.

Her mother did not answer. Then a nurse walked in to check her monitor.

'Do one last thing for me. Tell Jeff's parents I'm truly sorry for what I put them through,' she said softly and closed her eyes for the last time.

'Why didn't you tell her you'd do that for her?' the nurse said primly.

'Oh, I wish I could have but in the other car were his parents, and they're dead,' her mother cried bitterly.

Sarah Foster (13)
Newtownhamilton High School, Newry

A Fish Life

It was a beautiful, sunny, warm, colourful day in the glittering Barrier Reef. Home to billions of strange and wonderful species of fish, sharks, rays, jellyfish and many others. Thousands of tourists visit the Barrier Reef every year to see the fish they also can snorkel, scuba-dive and go on boat trips.

This story isn't just all about the Barrier Reef it's about a tiny stingray called Ray, his mum and dad were Spanish and were called Loco and Rico. Ray's best friend was called Flemo who was a small clownfish.

One day Ray and Flemo were playing among all the coral. Then Flemo spotted something glittering in the distance, Flemo approached it and saw a delicious, juicy worm squirming in the water. Ray saw what he was looking at, it was what his dad Rico had told him about, it was a hook to capture fish. Ray shouted but it was too late, he was already eating the worm then in a flash he was zoomed up through the ocean to the surface, Ray swam after him but it was too late, he was gone.

Then the boat with a roar took off across the ocean Ray rushed after it, but it was going too fast! Then it started to slow down and stopped at the harbour. Ray rushed back to the bunch of coral he lived in and burst in and told his mum and dad what had happened. They rushed off back to the boat with him. They reached the boat and started to circle it then a diver looked over at them and with one sweep of his net he caught all of them. He put them in a tank - it was massive with trees and coral and Flemo was there too, it was beautiful, warm water and knew they would like it there.

Neil Hughes (13)
Newtownhamilton High School, Newry

Earth's Invasion

It was Monday morning and the sun was shining and everyone was going to work. There seemed to be no trouble around the world but then, when it turned 10 o'clock, all radar systems around the world went mad. Thousands of UFOs appeared and locked into the mind of the most important man in the world and told him to give up now and no one would die. They gave him one week to stand down but first he had a meeting with all the head people of each country and they all decided to fight against the threat.

The day before they were to come back every country got ready with all the weapons they had. The Threat had seen this in their crystal ball and put a protection on their ship.

The final day had come and Earth attacked with their weapons but the protection on their ship made it indestructible. The Threat landed on Earth. They were giant slugs and snails with vaporising guns. They were also indestructible with gunfire. So they killed all in sight and invaded every home.

Some people tried to fight but with no effect until a family called the Reedymix ran into their house and threw everything at the invaders. The last thing in the house was the salt and it seemed to just melt them away.

It caught on everywhere else and the Threat was melted away. After this the world had to try to return to normal but with one billion of the world's population dead it was not going to be easy. So it was decided to have a day to mourn the death of all those people.

William Geary (13)
Newtownhamilton High School, Newry

My Brother's Funny Incident!

One day when my brother and I were up at my auntie's house we were told to go down and feed the cattle in the field below her house. We went down the lane as quick as you could say Bob's your uncle.

There was a hole in the ditch that you could fit through. Well Andrew jumped over and landed in the field so I followed. We both jumped as high as a bargepole.

We had finished feeding the cattle so I walked over to the gate and discreetly climbed over it but my brother, the smart Alec he was, and still he tried to jump back through the ditch. Instead of landing on the bank he landed in the shuck. I ran up the lane as quick as a bolt out of the blue, got my auntie and she came down with a rope to pull him out.

That didn't work so we had to use grandad's tractor. I was scared in case we couldn't get him out. It was like a fox cornering his prey. When my auntie came down I was relieved because she had brought help with her.

We hooked the rope around his waist and pulled as hard as we could. It was like a tug of war match. In the end we got him out. My mum was cross but gave out a sigh of relief that he was okay.

Norma McClenaghan (12)
Newtownhamilton High School, Newry

The Time Machine And The Diamond

My gran took me to visit the Stevenson Museum. I was so bored because the tour was dragging on and Gran was so engrossed in the history of it all.

We came to this magnificent diamond ring that sent a series of colours in different directions under the powerful lights.

The tour guide told us the diamond was very valuable and a plot to steal it back in 1801 had been foiled. He was beginning to give an explanation of this event when I wandered off to do a little exploring myself.

I was dallying down a narrow, dark corridor when suddenly I fell down a hole in the ground and sped towards a strange-looking machine.

I dusted myself off and noticed a plaque on the machine stating the manufacturer's name and date 'Louis Baker 1800'. There was a door to the front, which was half open and through the split I could see a series of flashing lights and buttons. I sneaked in very nervously, curious to know what would happen if I pressed the . . . argh! Oh no! What had I done? I made a rush for the door - *bang!* The door slammed shut and the machine rattled and banged, *whoosh!* We were off!

The years on the clockometer were whizzing back in time and eventually stopped on 1801. Everything went quiet. I rushed to the door and pushed it so hard that I fell out onto very hard ground. Just then a voice shouted, 'Stop thief!' I raised my arms in the air thinking he was speaking to me when suddenly a man was running towards me with a diamond in his hand. He was about to jump over me when I lifted my leg into the air, tripping him up. The diamond went hurtling into the air and landed, unharmed, on the ground.

The man who was chasing the thief quickly tied the thief up and retrieved the diamond. 'Oh thank you little girl, this diamond is the main attraction at the museum and is very valuable. Thanks to you, it is still the main attraction.'

I picked myself up and raced to the time machine. Pressed the other button to take me forward in time again. It rattled and banged its way back to 2004 again. When it stopped back in the same place I quickly ran back to Gran who was still engrossed in the tour.

She had never missed me and began to tell me the story of how the diamond had been stolen and then recovered thanks to some little girl. If only she knew who that little girl really was!

Aimée Chambers (12)
Newtownhamilton High School, Newry

Confinement

As I sit and stare at the walls around me I think about what could have been. If only I had not been caught, if only I'd been more careful. Looking back on it I see clearly where I went wrong. I became too confident. I could have kept my feet firmly on the ground. I would have been very cautious. If I had done this I could have been rich. I could have been free! To begin with no one knew I was selling speed, only those concerned, but then word got around. I should have never let that happen. Yet it did happen and that is when it all started to go very wrong. I was out on the street selling it and all of a sudden I heard sirens getting louder and louder. I threw all the drugs into a bag and ran in a tiny alleyway. I hid behind a big massive bin.

Then I saw a police car and a police motorbike going past the end of the alleyway. Just when I thought I was safe a police car blocked each end of the alley and the police motorbike came up the middle after me. I thought I was trapped, but there was an old derelict factory and I ran up the stairs and tried to get through the door, but it was locked.

I tried to break the door but it wouldn't move so I went through the open window and I ran inside and hid behind a big massive machine and the police came in after me. They caught me and put me in jail for 15 years.

Ryan Martin (12)
Newtownhamilton High School, Newry

The Mystery

One Saturday morning, a very dull morning, I got up and had my breakfast. As normal I just about took time to eat it, but something seemed to be wrong, but of course I didn't know what it was.

I passed no remarks but went on the way I normally would. Although I went on as usual I couldn't help thinking about what could be the matter. It was like there was magic in the air.

I got dressed, got my breakfast and went out. When I went out I found out what was wrong. Somebody or something had crashed into our wall at the front of our house and had crumbled the wall as if it was a biscuit.

The horrible feeling of not knowing what had gone wrong had vanished but an even worse feeling hung over me, that I didn't know if it was a ghost or a human in a car or something like that had crumbled it.

Eventually our neighbour Joe White came down the road and told us that he was very sorry that he had knocked it down when he had fallen asleep at three o'clock on Saturday morning. He said not to worry about it, that he would pay for it to be rebuilt.

That had solved my problems and I was as happy as Larry because I was all excited about getting it rebuilt.

Merlyn Hughes (12)
Newtownhamilton High School, Newry

Myth - David Beckham

David Beckham was one of Man United's star players who could pass, shoot and score!

He could always come up with an answer when his team were losing, and that was to score a goal. Everyone who supported or played in the team loved David Beckham's football, except for one man, Alex Ferguson.

United were drawn against league holders Arsenal in the fifth round of the FA Cup, a match neither team wanted to lose. When the big day arrived the two managers told their men to do their clubs proud by producing a win, but only one team could win.

The two teams lined - out and kicked off. It started off very rough with three yellow cars in the first three minutes. All calmed down after a while, and halfway through the second half Arsenal scored a goal, and Ferguson wasn't happy. Nothing changed until half-time. After the players had their refreshments and team talk, the players lined out once again and play resumed. It started off the same way as it did the first, with rough tackles and yellow cards. After 25 minutes gone in the second half Arsenal struck again with a goal that made it 2-0 to The Gunners. Ferguson was very cross, especially after he had run out of chewing gum. The referee blew his whistle and the match was over, and Arsenal had won.

Sir Alex walked behind his players disappointed with his team and cross with Beckham.

In the changing room Alex was very angry and saw a boot and Beckham in his way. Kicking the boot and hitting Beckham above the eye, Ferguson said, 'You played awfully and you did nothing David.' Beckham said nothing and walked out to his car. He jumped in and drove to hospital.

On his way he asked the football gods what he should do. They told him that he should prove to Alex what he could do in the Juventus game, in the midweek.

With his eye stitched and mended he was ready for Tuesday's game. He did prove to Ferguson what he could do in the match by setting up two of the three goals that United scored.

Sir Alex hasn't said anything to Beckham yet and the two men have never argued since.

Enda McElvogue (13)
St Ciaran's High School, Ballygawley

Oisin

Once upon a time there was a god called Hermes and a goddess called Fiona. Hermes was very tall with long golden hair that changed to fire when he was angry.

Fiona had pale skin, which shone, and brown hair that trailed along the ground as she walked. They had a son called Oisin who was very strong, but ever since Oisin was born, Jingo, their arch enemy, was trying to get him. Jingo had a scar down his right eye and black short hair; he had dark eyes that were as black as coal. Jingo and Hermes were friends all through their lives but three years ago they had a row which ended up leaving them hating each other for the rest of their lives.

Oisin possessed a power no other god ever had; he had the ability to control anything he wanted to, even the minds of the most powerful gods. If Jingo killed Oisin then he would possess the power. It was a friend of Fiona's who had a vision the day, before Oisin was kidnapped about a terrible slaughtering in Kingdom of Hermes.

It was a normal day in the Kingdom of Hermes, the day the kidnapping happened. Orla, Oisin's aunt, was looking after him in the nursery, when the doors were flung open and in marched about 20 men with the head of each guard that was protecting Oisin, in their hands. Orla screamed as they grabbed her and slashed her on the arm. She lay bleeding on the ground and the men parted to reveal Jingo. He strolled up to Orla and kicked her. Then he picked up the baby. Jingo stared coldly at Oisin as if remembering the scar Hermes had left on his face. Then with a flash Jingo, Oisin and the men were gone.

Hermes and his guards rushed in to find the place a mess. They saw Orla lying on the ground and asked her who had done this, with her last breath she replied Jingo and Hermes dissolved into thin air. When he reappeared again. He was in Jingo's lair, and around him was an army of soldiers. Hermes knew he had made a mistake so he tried to dissolve but couldn't. This was the end. He bowed his head and the army rushed in to kill him. But Jingo felt sorry for him and made him a slave. Hermes said he would only work for Jingo on one condition that he spared his son's life. So Jingo agreed, only he was ruling and Hermes was his slave.

Marie McKenna (12)
St Ciaran's High School, Ballygawley

Odin

Once upon a time there was a god called Odin. Odin's daughter was called Aoife. Aoife was the most beautiful girl in Ireland. She had long blonde hair down to her waist.

One day Aoife was on her way to the market to buy some food, when she came across a man telling her to come with him. He led her to a dark cave outside the town. In there was a man, a tall, powerful god called Hades. He was the god of the underworld. Aoife was frightened, she didn't try to escape because they had done nothing to her.

He spoke, 'Aoife, come live with me here in the underground and I will give you anything you want.'

Aoife didn't know what to say, she had just seen a man who she'd never seen before and he asked her to live with him. She replied, 'I'm sorry, I can't live with you, I will become the queen when my mother dies.'

Meanwhile, Odin was wondering where Aoife had got to. He went to the market to get her. He met one of Aoife's friends and asked her where she was. She told him about the man taking her to Hades. Odin and Hades were enemies ever since Odin became god and he knew he would be up to something.

So Odin went to Hades' cave to get Aoife. Odin burst into the cave and rushed over to Aoife.

'Get out of my world and go back to your palace!' said Hades.

'Aoife don't be fooled by him he's nothing but evil!' said Odin.

'I can make my own decisions Father!' demanded Aoife.

'She's right, it's her life, her decision,' said Hades.

'I have an idea, why don't we fight for her?' suggested Odin.

'That sounds great, so what are you waiting for?' said Hades.

'Don't! I don't want to live with you down here,' Aoife said.

'What? Why? I will give you anything you want,' said Hades shocked.

'I don't want to live with you either Father,' said Aoife.

'What do you mean? You can't live anywhere else!' said Odin, confused.

'I will create my own land and have it run the way I want,' said Aoife.

'You couldn't do that, you don't have the power!' said Hades.
'That's fine with me, I will give the power to do that,' said Odin, happy that she didn't choose to live with Hades.

And that's what Aoife did.

Emma O'Neill (13)
St Ciaran's High School, Ballygawley

The King And His Three Children

Long, long ago in the land of Navan there was a king called Stephen who had three children. They were Prince Dara, Princess Rachel and Prince Conor. All four of them lived in a castle on the top of a hill overlooking the village. People liked the king but sadly his time had come and he was going to die. So one night before dinner the king called his three children into the family room. He said to them, 'I am going to die soon, so I will have to decide which one of you will become next king or queen.'

They all thought for a while and then Prince Dara came up with an idea. He said, 'Whoever can fill every room in the castle will become next queen or king.'

During dinner they were thinking of what they could do.

The next day they all went out to buy stuff. Prince Conor came upon a man with a cart full of feathers. He said to him, 'I will pay you three silver coins for your feathers.' This was fine and they traded.

Then Prince Dara was out on the streets and he came across a small boy with a tin whistle. He said to the boy, 'I will pay you two silver coins for your tin whistle.' This was acceptable and they traded.

Then it came to Princess Rachel and she was at the market. She bought 80 candles of all different shapes and sizes.

It was the day of the contest and the king gathered them all in the hall. He said to Prince Conor, 'What have you got for me?' Conor took out the feathers and got the maids to go and fill the rooms but they only filled 20 rooms. Then the king said the same thing to Prince Dara and he took out his tin whistle and started blowing it. The king then said, 'I think we have our next king.'

Suddenly Princess Rachel said, 'Let me have my go first Father.' Rachel then took out the feathers and everyone laughed. She gave the candles to the maids to put in every room and light. It lit up every room. The king was just about to say it was a draw when one of the maids came up and asked when Prince Conor was going to blow his tin whistle.

'It looks like we have a winner then,' said the king. 'The new queen will be Princess Rachel.'

Some months later King Stephen died and Rachel became queen. The village was very happy and they all lived happily ever after.

Megan McDonnell (12)
St Ciaran's High School, Ballygawley

Persephone Falls In Love

When Persephone returned from the Underworld her mother Demeter welcomed her home by throwing a party for her. Everyone was there. Hercules asked Persephone for a dance and they spent the rest of the evening together. They had so much in common that they decided to meet again. Persephone told Demeter about her wonderful night with Hercules. Demeter thought this was great but when Zeus and Hades found out there was trouble. Demeter told Zeus and he was furious.

When Hercules and Persephone met up again Hades spotted them together. He went and confronted them. 'Persephone what the heck are you doing romancing with this young man?'

Persephone replied, 'Hercules and I are in love.'

Hades then went and had a talk with Demeter and Zeus. Demeter was the only one who thought that their relationship was a good idea. Persephone returned home to a house of anger. Zeus and Hades tried to convince Persephone to end her relationship with Hercules and she would not listen.

Demeter then took Persephone and herself outside for a walk. Persephone immediately saw a huge sign that said *Will You Marry Me Persephone?* on it. Persephone ran up to Hercules and said, 'The answer is yes!' But when Zeus and Hades found out about their marriage Hades told Zeus that they would abduct and threaten to kill Hercules if the wedding went ahead.

The day of the wedding finally arrived and Hercules did not turn up for it so Persephone and Demeter sent out a search party for him. Persephone went home and cried in her room. She overheard Zeus and Hades talking about the way they had abducted Hercules. Persephone slipped out unnoticed and headed for the Underworld to rescue Hercules. When she got there she saw Hercules tied up with a rope. She went and got a sword but it was no good. So she started to unravel it. It was too late. Hercules had been stabbed too many times for him to survive.

Ciara McGoldrick (13)
St Ciaran's High School, Ballygawley

The Cursed Gift

Shane woke up to his alarm clock ringing in his head. He knew he had to get up then he fell out of bed. He knew he was going to have a bad day. He got dressed, had the usual hot buttered toast and coffee, and then got into the car to drive to work. He turned on the news on his radio. The reporter said, 'Good morning it's 10 o'clock.' Shane looked at his watch. It said nine o'clock. He wondered a moment. He'd forgotten to set the clocks forward. He was late for work.

His boss gave him a lecture about how if he wasn't there on time he could find himself another job. 'Take the day off. You're obviously having a bad day,' Shane's boss offered.

'Thank you, Sir,' Shane replied.

When he walked down the steps of the office block, a voice from an alley called his name. He went over to check it out. A bony, wrinkly hand came out from a hole in the ground and pulled him in.

Where was he? Whose hand was it? These questions raced through his mind as he lay there in darkness. A candle was lit in the distance. He made his way towards it. An old woman appeared. She stood staring at him a few moments and then lifted something off the ground. It was a cat. Then she drew breath to speak. 'Here,' she said in a low tone. With that she gave him a book, only a few pages though.

Whoosh! He was back in bed. He was confused. He turned on the TV. 8.30. He checked his watch. 8.30. He was early getting up. The cat was sitting there, staring at him. Then Shane took the book from his back pocket. All it said was, 'Be good to the cat and you will have good luck but if you are bad to it, you will have bad luck'.

For months Shane looked after the cat well and he got promoted at work and a bigger pay. He won competitions and prize draws and became rich. Without thinking, he literally kicked the cat out through the door and it went flying over the hedge. When the letters came the next morning, they cut off his electric. This was from the Electricity Board. The next letter was about his house being repossessed from the council. He had 24 hours to get his stuff and get out. He was out on the street and for the rest of his life he sat on the street begging for food and money.

Edward McClenaghan (13)
St Ciaran's High School, Ballygawley

Fall Of The Philippines

My name is L Griffin. I used to be a mechanic in Pennsylvania, until I was drafted for the US army. My mother was proud of me, although I knew she was scared at heart. A few months later I was shipped out to The Philippines.

Now here I am, surrounded by my fellow infantrymen. Although there are so many of us, I can't help but think, *what lies in wait in these bullet-ridden streets?*

Firstly, I check ammo, a must for all marines, and then set off speedily yet always aware of the ever-present danger of an ambush. My division meets up with the men already here holding back the Axis troops. The Japanese empire is moving into position with the Germans as an armed force. The sense of danger is a real one and I am scared. I don't often say that either.

I take my gun in both hands and make a run for the sandbags in front of me. Already I see many dead bodies, American and Japanese alike. We are taking heavy sniper fire but I quickly disperse them with a few rounds of my Browning automatic machine gun, the infantryman's best friend, or so they say. I am called to 'escort' a tank to another part of the town. It drives on and I easily take out any threat.

I remember that I have to take out a control tower that is directing the Japanese what to do.

I walk in and there are only two guards, one man sleeping on the ground and one pretty much dead.

Better not disturb him, I thought. Instead, I put 4 c4 charges down, one in every corner! I ran outside but pressed the detonator a bit too soon. The sound of the explosion ripped through my ears like a knife! I was stunned and could not see for some time!

Anyway, as planned, the tower was down, along with the Axis Navigation. My mission was complete. I would now make my way for the LZ. That explosion was enough for anyone to hear! The last thing I needed was to attract unwanted attention!

Pearce Cullen (14)
St Patrick's Academy, Dungannon

The Waiting Game

I can remember that day like it was yesterday, it was just a few weeks after my 11th birthday. That day, the sky was lit up with fluorescent rays of sun and the birds were humming together in harmony, it was just an average August day, but in reality it wasn't.

The bad news came a few days prior. My mother's jaw almost bounced off the floor when the phone call came, we knew it had to be bad news, no one ever rings at teatime.

I couldn't remember Aunt Sheila, I tried to refresh my memory by looking at old pictures, hidden on top of the kitchen in a tattered old biscuit tin, but to no avail; it was like she never existed - or, she was very camera shy.

The morning of her arrival I awoke extra early to help tidy up the house. There was feeling of anxiety around the house, Dad didn't even have something to say, he was too busy polishing one of his prized golfing trophies.

Mum seemed to be harrowed by the thought of Sheila's arrival, I couldn't help but think Aunt Sheila was a hysterical, age-old woman with a blue rinse to match her favourite two-piece suit.

The scones that were bought especially for the visit were laid out on the coffee table, Mum's best china cups were even allowed to escape the dusty old cabinet.

Mum wouldn't tell me anything about Aunt Sheila, maybe she felt the walls had ears, or maybe she just was trying to divert her thoughts to something more pleasant.

As our definite Armageddon drew nearer, I noticed Mum was getting edgy; she even started to bite her nails, something she had forbidden in our house since, I can't remember!

The small hand hit four, and a lull engulfed the house, you could've heard a pin drop, five more minutes passed, and still nothing happened, we started to thank our blessings.

Mum was about to wipe her brow, when a feeble tap came to the door, the three of us sat looking at each other, I decided it was up to me to answer the door.

I left an imprint in the slimy green sofa and walked ever so slowly towards the door, I thought about saying a few prayers, but I determined it would be better to get this over with.

As I reached the front door, my arm moved towards the doorknob, I felt a cold shiver run down my spine. In a flash of a second I opened the door at the speed of light. I refused to look outside at first, but in time my reluctant eyes met a frail old woman in a wheelchair clutching her handbag in her hands as tight as she could.

Was this meagre old lady what Mum and Dad were scared about, or was I judging a book by its cover?

Shane Telford (14)
St Patrick's Academy, Dungannon

A Day In The Life Of John Patterson

John Patterson was a regular postman in Boston, America, until one day things changed. He came home from work to the news that he had been drafted into the war in Vietnam. He didn't want to go but he knew if he didn't that his father would never speak to him again. His father had been a soldier in World War II and had lost his right leg, 'A small price to pay for your country'. So, reluctantly he packed his bag, said his goodbyes and left for an army camp called *'Tiger Land'*.

When he arrived he was signed up to Colonel Labtec's Platoon. John met a man called Sam Scogin who became his partner for the daily 20 mile jog. When he got back to camp he got his food in the mess then John and the rest of the platoon were allowed some free time. Most of the men wrote a letter home to their family including Sam so John decided to write home as well. He wrote to his mother and father and a separate letter to his wife who was expecting their first child. It said:

'Dear Ruth,

It has only been a week since I saw you last but it feels like months. I am hating every second that I have to be away from you. I have been assigned to Colonel Labtec, one of the most strict men here, but I think I am managing. I have made a friend. His name is Sam Scogin. He is really nice, you'd like him. We have to go on a 20 mile jog every day. I know it sounds tough but it's getting easier. I probably won't be saying that in the morning. Write back soon.

Your loving husband, John.

PS I love you'.

When John had finished the letter he went to his bunk. It was 2100hrs, early for some, but sleep was precious. They could be called into battle at any time.

Daniel Toner (13)
St Patrick's Academy, Dungannon

Coma

I'm here, wherever here is, and I'm with me, whoever I am. How long I have been in this transmogrified state is unknown to me. Little snippets of a 'past', manoeuvre and inveigle their way to float before my closed eyes, challenging me to embrace and reclaim them.

Eidetically, the sound of children laughing and jeering, the fetid stench of burning and the surrealistic terror of pain, compound and haunt my conticent world.

There are names that resonate throughout my head. Names from somewhere, but nowhere. Names like Edith and Edward, Catesby and Percy, Johnson and Tresham. They semaphorically waver before me, as if taunting me with their alien significance.

I try, in my own way to pray for guidance in this infernal slumber. Yet I am filled with ineradicable turmoil. My religion offers little solace. I have been forsaken, abandoned in limbo.

. . . Vaguely I can hear something and I am filled with an insurgent hope. I am aware of some tangible force. With Herculean effort I manage to groan. My mouth is so dry, yet I'm afraid that if I don't formulate something coherent, my chance of awakening will have gone.

Gradually my eyelids flicker open to reveal a hazy globular outline. I hear words emanating from this vicinity, indistinct at first.

'. . . Therefore Mr Fawkes, due to the severity of your burns, you will remain with us indefinitely. I get the feeling that we'll be seeing a lot of you, and your pyrotechnical friends. I would even guess, *annually!'*

Richard Fox (14)
St Patrick's Academy, Dungannon

The Rocktown Banshee!

In the town land of Rocktown on the fifth of November in nineteen hundred and three, a terrible accident happened to a man called Franciejohn Convery.

A man called Williejames O'Kane was the local potato merchant. He came about every single month to collect Franciejohn and his wife's so-called delicious potatoes for the past twenty years. This month Williejames O'Kane came round as usual to purchase some potatoes. But the thing he didn't know was that the Converys had a terrible month because blight had hit their crop and Franciejohn went on ahead and sold the potatoes for the usual price.

When Williejames O'Kane got home he took the potatoes straight to the market, as he had never had any problems with the Convery's potatoes before. Then when a customer confronted Williejames with a complaint that he'd fallen ill and the customer demanded all his money back plus a few extra pennies.

Williejames O'Kane was furious and barged into Franciejohn Convery's house with rage like no one had ever seen before and it was to be believed that Williejames O'Kane murdered Franciejohn Convery. Sarah Convery witnessed the brutal attack of her beloved husband *Franciejohn Convery*. It was also to be believed that Sarah Convery cried for one whole solid year until it came round the anniversary of her husband where she could take no more and gave up and died of a broken heart. And still to this day you can hear the wandering cries. So beware if you're out on the fifth of November in the town land of Rocktown to listen out for the haunting cries of *Sarah Convery*. You have been warned. Remember the fifth of November.

Fearghál O'Baoill (13)
St Patrick's College, Maghera

A Day In The Life Of Beyoncé

05.30: My harsh wake up call as normal! I get up and go to get washed and dressed. I put on my old velour tracksuit, it reminds me of back home with my mom and I miss her a lot! I do about 50 press-ups and head downstairs.

06.30: As I go down the stairs I meet Jimmy (my tour director). 'Big night tonight Beyoncé!' he says which made my fluttering nerves suddenly come back to me. The thought of doing something wrong in front of a screaming crowd made me squirm. I told Anna and Heidi (my make-up artist and fashion co-ordinator).

08.30: After two hours of fashion and make-up we arrive in HMV record store, Belfast. Just as I thought a large screaming crowd welcomed me (which isn't a bad thing of course though it can get scary!) After signing a whole load of autographs and singing three songs I get back on the tour bus again.

12.30: I now have a dancing session with my choreographer Levi (girl) which is pretty exhausting work! I have 30 dance routines for 30 songs and try to remember them all! I now have to go and check out the venue, the Oddessy Arena, Belfast.

15.15: We are now in the arena checking out the lighting and sound, how I look on stage and revising routines with the backing dancers but we got held back with a fused bulb but fortunately was easily repaired by our handyman, Mark.

18.30: I head to my dressing room and get my make-up, hair and clothes done with about 50-odd people around you in one small dressing room, it can get pretty hectic. I can hear a few of the screaming fans starting to arrive and the arena starting to fill up. I suddenly get a cold shudder up my back but no time for nerves now I've got a show to put on!

20.30: I am about to step on stage. I can hear the crowd screaming, suddenly they start to chant 'Beyoncé' and clap their hands. The buzzer sounds, the curtains go up. Here it goes. Talk to you later!

Lauren Agnew (12)
St Patrick's College, Maghera

A Day In The Life Of Thierry Henry

I woke to the patriotic sound of the French National Anthem, only to realise it was the day of the 'big match'. I was feeling very tense as I usually felt quite nervous. I was the captain of Arsenal in the FA Cup final replay between Arsenal and Manchester United.

I went down the stairs and opened the curtains, to see what kind of a day it was, and to my satisfaction it was warm and the sun was shining.

I got my breakfast and my gear, and headed off to my home ground. It was now coming nearer to the match as there were only ten minutes left. It was time to go. So I led the Arsenal team out through the tunnel and then there was a minute's silence for an old member of the Football Association.

Patrick Vieira and I took centre. After 20 minutes Robert Pires flicked the ball across to me and I took it round van Nistelrooy, Scholes and Keane, and shot. I scored in the top left-hand corner and the referee blew it up for half-time.

Three minutes into the second half Antonio Reyes was fouled in the penalty box and we were given a penalty. I stepped up to take the penalty and struck it with all my power. I thought I missed but somehow the ball found its way past Tim Howard and into the net. Six minutes from the end Sol Campbell took a corner and I headed it in the net. The feeling was brilliant to have scored a hat-trick. Just when the referee went to blow the match up Manchester United scored - too little, too late. Arsenal had won the FA Cup and they were about to present me with the most coveted trophy in football.

Ryan Conway (11)
St Patrick's College, Maghera

The Legend Of The White Child

The legend of the white child begins with, how this young girl, just thirteen, became the ghost called 'The White Child'.

At the young age of thirteen Sarah Marshall was at a sleepover with her friends. As usual their monthly sleepover started with a game of truth or dare. Now, like every other time they played this game, everybody picked truth and the same questions were asked and the same answers given. When it came to Sarah's turn, she decided to be original and picked dare. Her friends thought about it for ages and finally came up with what they thought was a world class dare. They dare her to go up into the local haunted house and stay there for half an hour. She, so not to be known as a chicken, took up this challenge and they sneaked out of the house and secretly began to make their way up the crooked, overgrown path to the haunted house which was on a massive hill.

Her friends stood outside while she opened the squeaky, rusty door and stepped in. Her friends waited for exactly twenty-nine minutes and then hid waiting for her to come out - thirty minutes, thirty-one minutes, thirty-five minutes - still no sign of her. They ran up to the door but became frightened and ran away.

They told their parents, teachers, friends and neighbours what happened and spectacular search parties went out, but nobody would search the house. Nobody knows what happened or what she saw in that house, but it was something so terrible, so frightening, that it turned her pale with fright and even her hair, clothes and eyes turned white.

The legend now goes that Sarah Marshall still roams the empty house, warning anyone who enters to get out quick, before they suffer the same fate as her.

That is how Sarah Marshall became 'The Legend of the White Child'.

Marianne Carey (11)
St Patrick's College, Maghera

A Day In The Life Of Ruud Van Nistelrooy

Today when I woke up I thought I was going to be sick because I knew we were facing Arsenal, who are at the top of the league. I recovered very quickly and I wasn't as nervous as I had been because it was a home match and none of our players were injured.

I lay on the sofa for a while to rest and at 1pm the whole team went to Old Trafford for an half hour of training. I went home for lunch at 2pm. I was ready for lunch because I had breakfast at 9am.

After lunch I lay down on the sofa and played on the PlayStation 2. A 3pm I lay down on the sofa and thought of strategies to score goals. At 4.30pm I went for a jog. I normally jog before matches to be more relaxed. At 5pm I had my dinner. I had it early because I didn't want to play on a full stomach. I relaxed again for a while and then I got all my stuff put into a bag for the match at 6pm. At 6.15pm I left for Old Trafford.

When I arrived at the ground at 6.30pm the rest of the team were there and we all got ready in the changing rooms. Alex Ferguson came in and he give us a big talk.

The best part of the day was running out onto the pitch. Then we all stood in a line and shook hands with the other team. We then had our pictures taken. As I was picked as the captain, I went up to the referee and flipped a coin. I picked heads and head it was. Ronaldo and I had kick-off! After half-time we were beating them 1-0. When the match was over the score was 1-1.

When I went home I was happy because we drew with them, we didn't get beaten. At home I got dressed up and then went out to a club with the rest of the team. When I got home from the club I was dead beat and went straight to bed.

Michael Corrigan (11)
St Patrick's College, Maghera

The Story Of Diarmuid, Gráinne And Fionn MacCumhaill

One day, Fionn MacCumhaill (one of the greatest Celtic heroes and the leader of the Fianna) went to ask Gráinne (the daughter of Cormac MacAirt, the high king of Ireland) for her hand in marriage and Gráinne accepted.

There was a great feast in honour of this. At the feast Gráinne noticed Diarmuid, one of Fionn's warriors. Gráinne wanted to run away with Diarmuid, so she put a sleep draught in everyone's drink but Diarmuid's.

When everyone fell asleep Gráinne pleaded with Diarmuid to take her away but Diarmuid was loyal to Fionn so Gráinne cast a magic spell on Diarmuid to take her away. Gráinne told him if he didn't marry her he would die. Also if he did go Fionn would kill him. Diarmuid knew he would die if he went or stayed but he left all the same.

As they left Tara on Gráinne's horse, they came to the River Shannon and they crossed it. Oisin (Fionn's son) warned Diarmuid that Fionn was coming but Diarmuid didn't listen.

As Diarmuid and Gráinne travelled south-west, a warrior named Muadham became their servant. Meanwhile Fionn hired three soldiers with three poisonous hounds to capture Diarmuid. After Muadham left, Diarmuid and Gráinne travelled north again. Diarmuid finally gave up being loyal to Fionn and he married Gráinne.

Soon Gráinne became pregnant. One night Gráinne heard the sound of a boar from the forest. She told Diarmuid and he went into the forest.

Diarmuid killed the boar with his sword just as the board struck him with his claws. As Diarmuid was dying he asked Fionn for a drink of water which had curing properties, if drunk from the hands of Fionn. Fionn refused twice. Oisin threatened to kill him, so Fionn got the water but Diarmuid had died by that time.

Rachel Gribbon (12)
St Patrick's College, Maghera

The Legend Of Norbert

Norbert the dragon was walking to the volcano for his daily drink of lava. On the way, in the distance, he could see smoke coming from the local village. He flew over and to his surprise it was on fire.

The locals of the village knew Norbert well. One of them, called Harry, yelled, 'It was caused by a dragon that was black and had pink spots.'

Norbert knew who it was, it was his evil twin brother Fuzzil-Bottom. His cave was outside the next village. So Norbert spread out his wings, took one big leap and glided over to Fuzzil-Bottom's lair.

When he got there Fuzzil-Bottom was asleep, so Norbert thought for a moment and then came up with a cunning plan.

Norbert went to the forest and gathered up some wood. When he got back he tiptoed into his brother's lair. He set the wood that he gathered at his tail and with one puff it was set on fire. He tiptoed back out and flew back home.

When Fuzzil-Bottom woke up the next day he snorted, 'Is it me or is it hot in here?' Then he realised his tail was on fire. He sprinted to the nearest river and put out the fire. Then he thought to himself, *this must be the work of the village people.* He never set the village on fire again.

Eoghan Mulholland (12)
St Patrick's College, Maghera

The Loch Ness Monster

A few thousand years ago the Loch Ness Monster got so annoyed by the fishermen killing the fish, that it decided to come up from its home to kill everyone who came to the loch in a boat. Every fisherman got eaten alive.

When the townspeople heard about this monster, they panicked and decided to drop bombs in the lake and try and kill it. This enraged the monster and then it came out of the water to end it once and for all.

The monster was 172 feet long and 78 feet thick. The monster destroyed all the docking bays for miles. It declared that it would not stop until everyone left the fish alone. Therefore if it heard and saw that they were still fishing it would come back and kill every last one of them.

For hundreds of years the words of the monster stayed in the hearts of the people. Until one day a man and his son went directly into the centre of the lake and without knowing, they started fishing. The monster leapt out of the water and roared. The man got out a gun and aimed it at the monster and shot. He killed the monster and came back to the town as a hero.

Michael Diamond (12)
St Patrick's College, Maghera

The Diary Of Gareth Gates

Woke at 7.30am, breakfast at Soho Restaurant, interview for Radio London at 9.00am - asked the same stupid questions I have been asked a dozen times before. Photo shoot for Smash Hits magazine at 10.35am. Lunch at one o'clock back at the hotel.

From 1.30 to 3.00pm I signed autographs for fans at Virgin Megastore in Piccadilly. Now got a severe case of writer's cramp. Spent two hours, 5-7, doing over-dubs on already recorded tracks, at the recording studio in Knightsbridge.

Recorded a Top of the Pops session for BBC2 at 8 o'clock. A quick snack, then off to Carlton Studios to be interviewed by Graham Norton for his Channel 4 programme. Another interview for a small local radio station.

My sessions with a speech therapist helped my confidence and practically banished my stutter. This time last year I would have been unable to string words together, never mind sentences for interviews.

Back to the hotel for another light meal and a few drinks. Attended a late night party with show business colleagues. Had a little too much to drink. Didn't get back to the hotel until four in the morning. I don't know how I will be able to rise at 7am. I have to do yet another radio interview!

Turlough Hendry (12)
St Patrick's College, Maghera

Myths And Legends

There is a legend that there is a mysterious creature called The Sasquatch. The Sasquatch lives on the rocky mountains in a cave with his family.

The Sasquatch is a 15 feet tall bear-like creature. He can bite through metal and tear through a human in fifteen seconds flat. Only a select few people have seen this mysterious beast, so it is unlikely that it would happen to you.

When a person sees the Sasquatch or even finds a Sasquatch bone it is on the worldwide television news in no time flat.

Fans of the Sasquatch will stay in the rocky mountains for weeks and weeks just to catch a glimpse of this mysterious creature. The people just want to brag to their friends, 'I have seen the Sasquatch!'

One day a father and his son were driving to a place where the father worked. The place was between the cities of Duncan and Victoria. It was called Malahat. At Malahat there was a forest called Fort Bamberton.

The father and son were exploring the forest on foot when suddenly a brown hairy thing ran across their path. The father and son followed the footprints left by the brown thing, until they came to a cave. They both went into the cave and couldn't see anything. The father wanted to explore the cave further but the son was becoming increasingly scared, so they left the cave.

The father and son ran back to the truck and jumped in and drove away as fast as they could. The son looked back and saw the mysterious, huge, hairy brown beast - the Sasquatch - chasing after them. The son was so scared, yet so excited that he could now tell his friends that he had seen the mysterious creature - the Sasquatch.

When they returned home, they phoned the RSPCA and asked if there were any rare bears that had escaped in the area. They were told, 'No'.

This is the best story in the whole world, because it is true. The son saw the mysterious beast the Sasquatch, with his own eyes.

Ryan Convery (12)
St Patrick's College, Maghera

A Day In The Life Of Cristiano Ronaldo

I went to bed and fell asleep, then suddenly. I saw myself in Old Trafford training with all the United stars the day before The Champions League Final. We were all ready for it. Then I went home in my Ferrari.

The next day I woke up and went to the ground to get the coach to get to the match in Liverpool. That day we were playing Barcelona. We had won the same amount of Champions League Finals so it was a big day in football for us.

We were running out onto the pitch when Gary Neville tripped and hurt his leg. That was the end of him. He had to go to the hospital.

We got the kick-off. It was Ruud van Nistelrooy and me. I kicked it to him and he bluffed it. It went to a Barcelona player. He went on a run and then out of the blue he shot. It was hard and direct into the top left-hand corner. The crowd roared with joy. What a start for us.

We battled hard for the rest of the first half but could not score another goal, however we had five good runs.

It was the second half and they had kick-off this half. Ryan Giggs was on a run, he was heading for the net. He turned and then passed it to me. I gave him it back. Then he shot at goal. It was a goal. We celebrated. We were going mad but we still had a game to be won. Just as things were looking up Ruud van Nistelrooy put in a bad tackle and got a red card. The match went on as normal to the last five minutes. We upped our game and we were on the attack. John O'Shea was on a run. He was heading for goal when he was brought down on the edge of the box. It was a free kick. I was to take it. I kicked it up in the air over the wall. It was going for goal. It was a goal! Top right-hand corner. Everyone jumped on top of me. We had won. I got to lift the cup.

We had a great party that night and the next morning I woke up to find it was all a dream - but it was a good one.

Kevin McKeefry (12)
St Patrick's College, Maghera

School Of Horror

In class the pupils were listening to Miss McKay tell them about the legend of their school. She told them about how a pupil was brutally butchered whilst waiting for his lift.

Two of the pupils dared Doey and Natasha to stay the night at school. They fearfully accepted.

The pair were walking wearily to the school and the silence of the night spooked the two and they began walking faster until they reached their destination - the school.

They were sitting in the hall, as quiet as mice, but suddenly out of the blue, the doors started banging, the lights flickered and Natasha and Doey began screaming! The door was flung open and two shadows stood at the doorway, laughing. It was none other than Julie and Danny.

The gang all decided to stay together, but Danny had to go to the toilet. Natasha followed him to make sure he didn't pull any more pranks. After about 15 minutes Natasha decided to go in and get Danny.

Back in the classroom Julie and Doey, blissfully unaware of what was happening, sat chatting until they were abruptly roused by a violent scream. Shaken, but fuelled by their friends' well being, they ran to the toilets where they found the pair side by side on a blood-soaked floor. Julie was paralysed with fear, but Doey lifted the knife just as Miss McKay walked in. She couldn't believe her eyes, but it was all an act. Miss McKay grabbed the knife and stabbed Julie several times until her lifeless body dropped helplessly to the floor. Then, as proud as punch mother and son walked off.

Mandy Scullion (13)
St Patrick's College, Maghera

Hide-And-Seek

Bruce was walking home from work very briskly because he knew what would happen if he didn't. About twenty years ago it was discovered that werewolves existed. The werewolves then left their underground habitats and found new homes in run-down flats. At night the werewolves came out to hunt.

Bruce was about half a mile from home when suddenly a creature landed on the pavement in front of him as if it had fallen out of the sky. The creature had sharp, pointed teeth and claws, it was covered in hair and stood at least seven foot tall. He immediately realised it was a werewolf. He turned sharply and sprinted in the other direction. The werewolf dropped onto all-fours and began to chase him.

While Bruce was running he remembered that werewolves always hunt in packs and the others wouldn't be far behind. He then saw five other werewolves not too far in front of him. He had to find an escape. He took a sharp left down an alley, he saw a dumpster and hid behind it. All the werewolves had stopped, standing at the end of the alley, sniffing the air. Slowly they all turned and stared down the alley. Bruce immediately got up and ran shoulder first at a door to a flat. Unknown to Bruce this flat was inhabited by werewolves.

Bruce began to run up the stairs and there was about a hundred werewolves grabbing at him while he was running. Amazingly he made it to the top and he burst through another door. He was on the roof surrounded by werewolves. He wanted to jump but couldn't bring himself to do it. Suddenly a werewolf pounced on him and ripped his head completely off his body, killing him instantly and the rest began to feast on his dead body.

Stephen O'Kane (14)
St Patrick's College, Maghera

Don't Lock The Door

Sarah was sitting alone in the house as her two children were at the Elk. She was exhausted so she went to bed at ten and fell asleep almost immediately. A while later she was wakened by a rustling coming idiosyncratically from the kitchen. She thought it was too early for her kids to be home so she inquisitively trudged downstairs, looking round the kitchen through her tired eyes. Satisfied there was nothing there and the noise must be from outside, she locked all the doors and went back to bed.

She used her last ounce of energy to clamber the stairs and back to bed. She had only just time to pull the sheets to her head when she heard the distinctive noise again, only this time it was coming from the living room. She heard it again, it was footsteps! Suddenly she realised that whatever was down there she had locked in the first time she was down.

She didn't know what to do. She wanted to hide but her body lay on the bed like a heap of bricks. She screamed but she knew it was no good. She kept screaming in the hope that someone, anyone, would hear her. The footsteps were coming up the stairs at a faster, heavier pace. She started to look around the room, the pasty walls, the dreary curtains; this was the room she was going to die in.

The footsteps were coming closer. She couldn't move, the only thing she could do was pull the sheet up over her head. She waited. Everything went silent; then she heard a loud, hoarse breathing coming from right beside her. She panicked. All she could do was cry hysterically. She felt a hand cover her mouth, she was struggling to breathe. She was trying to escape his grasp but he was too strong. During the struggle the sheets were thrown off the bed. Taking her last breath she looked up and saw her son standing there with a sick smirk on his face.

Claire Rice (14)
St Patrick's College, Maghera

The Hand

One day a boy named Will was playing with his latest in stock toy, the absolutely awesome 'Andy Asteroid'. He played and messed about with it. After a while he got bored and couldn't be bothered playing with it. He got up and went up to watch TV. As he was running up to watch TV, he stumbled over and collapsed to the ground. This didn't bother young Will.

Little did Will know that dangerous little bugs had got into a cut in his hand. As young Will was watching television he began to get pains in his hand. His hand looked extremely bizarre as it looked like it had minute white things climbing from the cut.

Later when Will was having his dinner, he noticed the things in his hand were a lot larger than they were before. They seemed like sharp canine teeth. Will was growing very concerned. Will then feared for his life. He hit his hand several times. His hand retaliated and attacked Will. Will just held his arm with his other hand.

Finally Will lost control of it and his hand bit his other hand. His other hand seemed to have enormous-sized teeth coming through as well.

Will didn't know what to do so he thought it was late at night and he would sleep on it. He believed it would all be gone in the morning. Will went to sleep and woke up to the sound of a cockerel. He felt so happy but when he looked at his hand it was 10 times bigger. Will screamed and hit it, but it got fiercer and fiercer and it bit Will on the face. Will tried to get it off but nothing happened. It was too much for him. It was physically stronger and gobbled Will up. Will was gone for good.

Odhran Scott (13)
St Patrick's College, Maghera

My Shocking Shoes

My shoes are haunted by ghosts, they have been for practically eight months now. I initially discovered the existence of these see-through sheets when my feet took on an irrepressible intelligence of their own. They have caused me to do many eccentric things, some advantageous but many remorseful.

The colossal steel toecap boots, which had been handed down to me by my grandad, turned me from a hopeless dancer to European champion. As an award for my recently revealed finesse I was given a complimentary holiday to any destination on the globe. I elected to voyage to the south of Uzbekistan to accomplish my lasting aspiration of swimming 1,500 metres.

When I arrived in the dilapidated Toshkent airport my shoes were so energised about swimming 1,500 metres they forced me to scurry the 53 miles to Uzbekistan's only pool on foot.

The following day I was preparing for my swimming lesson, however when I tried to detach those irritating, paranormal boots from my malodorous feet, I realised they were steadfast. They began to resemble something which was overflowing with super, super glue. This caused me to experience great trauma and anguish.

Nevertheless I decided to go to my swimming lesson which was scheduled for daybreak. Regrettably my malevolent swimming tutor saw my exquisite boots and declined to let me in the pool. When my boots heard this they became very abhorrent and spiteful. They stuck their tongues out at my vile swimming mentor. When my atrocious swimming trainer seemed oblivious to their mischievous conduct, they took matters into their own laces by forcing me to kick my obnoxious swimming coach so relentlessly she breathed her last. I now find myself absconding from the Uzbekistani authorities.

Michael A Toner (14)
St Patrick's College, Maghera

Rising Of The Underworld - A Day In The Life Of The Grim Reaper

From the light I bring darkness, to the world I bring death, in the shadows I lurk. For every death in the world, I am responsible. I have many names in all religions but my role remains the same.

Every creature on Earth has been given a number in which order I strike.

From number 1 there was nothing planned for the future until I reached a certain number. An old story told to me by the world's creators stated there would be one who would change the world and in time bring forth Judgement Day and the Apocalypse. Instead of claiming the life of this individual I sealed him in a grotesque land as I thought it would be worse than death. However, it proved not to be. In time he grew strong, developing abilities this world was not meant to witness. His number was 666.

When the creators heard of my mercy towards him, they showed none to me.

I was to be stripped of my immortality and burnt alive. As I was placed in the fire, my short life flashed before my eyes. I felt my body heat up, my heart slowed, I started to inhale the fumes. I felt the skin being burnt from my bones. I'd held the pain long enough, I could no longer bear it, I let out a roar and opened my eyes, my surroundings had changed. I was now in a dark place surrounded by fire, endless pits and streams of magma.

This place was oddly familiar, then I realised this was the grotesque land I had condemned number 666 to.

I raised my hands before my eyes to see only bones. I looked down over the rest of my body to see only a few patches of scorched skin, the rest was bones.

Was I dead? For sure this was not Heaven.

An answer came. 'Welcome to Hell.'

I turned around to see none other than number 666.

He said, 'We haven't been introduced yet, I'm Baltlasavr.'

I replied, 'I have many names, but my human name was Loki. As you can see I am no longer human, only bones.'

'It was the least I could do. You saved me from death so I did the same for you to a certain extent. I have a proposition for you. Become my right hand man, become Reaper of the Underworld. Let Heaven have the saints, we will take the sinners. When the time is right we will raise an army like none other and take the heavens and the Earth. I can give you powers beyond your dreams. What is your answer?'

My heart began to beat faster and faster. 'I would very much like to have my vengeance of the creators and the heavens.'

With my appearance I will strike fear into the hearts of many, that is my role in this world.

I am the bringer of death,
The reaper of souls,
Your time will come.

Shéa Flanagan (13)
St Patrick's College, Maghera

The Short Cut

On one dark and misty evening on the last day of the winter term, James and his younger brother Paul decided to take a short cut home through the woods. They departed from their friends at the bottom of the park and headed into the woods.

Paul whispered, 'I don't think that this is a good idea James.'

As they strolled through the trees they noticed an old abandoned house in the middle of nowhere.

James and Paul walked nervously towards the deserted old house. James opened the door slowly. As he peeped through the corner of the door he observed the old staircase. As Paul observed the three rooms downstairs James made his way, bit by bit, up the rotten, aged staircase. James moved gradually towards the main bedroom. At this stage, Paul noticed it getting pitch-dark and the mind was gradually building up. Paul went in search of James. Suddenly James came through the ceiling like a ton of bricks on top of Paul. He had fallen to his death.

Paul went into a frenzy; he ran out of the house but could see nothing. The mind was swirling around him. He sharply ran over the hill and hoped to reach the road but as he reached the top of the hill he heard a rustling behind him. He ran as fast as he could. He didn't know what was happening or where he was going!

James was never found . . .

Stephen Quinn (13)
St Patrick's College, Maghera

Banagher Old Church

There is a legend about Banagher Old Church. The ruins of the church are situated at Magheramore Road. This is where Banagher Glen is beside. It is about 1,000 years old and it is well preserved. The roof and some of the gables are gone. It was built by a holy man called Muireach O'Heaney. He died and was buried, but the next day his coffin was risen and he was placed in a tomb. The tomb is beside the old church.

At the bottom of the south-west corner of the little tomb is a hole six inches wide from which a member of the O'Heaney family has the right to withdraw some Banagher sand. This is known to ward off all evil. It is called lucky sand. People are known to have taken it to football matches and the race track. It has even been taken across the Atlantic to emigrants to secure success and by prisoners to secure acquittal. It is supposed to lay ghosts to rest.

There are sandpits dotted around the old church, which are still going. I live very close to the remains of the old church. I have been down to it and I have taken some sand from it. It is a beautiful place. People say that this legend is true, and I have found some of the information about this legend from a book and video.

Rose-Marie Murphy (12)
St Patrick's College, Maghera

The Loch Ness Monster

'Do you know about the Loch Ness Monster?' asked Granny.

'What about the Loch Ness Monster?' I said.

'Do you know why he's in Loch Ness?'

'Yeah, wasn't he a descendant of the dinosaurs or something? I read about him in school.'

'School, schmool!' said Granny. 'You don't learn nothing in school.'

'Well, why is he in Loch Ness?' I asked.

'He's in Loch Ness because, centuries ago, there were things like witches running around. It was a giant that put it there; a huge big giant. Taller than the tallest tree he was.'

'But what does that have to do with the Loch Ness Monster?' I asked impatiently.

'Hang on, I'm getting to it!' she continued. 'Well, this giant, Coln Sesh he was called, he was special as well as being the tallest. He had magic! See, giants don't usually have magic. He was the biggest giant ever and he wanted a pet.'

'A pet?'

'Yes, a pet. So he got himself a pet hobgoblin. They're a bit like fairies, only different. They happen to be a favourite pet of witches who are allergic to cats.

Anyway, soon after, he got bored of his hobgoblin and Coln tried to turn it into a worm (because he liked worms) and he went and got the spell wrong! Instead, it changed into a huge, snake-like thing. It didn't look much like a worm, so he threw it into Loch Ness. It lived there for a few centuries until people in boats started seeing it. So there you have it! All about the Loch Ness Monster. Tell that to your teacher!' Granny smiled.

I didn't see her. I was asleep.

Áine Quinn (12)
St Patrick's College, Maghera

A Day In The Life Of Roy Keane

Although I am a well-known professional footballer, an active young man like myself can find many ways of living any day to the full. Being a married man with a family and a few pet dogs, a day in my life has to be structured so that I can combine my work and my social life. Being able to afford many extras, I live in lush surroundings in a green belt area of Greater Manchester. My programme for a normal day would consist of something like this.

I get up at 6.30am and normally go jogging for about an hour. When I return home my wife is usually preparing breakfast for me and the children. While she is doing this, I normally have a quick dip in the indoor pool. We then have breakfast together and my wife prepares to get the children to school.

When I see them safely off, I prepare my dogs for their morning exercise in the park. I usually spend at least an hour with the dogs.

It is then time to attend the training ground in my career as a professional footballer. When training is over I have a shower, discuss team tactics with the players and the staff. I then drive home. To relax I watch a bit of TV. Quite often this is about football. On match days I have to sort out my travelling times depending on whether we are at home or away. I like to get to bed early at night.

Kevin O'Kane (13)
St Patrick's College, Maghera

A Day In The Life Of Thierry Henry

I get up every morning from my four-poster bed with my servant knocking on my bedroom door with a ludicrously tasty full English breakfast. I get up out of my bed at 11am and talk to my wife. She had got up early this morning to go and meet her good friend, Jennifer Lopez. I was talking to my wife about how she got on in town when my phone rang.

My wife, Kate, answered it but it was Arsene Wenger, my football manager, wanting to speak to me. It was not serious, it was just to tell me that I had football training at 2pm today. My plans were to go to the gym from 12 to 1pm with my wife. It is only half a mile down the road. We arrived at the gym at 11.40am and we both got drinks of water from the machine. We departed the gym at 1.10pm and went back to my house in my brand new Lotus Elise.

We arrived home to see a crowd of press outside our house. There was a rumour that I was moving to Real Madrid. We managed to push through the press to the front door of our house. It wasn't too long until I had to go to training so I had to leave earlier to beat the paparazzi. I came to Highbury ground at 1.50pm and I met Robert Pires on the way in.

When training was over, I was quite tired so I decided that Kate and myself would go out to a fancy restaurant that no press could get in to (to annoy us).

When I got home the press were still there. I told Kate to come quick, as we were going out for dinner in town. It was a nice, peaceful meal with no press. We got home at 7.40pm and Kate wanted to watch a video on our 52-inch TV screen. I was so tired after all I'd done today, I went straight to bed after the film.

Kevin O'Neill (12)
St Patrick's College, Maghera

A Day In The Life Of Sarah Jessica Parker

I got up at 7am and went to the gym to work out with my trainer, Joey. I went training for an hour and a half.

When I came back at 8.30am, I had a large healthy breakfast.

At 9.15am I got ready to go to the 'Sex and the City' filming studio to film the last episode.

I arrived in New York City at the studio at 9.45am and I got my hair and make-up done. While I was getting my outfit on, I quickly read over my lines. At 11.30am they finally started filming.

I took my lunch break at 1pm and went to the Plaza for lunch with Halle Berry and Jennifer Aniston.

I arrived back at the studio with my cast members at 2.30pm and I filmed the rest of the episode. The filming finally ended at 4pm and I went shopping with my stylist for a while.

I headed home at 6.30pm and went out for a run with Joey again.

When I arrived back home I got ready for the 'Sex and the City' cast party and awards.

At 9.30pm I arrived in New York at the Hilton Hotel for the party.

When everyone was seated we got dinner and the awards were handed out. I got an award for most devoted actress.

I finally got home at 2am and I went for a swim in the pool.

At about 3am I headed to bed. In the morning I have to get up at 8am for a photoshoot for 'Cosmo' magazine.

Caitlín Kelly (13)
St Patrick's College, Maghera

The Gem Of The Roe!

There once was a family, the O'Cahan family. The father was the chieftan of a little town called Dungiven. In this family there were 12 boys and a girl, her name was Finvola, also known as 'the gem of the roe'. Everyone thought that this girl was the prettiest they'd ever seen.

One day a Scottish man called Angus came visiting Dungiven.

Suddenly Finvola's heart began to pump very quickly. From that moment on she knew that he was the one for her.

When Finvola's father found out that Angus was courting Finvola he was very angry, but decided to move to Scotland where they would get married. Finvola's father would only allow her to do this on one condition: if she died she was to be buried in Dungiven. They agreed.

That night they set off in a boat across the ocean to Scotland.

Years later, Finvola's brothers were out in the garden when they heard the Banshee (the woman of the dead) crying. Then they knew that Finvola must have died. They rushed up to the castle and told their father. They all went across the ocean to Scotland where they found Finvola lying in a bed, dead!

Finvola's father was so mad that he killed Angus. The 12 brothers lifted Finvola onto the boat and when they got back to Dungiven they took her to the old Priory and there she was buried. From this day on no one has found her grave again.

Áine Kelly (13)
St Patrick's College, Maghera

A Day In The Life Of A Fish

Hi. My name is Goldy! You may think that I'm a goldfish because of my name, but I'm not. I'm a catfish. I'm called Goldy because I have a tint of gold on my scales. Catfish don't usually have a gold tint but I'm different, that's why I'm called Goldy.

Today I thought I would go for a swim up by the surface, so I went up, it was still daylight by the time I got there.

Then the scariest thing happened, I was swimming around, admiring the huge beam of light up by the big fluffy things up in the blue sky when all of a sudden I saw a white net coming towards me. I was so stunned, I didn't know what to do, so I swam away with my heart still pounding. I opened my eyes and to my amazement I wasn't caught in the net. I swam fast, still making sure it didn't come back for me. It had got some of my sea friend creatures. I didn't care, I had other friends.

As I was getting closer to my home a big shark was in my way and if I made a sudden movement he would eat me alive. I was frozen still. Then I saw a rock with a crack in it big enough for me to fit in. If it was any smaller I wouldn't have fitted in. I swam as fast as I could to the rock while shivers went up my spine. He came after me and tried to catch me. After half an hour he went away.

I'm still in the rock, too terrified to come out in case he's there waiting for me.

This is the most dangerous, scariest and adventurous day I have ever had. I hope I never have another day like this again for a long time.

Siobhán Barry (12)
St Patrick's College, Maghera

A Day In The Life Of A Hunger Striker

I was wakened today by the determined chants of my fellow prisoners. At this very moment they are the only ones keeping in this, God bless them! As usual the guards came to my cell, but the same answer I gave them - no. I wondered if I would be saying this in a few weeks. Mentally I am dying for I know that I am breaking my mother's heart and all of my family. But inside I believe that every Irish man and woman deserve independence and freedom. Foremost in my tortured mind is the thought that there can never be peace in Ireland until the foreign British presence is removed.

Once again I was woke by the prisoners but their chants are getting considerably dull! I went to see the doctor. I now weigh sixty-four kilograms. I don't have any other problems.

I received several letters today. I have only read one of them, this is what I needed. Mother has regained her fighting spirit - I am happy now. I wrote some letters today to my mother and will write more tomorrow.

The boys were all washed, but I didn't get washed. They were still trying to get the men their first wash. They put a table in my cell and placed the food in front of me but I was still refusing to eat. The boys were saying the rosary twice a day. I got my hair cut today. I feel quite good, the boys say I look ten years younger!

I now weigh fifty-seven point five kilograms. This may be my last note as I am getting very sore mentally and physically, so here's one of my poems:

'Doesn't seem quite so long ago
The last time that I saw you
Ain't it funny how memories grow
They always fold around you
They tried to break you in a living cell
But they couldn't find a way
So they killed you in a H-block cell
And hoped all would turn away
Thought that your spirit could not rise again
But it dared to prove them wrong
And in death you tore away the chains
And let the world hear freedom's song'.

Joseph Bradley (11)
St Patrick's College, Maghera

The Swaski Cult

In Egypt, still here today lives the Swaski cult, it lives a history of torture, violence and cruel massacres.

Bovonia, a young black American, was on a foreign exchange programme.

One day she was walking in the village of Ammon-Ra in which she arranged to meet her brother, Macha. They were walking along the street when they met the young man she was staying with, Anuka. Anuka was acting strange; wearily you could say, as if something was bothering him.

That night her brother stayed with her and Anuka. Bovonia needed to ask Anuka something but he said he was busy and not to come in.

At 12am she was woken by large, strange men. They told her to 'get up, now!'. Bovonia was petrified so she did what she was told.

She was led to a strange room. Anuka was in it. He was laying out something; Bovonia craned her neck as she was held down on a chair. She saw a scalpel, butcher's knife . . . Anuka turned round.

'What's going on?' she said.

Her requests were answered, in the worst way possible. On a table, held down with leather straps was Macha, screaming. Bovonia was powerless. They cut open his stomach; he lived 30 seconds after all his major organs were cut out. Bovonia was next. Another grisly ending . . .

10 years on her parents wait in hope that'll last for the rest of their lives.

Donna Toland (12)
St Patrick's College, Maghera

A Day In The Life Of The Grim Reaper

I arose early this morning to finalise who I was going to do away with and decide which method of death they were going to suffer. All the finer details still had to be arranged! I lifted my cloak and scythe. I walked to work, clocked in and paddled down the corridor into my office. I then got myself into Grim mode.

I spun my globe to see where my first target was going to come from. Slower, slower the globe got, I lowered my thin, spindled finger. My first victim will be from . . . the continent of Europe, Ireland, Co Derry, Swatragh to be precise.

First kill of the day is always the best, and now it was going to be ten times better because my first kill was a girl and I love the sound of a terrified girlish scream! I got great pleasure from that kill. Then next came a man in California, he was one of the type that make my job easy, you know, middle-aged, balding and depressed.

Lunchtime and I would be working over lunch today as I had a call in South Africa. I hate those tribal leaders, it takes just a little too much work to scare them. I usually have to end up showing them my pictures of me on holiday. They hate to see such a white body!

Five to five, thank goodness, clocking off time was coming up and I couldn't wait to get home to a nice bath. All that scaring and pulling faces is bad for the frown muscles so I think I will have a massage and an early night tonight.

Five o'clock came and I was the first to clock off. I went around the corner where they had the local pizza shop. I was famished from lunch. The cashier seemed astonished to see me and gave me the pizza for free: happy days for me!

After dinner I slipped into a hot bath and relaxed into Gerald mode, you see Grim's just my work name! I had a massage and watched some prime time TV. Then I thought that I would have an early night and hit the sack. I wanted to look fresh in the morning. It's a drawback of the job but I can hardly complain because the job takes you all over the world. The life of Grim isn't as bad as it seems, plus the wages are good!

Christina O'Hagan (13)
St Patrick's College, Maghera

A Day In The Life Of David Beckham

'Good morning listeners.'

'No, not 6am already, it is too early for training.'

I got up and went out to the balcony to view my 63 acres of a garden. There were my gardeners who were getting the lawn ready for the spring. My butler then brought me out my champagne breakfast, complete with sausages, toast, bacon, eggs - the whole works.

After I had finished it was about 7am and then I went to the shower and got dressed. As it was a training day I decided to wear black Adidas tracksuit bottoms, a white Adidas T-shirt and a matching jacket.

After saying goodbye to Victoria, Brooklyn and to Romeo, I left for training in my silver Mercedes-Benz convertible.

'Hello Victoria, training was tough today, I need to cool off in the pool.'

I had turned off the water heater earlier and now I am glad because it is lovely and warm today and the pool is heated by the sun.

I stayed in the pool until 5.30pm and then went into the kitchen to have dinner. My cook had prepared chicken, steak, potato salad, pasta and mayonnaise served with Coke and lemon.

I was called out for a photo shoot for next week's magazine which took three hours and by the time I got home it was 11.30pm so I went to bed because I had an early start the next day.

Orlagh O'Hare (12)
St Patrick's College, Maghera

A Day In The Life Of Christina Aguilera

I got up today and went downstairs to make breakfast. I was in the middle of making toast when my phone rang. 'Private number! Great, another manic fan!' But no, it was my lovely manager looking for me to do another video shoot for 'The Voice Within'. *Lucky me!* So there's me leaving my fantastic, massive, 3-storey mansion at 7.30 in the morning going to shoot a video and me thinking it was my day off. Think again!

I stopped at the food store and bought some breakfast. I got mobbed *again* and had to sign *more* autographs. They just love me *sooo* much. Well, who doesn't, apart from that cow Britney.

Anyway, I arrived at the shoot and finished the video. It didn't take that long as I wore the same thing for the whole video.

It took a whole day. Usually it would take about 3. Thank God it didn't take that long. I left the shoot and went to the mall, then home to a nice warm bath and a warm, cuddly bed.

Karen Diamond (13)
St Patrick's College, Maghera

A Day In The Life Of Michael Collins

8.30: My servant knocked and walked into the room and gave me my breakfast.

8.45: As I washed, I heard a great bang at the end of my street. I rushed to get changed and rushed to the scene. It was a bomb explosion and my friend Brendan was lying down on the ground after his lungs had been blown out of his chest.

9.55: The doctor came out to tell me that my friend wouldn't make it and my three other friends were found dead: Conall, Steven and Peter. Paddy and Brian jumped out the door just in time.

10.24: I met with the bomb expert secretly so the English would not find out about my plan. My plan was to plant a bomb in the Queen of England's car so it would blow her to smithereens.

1.05: I was having lunch and the English attacked! They got to the bomb expert and found out my plan and we had to get out and fast. Bullets were going and cannons were firing.

3.36: We got out of Dublin and hid in a small farm outside Donegal town, Toomebridge, Antrim on the Carlane Road.

7.38: The farmers brought us food and blankets in the shed. The cattle and sheep stunk and it was feeding time so all we heard was 'plop' and 'drip'.

11.30: We're going to sleep now. We need our break. It was a bad day, from being chased and my friends being killed. We are forced to live in this shed with the cattle like the English say, 'the dogs we are'. Lights out for now anyway.

James Laverty (12)
St Patrick's College, Maghera

A Day In The Life Of Kerry McFadden

Today I got up at the crack of dawn and got dressed, gave Bryan a hug and a kiss. I woke up Molly and Lily-Sue and gave them breakfast. Bryan drove me, Molly and Lily-Sue to his mother's house. After that Bryan drove me to the airport because I had an interview in London.

I arrived in London at 1pm. As soon as I got on the set I had to go to the make-up room. Anthony McPartlin and Declan Donelly were interviewing me.

'It is so hard leaving my two little girls because I love them so much. Especially when family means so much to me.'

Declan asked me, 'How can you look after your girls and have a party life?'

I answered, 'I only go out for a drink at the weekend.'

Anthony asked me, 'Do you still meet up with the girls from Atomic Kitten?'

'Yes I do, actually. I am meeting up with them this afternoon.'

We finished the interview at 5pm. I went to my house in London and Liz, Jenny and Natasha met me up at my house. We decided that we would go to a restaurant for dinner. We had a four course meal. I had soup for a starter, turkey and ham dinner and I had a banoffe pie for dessert, and a milky coffee to drink. After we'd eaten we chatted for an hour and a half. We talked about what we were going to do in the future. I said I was going to be a full-time mother to Molly and Lily-Sue. We went to a pub for a drink. I took a bottle of wine. We said bye to each other and I got a taxi to the airport.

I got on the 8pm plane home to Dublin. Bryan collected me at 9.30pm. At 10.30pm I went to bed because I was really tired.

Caroline O'Connor (12)
St Patrick's College, Maghera

The Giant's Causeway

A few days before his seventh birthday, Philip disappeared. His parents sent out search parties. They offered huge rewards for years, but there was no sign of the boy.

One night, Philip appeared in a dream to Robin Kelly, the blacksmith.

The boy was carried off by a giant, Manon McMahon.

'I've been a slave in the giants' court. I've finished my seven years here, and if you come to rescue me, my parents will reward you generously.'

The blacksmith thought to himself, *how do I know this is not a dream?* It was all very confusing.

Carrying only a ploughshare for protection, Robin set out for the Giants' causeway - this massive, rocky staircase from the seabed right to the top of the cliff where the giant lived. As the blacksmith made his way into a room, there sat three gigantic figures.

Manon McMahon, sitting at the head of the table, stone-like, whose beard merged with the table, said, 'What are you doing here?'

'I've come to collect Philip,' explained the blacksmith.

'Yes, you're right, let me show you the way,' the giant replied.

The giant led the blacksmith to a very large room where hundreds of children sat around a table. 'Very well,' growled the giant, 'you shall choose Philip from among the crowd and if you choose the wrong boy, you shall pay with your life.'

The blacksmith knew he could not possibly choose Philip out of all these children, a child he had not seen for seven years, so the blacksmith decided to soften the giant. He reasoned with him and handed him the ploughshare instead but, with the giant's grip it snapped, the children roared with laughter.

The blacksmith heard someone call his name, he took hold of the boy. 'This is Philip Ronan,' he announced. Immediately the room was plunged into darkness.

The underground shook their feet. Philip and the blacksmith suddenly found themselves at the top of the causeway - *free!*

Naoimh Glass (13)
St Patrick's College, Maghera

A Day In The Life Of Austin Powers

Hello, my name is Austin Powers, baby, yeah. I've just been back from getting my chest brushed and believe me, they look groovy. Today I've plenty of things to do. I have to get my teeth polished, then I need to get my tux from the dry cleaner's and save the world again and be back in time for tea.

I'm eating breakfast at the minute (I'm eating my own special brand, Austin 'O's, I swear). You'll never believe it but I have to save the world in last year's blue because my new one is at the dry cleaners, true story I promise. If this is getting boring for you I'll skip a couple of hours where I'm at my lunch break, this is where I met a scrumptious little number called Hannah. I asked her, 'Shall we make out now or later?' I was 25 years old than her, well I can't blame her.

If you want to know how I saved the world today, I tripped Dr Evil and he dropped his weapon of mass destruction, or as he calls it, Mini Me, down a drain and I defused it with my eyes closed.

Well, that's my day so far, up to now. Well now if you want to know what I'm doing, I'm in bed with . . . yeah, baby, yeah! Kids stay in school!

Conall Halferty (13)
St Patrick's College, Maghera

A Day In The Life Of Christina Aguilera

7am: Alarm goes off, (time to get up). Have to go to London recording studios to record 'Can't Hold Us Down'. Have to rush through breakfast. I get dressed and phone Shelly (my mum) and tell her to pick me up and drive me to London Studios. I have to be there for eight. *Beep, beep!* Time to go.

8am: I arrived (just in time). 'I'm here,' I gasped as I ran through the set to get changed. Got changed. Have to go to vocal warm up before entering the recording lounge. Finally, it's time to record. Finished recording, time to go home and get changed for photoshoot.

9.30am: At home, have to take a bath. 10 minutes later - out of bath, time to get dressed. (Got dressed.) Going downstairs to get hair and make-up done. Finished hair and make-up, time to order my limousine. 'Can I order my limousine? Thank you.' *Beep!* Time to go, limousine's here. (Can't wait.)

12pm: Just arrived at photoshoot, about to go and change into my fashion clothes. 5 minutes later - time to take photos. 1 hour later - photoshoot over. Really tired, thank God my day's work is nearly over. About to drive into town to get something to eat. Hope there's no traffic.

3.05pm: Arrived at Rockerfellas, ordered dessert (strawberry fruit cake) finished dessert. (It was lovely.) Just about to leave, until a group of fans stop for an autograph and photo. Finally home, Shelly (my mum) is washing dishes. I decide to help her and we both get tired very quickly. I run into the bathroom, take off my make-up and fall on top of my bed and finally *sleep!*

All in the day of a superstar!

Shauneen McAteer (12)
St Patrick's College, Maghera

The Gem Of The Roe

In the land of O'Cahan (Dungiven, Co Derry) a young woman named Finvola grew up in the castle. Finvola had twelve brothers, her mother died when Finvola was just a little girl.

When Finvola grew up she fell in love with a young man named Angus who was from Scotland. Finvola married Angus but before they set out on their journey across the sea, Finvola's father told Angus that Finvola must die in Dungiven.

Angus and Finvola moved to Scotland and there they led a wonderful life. They had two children, one boy and a girl, but short were the found years these lovers did share. Suddenly Finvola was diagnosed with a long-term illness. Angus did not inform her father.

One evening Finvola's father and her twelve brothers were out hunting on Benbradagh when they heard the Banshee cry low, it was the death of Finvola, the gem of the Roe.

When the family knew about this they got on their boats and rowed to Scotland and killed Angus. They brought Finvola back to Dungiven and buried her in the old Priory! Until this day she's known as the 'Gem of the Roe'.

Sinéad Kelly (13)
St Patrick's College, Maghera

The Children Of Lir, The Modern Version

In the year 2025 there lived a happy family in Ireland. King Lir, his wife Eva and their two children Fionnuala and Aodh.

One hot summer's day the two children had gone to school when they got an urgent text on their mobile phone, to say there were needed by their father. They rushed home in the limo and arrived at the hospital. They saw their father, who looked disturbed.

'Yo Pops, wazzup?' queried Aodh.

'You have got twin brothers but I am afraid you mother has gone to rest,' he replied.

It was to be that the boys were to be called Fiachra and Conn. Eva's sister, Aoife, was to marry Lir and was to bring up Eva's children.

In the month that followed, Aoife grew jealous of the children as she felt they were keeping Lir and her apart so she came up with a cunning and devious plan to get rid of them.

Next morning she invited the children to the amusements. Of course the children were very happy to go and at once jumped into the limo.

When they arrived they sprinted onto the bumping cars and didn't notice that there was no one else there. However they did notice Aoife who was standing beside them muttering something. It sounded like an incantation. Suddenly a bolt of lightning hurtled towards them and they were no longer human, but a bumping car, a roller coaster, a ghost train and a merry-go-round.

They had to stay with the amusements for 900 years, travelling all over the country. After the 900 years, a joker came and rang the bells on his hat. The children were human again. They looked so much older but that didn't stop them from having the best day they had ever had at the amusements.

Louise Doherty (13)
St Patrick's College, Maghera

The Legend Of The Giants' Causeway

A long time ago there were two giants, one from Ireland called Finn MacCool and one from Scotland called Bennadonna. One day Bennadonna heard about Finn MacCool and challenged him to a fight to see who was the strongest. So the two giants started to build a bridge from the end of Ireland to the end of Scotland, to get across to challenge each other.

One day, as Finn was training he heard that Bennadonna was much larger than him. He began to worry so he made up a plan. When Bennadonna came he would dress up as a baby and get his mother to say that he was Finn's son and that Finn was out.

The day arrived when Bennadonna came and asked his mother where Finn was. She replied, 'He is out running but if you want you can have cookies while you wait.' She gave him cookies but with a stone inside them. When he tried to eat them he broke his teeth. She also gave Finn some cookies without stones in them. He ate them easily. Bennadonna started to think, *if Finn MacCool's son is big and strong, what is he like himself?* Bennadonna was so scared he ran over the bridge so fast he sent it flying back on to Ireland. That is why the Giant's Causeway is there today.

Michael Hughes (12)
St Patrick's College, Maghera

The Myth Of The Roman Graveyard

There was a small cottage on the edge of a town beside an old deserted graveyard in which eleven Roman kings were buried. No one went near it because they thought it was haunted and they knew the cottage was. Many years ago an old man who lived in that cottage used to be an archaeologist but was retired. He spent most of his days in his back garden and from there he was able to see the graveyard. He heard of many rumours about the graveyard but he only believed one.

The Roman kings were buried in this graveyard with all their treasures and one, the highest king of all was buried with something that could make you rich beyond all your dreams. There was a catch though: if you dared dig up any of these graves you would pay with your blood.

The old man didn't believe that. *What can they do to me if they are dead?* he told himself. He decided he would dig up the High King's grave.

One night the old man got his torch and shovel and began to dig. It was nearly midnight when his shovel hit the coffin and he was pleased to get a break. He pulled his torch closer and cautiously pulled it open. It creaked as it opened and there inside was the remains of the High King and the old man couldn't believe his eyes. Lying in the coffin, with what seemed like hundreds of pounds worth of jewels, was a humongous golden plaque that was worth about £2,000,000.

The next day the old man was found dead in his house. No one, not even the doctor knew how, legend has it that it was the Roman kings.

Cara Cassidy (12)
St Patrick's College, Maghera

A Day In The Life Of Kylie Minogue

07.00: I'm up! Oh but I'm so tired from my late night out with my boyfriend out in a ravishing London restaurant. I'm really nervous what with my big day today.

I've just had my brekkie consisting of a fresh fruit salad and a piece of burnt toast all washed down with a glass of pure orange.

10.00: Now I'm dressed and I have my make-up on (Max Factor) and I'm just on my way to visit a six-year-old girl called Hayley Okines who sadly suffers from an ageing disease - Progeria. So I will be visiting her in her local hospital. Hoping to make her day that little bit happier.

11.00: I've just finished talking to Hayley, she was such a happy, polite and sweet child. The hour that I spent with her was really rewarding seeing how lucky I really am. It was really moving and it really saddens me to know that she will be dead in no more than nine or ten years. I feel it was a privilege to meet such a wonderful and unique person like her.

11.30: I'm on my way to the airport now! I hope I can squeeze my way onto the earliest flight to Paris so that I can be with the main man in my life, Oliver Martinez, and kick-start my world tour where tonight I will play in front of a whopping *thirty thousand people* so I'm really nervous and worked up about it!

14.30: I've just had the most delicious lunch with Oliver here in Paris. I feel quite queasy after that one and a half-hour flight but my stomach has settled now. I have now had my chauffeur escort me to central Paris where I will check into my hotel and unpack.

16.00: I'm going now to see my stage manager about tonight and make sure everything is OK for the gig.

18.00: I'm just about to go on stage and my backing dancers are already on. I am so nervous in case I forget a dance move or a song word, but I've got to go now, it's my cue.

00.30: I'm wrecked! Thankfully I didn't slip up too much! I missed one dance move but it's not too bad! It was a great crowd and it was brilliant singing to them, but I better go how - so tired! Night-night!

Elaine Convery (12)
St Patrick's College, Maghera

The Dragga Man

It was the 23rd of April 1996. My family and I were having dinner - mmm . . . delicious, thick, creamy potatoes, roast beef and gravy!

After my dinner, I went outside for a walk. I love the spring, the fresh air blowing through your face. We live down south and the weather is great!

I was walking along the road when I met these tourists with big rucksacks and bags! What were they doing here? One of the girls came up to me, they were 20-25 years of age. 'Hello,' I said.

'Hello, I'm wondering do you know where Maghera is?'

'Why do you want to go there?' I said nervously.

'Oh, nothing much, I just want to find out about the Legend of Maghera!'

'Wait, until I tell you about it!'

'The legend has it that 'it' appears every 23 years on the 23rd day of spring! It is known as 'Dragga' and is feared by all who believe his story. He comes to slaughter all his marked prey and God help anyone who comes in his way. He appears only at night with blood and torn pieces of flesh stuck between his razor-sharp teeth. It's like a gigantic bat with a wing span stretching to almost 6-feet in length and the blood-gurgling roars that make you quiver with fear. He has dark black eyes with dark ashy skin and leaves nobody alive who crosses his path.

He swoops down on unsuspecting targets and grasps them with his amazingly sharp claws whilst whisking them off to his hidden den where he devours them and they're never seen or heard of again.

So if you're thinking of taking a trip to Maghera, think again, won't you?'

Rachael Deery (11)
St Patrick's College, Maghera

A Day In The Life Of Beyoncé

Dear Diary,

I'm Beyoncé Knowles and I'm not like any other 23-year-old that gets up for work at about 10.30 or sometime like that. I have to get up at about 4.30 in the morning. I have about half an hour to get up, wash myself and to get dressed, go to the salon and try and avoid the paparazzi. I also have to get my hair done, get my tan on; nails and feet pedicured. I have to be out of the salon at 7.30 at the latest.

Next I meet my tour manager at Walshes Café at 8.00 for a meeting. I have to leave these at the latest 8.30. Flight leaves at 10.45, be there for 9.00 hopefully (that's if the meeting doesn't drag on). Get the jet over to England, have to be on CD:UK for 12.00 that's if everything runs according to plan, perform my latest single 'Naughty Girl'. Leave there before 13.00, get onto the tour bus. I then have a signing at Virgin Megastores on Brochure Road in England, that will probably take at least two hours. Leave there at about 15.00, go to get a bite to eat while doing an interview with GMTV's Entertainment Today. Leave there at about 17.30, go to the airport, have to be there for 18.15 no matter what. Get the jet the whole way over to New York for my concert tomorrow, which begins at 13.00. I'm Beyoncé Knowles and that's how I like my hectic life.

Clare O'Hara (12)
St Patrick's College, Maghera

A Day In The Life Of Jennifer Aniston

This morning I woke up full of excitement, as it was the premiere of 'Along Came Polly'; Brad was still sleeping as usual! I woke him up as we had so much to do. I went downstairs, got breakfast. I gave Brad a kiss and told him I would be back later, as I was going to pick up my dress for tonight, and also going to get my hair and make-up done.

I grabbed my car keys and put on my jacket. I was still very excited. I picked up my handbag and mobile phone and ran out the door. I arrived at Gucci to collect my dress and had a chat with the shop assistant.

After that I went and got my hair done, by this time it was twelve thirty. I had only five and a half hours left to get my make-up done and get to the premiere. I met up with my make-up artist. Then I went and got something to eat.

I went to see if Brad was ready, because knowing him he probably wasn't. To my shock he was! We had only an hour and a half to go, at this point my nerves were starting to play up on me big time.

Brad and I got into the limo and started off for the premiere. We arrived there and as usual there were loads of camera crews and photographers. Brad and I walked up the red carpet and photographers were shouting at us to smile and get out pictures taken.

It was a night to remember!

Orla Gallagher (11)
St Patrick's College, Maghera

A Day In The Life Of Stilian Petrov

I woke up this morning and thought that I was going to be sick. You see today is the day that Celtic play Real Madrid in the UEFA Champions League Final and I am playing. Today could be the day that my boyhood dream could come true. I am so excited.

I hopped out of bed, packed my bag and put on my clothes. The plane leaves for Barcelona at 2 o'clock. I left my three-storey house and jumped into my forty-thousand pound Jaguar. I drove into Glasgow and then out on to the motorway which takes you to the airport.

I was late for the plane, so I drove about 100mph down the motorway. I got to the airport, parked my car and ran as quickly as I could to the plane. It was just about to leave. I jumped on and breathed a huge sigh of relief. Everyone was talking about the match on the plane. I fell asleep and woke up to a big tap on the shoulder by Henrik Larsson. He said, 'We've arrived Stilian.' I felt really sick now. We got a bus and went straight to the Nou Camp Stadium. When we got there we saw thousands of people trying to push their way into the stadium's gates. The bus stopped. We walked down into our changing room. We put on our green and white kit.

When the match was soon starting we walked down the tunnel. There was a huge roar. Ninety-thousand spectators were watching us. It was fantastic. The match started. We played well for the first 43 minutes until Raul scored for Real Madrid. The first half ended. We went into our changing room.

About 10 minutes later we came out for the second half. We were determined to win. We were the far better team now and it paid off with a great goal by Alan Thompson from a free kick in the 62nd minute. The last twenty minutes were so nerve-racking. One mistake and it could cost us the cup. Probably the last attack of the game when Alan Thompson had the ball on the left wing, he crossed it in to me and I volleyed it into the top corner. I couldn't believe it, I had scored. Thousands of Celtic supporters were screaming in the stadium. Real Madrid kicked off. The referee blew his whistle, the game was over.

Myself and the team went up to collect our winners' medals and Henrik Larsson lifted the cup. We had won the UEFA Champions League and I'd scored the winning goal.

Gavin Downey (11)
St Patrick's College, Maghera

A Day In The Life Of David Beckham

I woke up and turned to look at my clock. It was 9am. Since I had woken there was a weird tingle in the pit of my stomach. It was nerves but why? Then it hit me, tonight, the 7th December, Real Madrid and Barcelona, the titans of Spanish league, would clash.

The day passed slowly and uneventfully. I knew that would change. It came to 3 o'clock and the rest of the panel and I gathered in the lobby of the grand hotel we had spent the night in. When the time came I stepped out of the door and into the scorching Barcelona sun. I strode confidently onto the team's luxurious coach and soon arrived at the world famous Nou Camp.

I then had a light warm-up followed by a meal to provide me with the energy necessary for my best match performance. Before I knew it I was in the dressing room preparing for the biggest match of my career in Spain.

I laced up my boots and slipped on a silky white jersey. The number 23 was painted on the back. I heard a familiar bell to signal that the game was about to start and made my way to the tunnel. Raul, our Madrid-born captain, led us out, much to the disgust of the home fans.

Barcelona dominated the first half and in the 45th minute Luis Garcia swung in a delightful cross which fell perfectly for Ronaldinho to hit home with an unstoppable overhead kick. The team went in at half-time ashamed but came out inspired by the words of Carlos Queroiz. It showed and finally in the 74th minute I hit a long ball in the direction of Ronaldo who turned in a way only he could and hit a clean, crisp volley into the top corner. The game ended in the 91st minute when Luis Figo tucked away a penalty. I had played my part and we had won.

Dominic Carville (12)
St Patrick's College, Maghera

Undiscovered

In years gone by there was a story passed down in time. On a lonely old hill stood a big, fancy mansion. On the day of Friday the 13th 1992 a murder occurred. Elizabeth and Tom had just been married a year and had lived happily for this year until that night took place.

Tom had just arrived home from mass. As he approached he took each stair two at a time. He opened the bedroom door expecting to see Elizabeth in bed: well she was but the only thing was she had a knife stuck in her chest and she wasn't breathing. She was dead. He saw a strange ring at the side of her bed. He picked it up but stood there horror-struck at the sight.

Tom ran straight down the stairs, out the door and down to the police station. He reported that his wife had been murdered.

The next day the story had spread around the local village. Everyone thought it was Tom because the house and hundreds of acres of land had been left to Elizabeth; so if she was dead he would get it, as he was the only family left. Tom was constantly telling people that it wasn't him but no one believed him!

On the day of the funeral Tom had expected no one to turn up, but most did with respect for Elizabeth. Not many people spoke to Tom except for a strange man who had never been seen before. Tom recognised a ring that he had found on the floor at his wife's deathbed. The man caught his eye and realised he was looking at the ring. Tom took his ring out, the man saw it and suddenly scarpered . . .

Kerry-Ann Cunningham (11)
St Patrick's College, Maghera

A Day In The Life Of Chad Kroger

Our tour manager came in and woke me up for we had a signing at 11.30am and it's 10.45!

We all have a big hangover from last night's party we had, because it was the first night of our UK tour.

We pulled up outside HMV in our tinted Land Rover, it was a surprise guest appearance but we still got surrounded with people screaming.

'What a useless signing, the mic's broken halfway through!' Chris said to me.

Believe it or not that did actually happen, I was in the middle of signing 'Figured You Out' when I heard a crash from behind the banner.

Today's going to be hectic because we've got to rehearse our show, in Dublin, we're now in London. And to make it worse we only have 4 hours to do it all in!

When we got there our back-up band were rehearsing already on stage. Then they moved off and 'Too Bad' came on, so obviously it's our first song we are doing.

It's 5 minutes 'til we're on and the screams from the crowd are ear-bashing!

'Now, who you've all been waiting for - Nickleback!'

We run on stage. 'Nick' flashes on one of the screams. 'Le' flashes in the middle. 'Back' flashes on the right and now the screams are *unbelievable!*

At the end of the night we're all hyped up ready for Belfast tomorrow night, but first we have *another* signing in the morning.

There's a day in my miracle of a life!

Éimear Birt (12)
St Patrick's College, Maghera

The Legend Of Glenariff Forest

Sport has never been one of my strong points. The more I tried, I always seemed to get worse. I thought there was no hope for me until one day my life changed. I was walking through Glenariff Forest to get to one of my favourite waterfalls. When I got there I saw a black, hooded figure standing by the bank. As I got closer I heard a voice calling to me, 'I know what it is you wish. I will give it to you if you can control the way you use it!' The figure disappeared.

The next day I found to my surprise that I could actually play netball. I never missed a shot and my friend Laura who was great at netball couldn't get the ball from me once. Soon I was playing football and all kinds of sports too. I got into loads of teams and I had a lot of trouble keeping up with them all. The fame got to my head and I loved it whenever people would come up to me and compliment my skills. This was all soon to change.

After many weeks I went back to Glenariff Forest to see the dark figure to ask for more talent. Instead of this it said to me, 'You got too carried away, the fame hasn't been worked for, you are a fraud!' And with that there was a bright, white light and I knew I would be useless at any sport I tried to play. I begged her to give my talent back and I promised to use it more carefully but she was gone within a matter of seconds. I realised I had been a great fool and that this had been a great lesson to me. I have never forgotten what happened and I never will. Be careful what you wish for and use it wisely!

Emma Dillon (12)
St Patrick's College, Maghera

The Rivals Clash

I woke up this morning very excited as today we play Rangers to see who clinches the league title. First of all I got up and my servant had my breakfast sitting ready for me. My servant who washes my boots (David Beckham) had them ready so I headed off!

I jumped into my Ferrari and headed to Parkhead. I arrived and entered the changing room after signing a few autographs. Now the nerves started to kick in! The team was called out and I was up front as usual so we went out on to the pitch and the stadium erupted with noise. Then the referee blew his whistle and the match began.

It wasn't until I got the ball I side-stepped two defenders and hit the ball in the top corner of the net. The fans started chanting my name 'Larsson, Larsson!' The match finished one-nil and the celebrations lasted into the night.

Brendan Donnelly (13)
St Patrick's College, Maghera

The River Roe Monster

Once upon a time, there lived a monster. It lived in a little town called Dungiven, but this monster didn't roam the streets nor did it fly over the roofs. This monster lived in the river and gradually became known as the River Roe Monster. It was a twenty foot long, dragon-like creature but instead of wings it had fins. This animal was so evil hell itself spat it back out.

The animal lived underneath a bridge and mainly fed on cattle and fish. But one day, a farmer went to look for his cattle when it leaped from the waters below, grabbed the farmer and with one bite, he was gone. The news spread across the town that the farmer had disappeared and no one ever visited the bridge. People were so frightened that they moved homes to be further away from the river.

One night a little boy called Stephen was asked to look after his father's cattle. He noticed that one was missing. He decided to search for it before his father found out. He heard noises coming from the bridge not so far away.

He went over and looked over at the bridge when he saw a shadow moving. He went over and the monster jumped out and grabbed him by the foot. It then pulled Stephen's shoe off by accident which gave the boy time to run away, the monster then actually climbed out of the river and went after the boy. It was then that the monster realised it couldn't breathe air and slowly suffocated. And thanks to that boy, Dungiven is no longer a town of fear.

Stephen Henry (13)
St Patrick's College, Maghera

The Dog

I stood there, the broken chain reflecting the glare of the moonlight into my eyes. It had escaped and now this killing machine was running loose. Or was it? What if it was just out to stretch its legs and was coming back to finish me off?

The bone in my leg was exposed from the flesh which was previously violently torn off, I tried to aid and conceal the wound as best I could but it was no good, my attempts were flawed when more blood continued to flood from my leg. They say there is silence before the storm. Suddenly the rain began to slow up and there was an eerie silence. Just then heaving breathing, at first I imagined it to be my own, but it kept getting louder as if the breathing itself was getting closer. 'Oh no!' I said in a low toned voice, I was right, he had come back that bloodthirsty, rage-infested, beast of a *dog!* Slowly I turned, the alleyway seemed to get smaller and close in on me. I turned only to be greeted by the sound of blood dripping from teeth, I could see his outline, surely he had killed again. But just then, 'No,' I said, 'it can't be,' the figure stepped forward. This was no dog, but what stood in my presence was a man, not just any man, it was my neighbour. Surely the dog's bite couldn't be contagious or could it?

Then I could feel blood dripping from my mouth . . .

Dominic O'Kane (13)
St Patrick's College, Maghera

The Man That Never Was

Lucie was running fast than she'd ever ran before. Looking over her shoulder she couldn't see him. Her view was blocked by the tall trees behind her and she was continuously tripping over the twigs and roots on the ground. The wind was blowing, her long blonde hair away from her face but she was still finding it difficult to see. In the distance she could make out rows of blurry lights and knowing she was near the motorway, ran even faster! With the sound of car after car, Lucie began screaming at the top of her voice, 'Help,' she shouted, 'can anyone hear me?' but her heart sank due to no reply.

Looking behind her once more, she stopped suddenly. There was complete silence for what seemed to her like an hour, but was actually about five seconds! Where did he go? Was he gone? No, he was too smart for that. Lucie could hear him breathing, heavy breathing coming from behind her but no one was there. She looked up and looked around her. Again, nothing. Lucie, feeling a sense of relief, ran to the motorway and frantically waved her arms, just wanting to get home. Many cars passed her but only one eventually stopped. She couldn't recognise who was driving, but she didn't care. He was in the bushes, she was getting in the car, she was safe.

Lucie opened the door but looked behind her just once more before getting in. She knew in her heart she wouldn't be able to rest until she saw him again but she just couldn't see him. She couldn't understand it but breathed a sigh of relief as the car drove away in the direction of home.

Hearing a noise, she looked up. The driver had locked the doors! Tears filled her eyes. *No, it's not possible,* she thought or at least she hoped. The car pulled over. Lucie tried to open the door but with no success. The driver turned around with a knife in his hand! It was him. Lucie stopped screaming, she stopped fighting . . .

Alana Johnston (14)
St Patrick's College, Maghera

My Story

I opened my eyes. I could hardly believe it, the morning of our holiday. We were already packed and ready to leave from the night before.

We got into the car and we were off on the journey to the plane. The plane journey was unbelievably long. Father went to get our luggage but to our horror he didn't come back. We went to look for him but we found him lying in a pool of blood.

The police came and examined the body. Their conclusion was that he had been struck over the head with a hammer. The police wouldn't let anyone out of the building. Police Constable Craig found the hammer with fingerprints on it. Everyone in the airport had to be fingerprinted. They found that Michael Calomel had the same fingerprints as the ones found on the hammer. He was arrested on the spot for murder. We hired Mr D Jones as a lawyer to sue this man.

On the morning of the court case I was extremely nervous. We entered the courtroom. There was such a tense atmosphere. I was afraid to move.

The day was both nerve-wracking and exciting. The most nervous period was when the jury went out of the room. The moment they came back I jumped off the seat with nerves.

'Jury, have you a verdict yet?'

'Yes we have found him guilty of murder.'

Michael Calomel got life!

Ronan Young (14)
St Patrick's College, Maghera

Mysterious Treasure

There were two children who were best friends, Stef and Christina. One Friday night they were really bored so they decided to go to the *ghost house*, which was a mile down the road. Stef and Christina told their parents that they would stay near home and be back at ten o'clock.

They were on their way to the ghost house to find the treasure that nobody could ever find. They thought it would be a piece of cake.

When they got there the gate was open and so was the front door. They thought it strange but walked on in anyway. As they got in the room they closed the door and shockingly, a light came on. They both jumped and screamed. The door had jammed so Stef and Christina went to a very bright corridor which had yellow doors and light green paint on the wall.

They opened the first yellow door and there it was, the mysterious treasure, the box was all golden. Stef ran to grab it but amazingly the box disappeared. They thought it was too much because they were so shocked and they knew now the house was haunted.

Suddenly the door at the bottom opened and there was a golden light coming from it. Christina ran towards it and Stef followed. They charged into the room without having the slightest idea of how much danger they were in.

The golden box vanished and a tall, dark shadow moved from the corner towards them. Stef and Christina were so frightened they were locked still and the shadow's eyes opened and its eyes were red and it produced a metal hatchet and slashed Christina in the leg. She fell to the ground. Stef, not knowing what to do, charged over to Christina to bend down and pick her up but the shadow hacked her in the back.

A loud screech came from the sky outside and a little girl suddenly appeared at the window and peered through it. The little girl burst in and began to eat Christina. Maggots soon fell from the ceiling and by this time the two girls were so paranoid they nearly died, but Stef found the courage somehow and hit the little girl, lifted up Christina and escaped through the smashed window.

They got home to their own houses to find their parents lying slaughtered on the floor.

They woke up, it was just a dream. But why did they both have the same dream?

Lisa O'Kane (13)
St Patrick's College, Maghera

A Day In The Life Of Jennifer Aniston . . .

Lying in bed, wishing that she never had to rise as she knows about the day ahead of her. After she wakes, she realises that her beautician will be arriving in just over ten minutes to do her fake tan for the premiere of her newly released movie, *Along Came Polly*.

She leaps from her bed like a frog leaps into water and rushes to her wardrobe and races to find something to wear. Before she knows it, there's a knock at her large Hollywood house door.

She runs and they start immediately as they are already running behind schedule. Just when she sits down to have a cup of coffee she gets another bang at her door.

This time it's her make-up artist coming fully equipped with everything from the best of foundations to the best of fake nails. When her make-up is completed and her fake tan is dry, she sits down to have a cup of coffee and a few moments to herself, but little does she know that her hair stylist is pulling up in the yard of her fancy Hollywood house.

As she gets her hair set she thinks that she has no time to spend with her husband Brad throughout the day. When her stylist pulls out of the yard she is gobsmacked to realise that by her watch she has only got just under two hours to be at the premiere in good time. Looking in the mirror she is becoming more excited about the fantastic night ahead of her and she realises what the whole rushed day was about.

Roisin Kearney (13)
St Patrick's College, Maghera

A New Bloom

Born in England, now living In America, Orlando Bloom is one of the fastest growing actors in Hollywood.

One of Orlando's first jobs as an actor was in 'Black Hawk Down'. Since then he has been working on projects non-stop. In 2003 he acted in 'Pirates of the Caribbean: The curse of the Black Pearl', also starring Johnny Depp. He also starred in 'Lord of the Rings', playing Legolas. He also starred in 'Troy', 'The Calcium Kid' and 'Heaven' will soon be released.

In 2004 he began the starring role in a major production, 'Kingdom of Heaven'. In 2005 a sequel to 'Pirates of the Caribbean' is planned. Filming is to start again in January.

A year before filming 'Lord of the Rings', Orlando fell three storeys off a porch, trying to open a jammed door. He broke his back. He was told he might never walk again, but luckily he recovered.

For Orlando, acting doesn't come easy as he is dyslexic. He has to get his lines earlier than everyone else as he likes to learn them off by heart so he won't have a problem when filming.

For 'Lord of the Rings', Orlando had to learn archery, how to ride a horse bareback while shooting an arrow and how to fight and wield two swords. It was 'Lord of the Rings' that made Orlando the big star he is today and I can safely say we'll be seeing a lot more of him.

Adelle Hasson (13)
St Patrick's College, Maghera

A Frightening Experience

There was once a man named Jim. He lived all on his own in a big, dark, scary house in the countryside. There also was Mickey Joe. Mickey Joe was married with two children. They lived on the outskirts of the town. Jim and Mickey Joe were very good friends. They also liked to drink.

One night the pair of them were down at the local pub and got really drunk. They were that drunk that the owner of the bar had to kick them out. They were both walking about without a care in the world. They had not a clue where they were going. However, when they were going to cross over the bridge, Jim accidentally pushed Mickey Joe and he plummeted to his watery grave.

It was about six months later. Everything was going fine for Jim. He forgot about the incident until one night in late November in which Jim got a big surprise. Mickey Joe's ghost had come to haunt him. Jim was frightened to death. He could not move. He felt numb. It then sank in and he sprinted as fast as he could to his car. He tried three or four times to get it started. Jim's heart was beating at an unbelievable rate. Mickey Joe came through the door of the car. He had a knife. He stabbed Jim in the chest.

Then Mickey Joe woke up. It was all a dream.

Kevin Rogers (13)
St Patrick's College, Maghera

The Story Of Blind Man's Pass

The cavalry sergeant sat astride his horse, bathed in the eerie glow that radiated from the pale moon and glinted through the trees. He had arrived at a split in the winding, mountainous road. He hesitated, thinking back to the smoky tavern in the isolated town he had just left.

'Beware of Blind Man's Pass,' the old man had whispered, 'a cavalry officer, much like yourself, traversed the pass one night long ago. He was attacked and murdered by a highwayman. His eyes were gouged out. They say his ghost still roams the mountain.'

The pass clung to the mountain like a serpent, disappearing into the mist. The sergeant started forward, almost smothered in the shadows of the trees. It was plain that no one had ventured along this lonely way for years. As he passed further into the darkness, a feeling of dread spread slowly over him. Suddenly, the ghostly neigh of a horse floated to the sergeant over the treetops. Fear gripped his heart in an icy grasp. Then, the steady beat of a horse's hooves echoed in the darkness, drawing steadily closer.

The figure of a man on horseback melted the gloom. He was dressed in an old officer's uniform and his head hung limply forward, an old, pointed hat covered his face. Another bolt of ice-cold fear coursed through the sergeant. The man raised his head, revealing a scarred, mutilated face. The sergeant stared into the dark voids where the man's eyes should have been, petrified. Then he felt himself falling as if a gaping, black chasm had opened beneath him to carry him into a dark, evil subterranean world. His soul fled, never to return.

The sergeant now wanders the pass, awaiting release, fated to haunt it for eternity.

Michael O'Kane (14)
St Patrick's College, Maghera

Screaming Shrills

Running along, panting, out of breath. Panic overcame Jane. She stopped for a minute to catch her breath. She turned around to see if the man was coming after her.

Jane ran down a dark alley. She tripped on something and went down head first, knocking herself unconscious.

When she woke up she found herself in a dull, damp room attracting flies due to the smell. She looked out the window to find she was in isolation. There was not a building in sight. She screamed so loudly she heard her high-pitched shrill echo.

A man came in but his face was confused.

'Where am I?' cried Jane. There was a long pause.

He didn't answer.

'Well, where am I? Answer me please!' begged Jane.

He did not answer, but left her a glass of water as he slipped out again. Jane took a frantic attack, kicking everything that got in her way. She yelled for the man to come back. When he finally came back two hours later, Jane screamed hysterically in his face. 'Please, why am I here? What did I do?'

There was no reply. She then started hitting and spitting at him.

The man grabbed her and threw Jane against the wall. 'The name's Mike!' he yelled.

'What do you want?' screamed Jane.

'To see you suffer. Do you not remember me from school? You made my life a living hell and now it's your turn!' Mike didn't give Jane a chance to answer and wrapped a rope round her neck and bit by bit, tightened it until it finally strangled her. He then left her there and never came back.

Claire Sweeney (14)
St Patrick's College, Maghera

The Headless Ghost

With every crack of lightning a shadow was thrown against a gravestone. Lightning covered the graveyard for a split second before being covered by a blanket of darkness. The icy night wind swirled through the graveyard bouncing off the tombstones and down the overgrown path to the old house at the bottom of the hill.

Inside, the house was in total darkness, and it is said you can still hear the screams of the young girl who was murdered there two hundred years ago.

You see, years ago a young woman moved into the house with her fiancé, dog and four cats soon after, they'd got married. It is said that Henry, her husband, had an affair with their maid, Martha, who was just 21. He himself was 49, and his wife Angela was 29. After a year or so, Angela began to get suspicious. He tried to deny it, but she caught them one night while she was out. She carefully planned her murder. She was going to poison Martha, a few nights later at the dinner table. As Henry was off working, this was the perfect opportunity for her. Before he left, he saw her plans and so he and Martha cut off her head whilst she was asleep. The neighbours heard her screaming and soon called the police. They investigated her murder, but before they had any evidence, Martha fled. Henry was arrested and was sentenced to execution.

The morning of his execution, the prison guards went to get him, only to find he had hung himself in his cell. They went to the house to examine Angela's body, but when they got there, they only found her body . . . but no head! People say she roams about the house looking for her head. They say she is going insane because she can't find her head. Every year on the 12th November, it is said that Henry comes back to try and finish her off! That's why you can still hear her screams! 'Aaarrggghhh!'

Kathryn Shiels (14)
St Patrick's College, Maghera

Finn McCool And The Giant's Causeway

Finn McCool was a huge giant from Ulster. He was known as the greatest giant in Ireland and the UK, but there was only one giant who was bigger and stronger than him. This giant's name was Hemish and he came from Scotland.

When Hemish heard about Finn, he decided to build a causeway from Scotland to Ireland to fight him. Over in Ireland, Finn heard about Hemish so he started building one in the opposite direction.

The two giants began their causeways and built for months, until one day Finn saw a huge figure of a man coming charging across the sea at a tremendous rate. Finn ran home as fast as he could to his wife who was carrying his child at the time. He told her what he had seen and she quickly came up with a plan to scare Hemish away.

She told Finn to go and hide in the baby's crib under the blanket. They both waited until a huge, thunderous knock came on the door. Finn's wife went and opened the door and there was Hemish standing tall. He asked for Finn, but his wife told him that he was out and told him that he should come in for a cup of tea and a pancake. He could not refuse, so he went in and sat down. Then he went over to the crib and looked in at Finn. He asked how old the child was and she said two years. When Hemish was not looking, she threw some stones into Hemish's pancake. As soon as he took a bite, he thought to himself, *if this is what he eats, then he must be tough and if that's the size of his child, what size is he?* Hemish started to get worried and ran home back across the causeway, scattering the blocks into the sea.

Hemish never came back, and Finn and his wife and children lived long and happy lives.

Orán O'Kane (13)
St Patrick's College, Maghera